MW00943843

Whispers in the Shadows

Tucker Hood

Book one of The Last Flame Series

This is a work of fiction. Names, characters, places, and incidents either are the product of the author's imagination or are used fictitiously. Any resemblance to actual persons, living or dead, events, or locales is entirely coincidental.

First paperback edition August 2020

ISBN: 978-1-7354723-0-0

Thank you Mom and Dad

for always supporting me

Contents

Prologue:

Bard's Tale

Long ago, eons before the time of your father's father,

An evil shadow of a king ruled the land.

Where he came from none remember,

But the memory of his tyranny still stands.

His kingdom spread like a dark cloud over the sun,

A plague that destroyed free will as it grew.

One man found the strength to stand up to his rule.

To the North, a rebellion he began to brew.

They say his eyes burned with a white fire,

That his soul was deadly strong,

He wielded two fatal steely blades,

And a blinding glow leapt from his body.

His name is now long forgotten,

But his bravery lives on.
As he led the final battle toward the king,
He fought through hordes of the enemy,
Hundreds, perhaps thousands of them - gone.
He pushed back the shadowy reign of the King,
A task thought all but impossible.

His army was fueled by desperation and love,
A force that the King found to be unstoppable.
Even with the burning love for country and family,
The rebels were still mortal men.
Many died as they seized the King's castle,
Each giving everything they could in the end.

The hero led the way fearlessly,
His arms swung sabers with deadly power.
He fought throngs of the enemy, saving many lives,
And his bravery was unparalleled in the final hour.
As the death toll grew, he forced his army to retreat,
While he stayed to finish the fight.

The people spoke of booming cracks of thunder,
Brilliant flashes of light,
And the screaming of the countless strætae.

How he managed to do it is a mystery,
But in the end he stumbled back to the remnants of the army,
"It's done," were his last words before he collapsed completely.

He forced the lingering Shadows out of this world,
Leaving its creatures to live in peace.
But even as the last of the shadows slipped away,
Rumors spread about the Shadow King's release.
A whisper of a time when the King would return.
A promise that he would not be stopped at his next turn.
A prophecy that against him could stand only five:
One of Water,
One of Fire,
One of Earth,
One of Lightning.
One of Mind,
And so the darkness left this world for a time.

The bard ended his story with an odd flourish of his hand then blew out a candle on the nearby table. "There you have it." His gaze wandered the old taproom and examined his patrons' hard faces as he spoke. "The tale of the Shadow King."

He stood for a moment on the edge of the stage and waited for a reaction as the audience let the last few lines resonate through the dim room. After a slight pause, the gruff crowd offered the bard a few seconds of praise. It wasn't much, but the bard had expected less from the few young men and drunken travelers gathered in the tavern tonight. After the brief show of respect, they went back to talking amongst themselves about the goings on in this small corner of the world.

The bard hopped off the stage. *By the goddess, I wish I was back at home now,* he thought. His small cabin was to the north a few miles beyond the city of Galleon, just far enough removed that politics didn't bother him but close enough that he could reach the city in the event of an emergency. Unfortunately, the price of his remoteness was the loss of a stable job, which had forced him to either move or take up barding. Obviously, he chose the latter, which brought him to the current tavern. Here, in the southernmost region of the kingdom, lawlessness ran rampant, people went missing on the streets, and even the wildlife seemed more dangerous. His father, a casual musician and storyteller, had often warned him of the perils that came with the life of a bard and encouraged him to take up a more reliable profession. All things considered, he couldn't help but think that he had made the wrong choice. He probably should have left years ago and settled in more habitable regions of the realm.

The bard's thoughts shifted from his home as an argument broke out at a table near him. "I tell you, I seen one of 'em, all shadowy and mist-like." The speaker was an old man with one eye. "He was just stan'n there on the side o' the road. One second he was there, the next... Poof." The old man made an explosion motion with his hands and looked at the group of young men crowded around him.

"What'd you see em with?" asked one of the rowdier men, bringing a handful of chuckles from the others.

The old man frowned. "Laugh all ya want, but when one of 'em comes fo' you in the night don't say I didn't warn you."

Another one of the boys saluted the old man. "I'll be sure to watch out for shadows in the dark, sir."

The old man's face grew red and his eye bulged. The bard turned away his attention as the conversation devolved into a battle of insults. He stared into his mug, letting his mind swirl like the remnants of froth on the dark liquid. He thought of his daughter, waiting for him to come back from his adventure with some grand memento for her. He chuckled to himself. Then the familiar tears welled when he thought of the good times they had had before her mother left: walking hand in hand along forgotten paths in the woods surrounding their house, running to and fro in the front yard laughing, days spent playing in the cool water of the nearby river.

Those had been the days, the time when they had been a family. One day she had just disappeared. The only thing she left behind was a note: *"I'm sorry, but I have to go. I love you both so much. It breaks my heart, but I must leave."* With those words, she had abandoned them.

A tear spilled out and rolled down the bard's face. It was filled with the sweet sorrow of the past and carved a burning path along his cheek. The salty droplet of pain and love continued its slow journey, the moist remnants of its travels a scar on the bard's face. He sniffed but couldn't bring himself to lift his hand and wipe the droplet away. Something deep inside prevented him from rubbing away the memory; he let it be. He was content with the temporary scar it would leave. The bittersweet tear carried with it a trail of memories until it disappeared into the bard's thick beard. Nothing but a distant ache remained. "I'm sorry I couldn't be there for you," the bard whispered to himself as he closed his eyes.

The pain, both hated and cherished as all that remained of his past life, had started to slowly dissipate when a strange voice twisted and writhed, like smoke and shadow, quietly into his mind. "A sad tale indeed, although it's only partly true." The bard opened his eyes and looked lazily over toward the figure who spoke. The person's face and body were covered by a thick cloak that was dyed either black or the darkest blue in the world. Thin veins of red were woven, web-like, into the fabric. The cloak was closed with a gold button in the shape of a wing. The only thing visible under the hood was a pair of burning red eyes.

The bard rubbed the scar of memories from his face, careful to make it look like he hadn't been crying. This man was surely out of the ordinary, but what did it matter? To the bard, lost in a shroud of melancholy, the outside world was faint and distant. He shrugged, "Truth, lies. It makes little difference as long as the story is good." He turned his head away, "Besides, it's not something I made up."

There was an odd movement under the man's hood, a flicker, like a shadow passing over a field. "I do believe that you have only heard part of the story, for there is much more to it if I remember correctly." The figure's voice flickered in volumes, fluctuating unexpectedly from barely audible to piercingly loud. The bard strained to follow the words that spouted from the deep cowl. "Tell me, did you happen to hear the story from a man by the name of Corbin?" The figure crept closer to the bard; a wide sleeve of the cloak moved smoothly toward the bard's bare arm.

"Corbin… Corbin…" The bard could hear his voice as if it came from a long way off. "Yes. That was his name. But…" The bard paused and tried to rouse himself. He shook his head, bewildered by the sudden sluggish feeling that had crept over him. "But why do you care?" The bard recognized the great weariness that had settled on him. It was similar to the despair he had fought for so long. He shook his head. He could not give in to this powerful sorrow, yet it loomed before him like a great chasm. "You say that there is more to this...story. It's a favorite here. What would it take for you to tell me the version you know?" Among the traveling bards, it was considered rude to request the telling of a new tale without offering an exchange of some type.

The figure's hood partly lifted, revealing red eyes in a smokey, black face that seemed to be constantly shifting. Of course, the bard thought, the room was very dim. He had just blown out the candle nearest his table. Nevertheless, the bard's gaze shifted quickly away from the strange eyes. "I require nothing much," it said in the same flickering voice. "But this isn't quite the right...atmosphere for such a story, wouldn't you agree? Follow me outside and I can tell you all you want. And I want to share something, too, a … trick, to truly show the audience what kind of storyteller you are." With its last sentence, the figure's red eyes gleamed greedily for a moment through his hood. The bard nodded, entranced. He was gripped with a desire, soft at first but growing more intense, to acquire whatever the figure in the cloak possessed.

"No harm in learning something that could make me some money," he muttered and stood unsteadily, a wave of drowsiness numbing his movements. The ground seemed far away and unstable under his feet, but his heartbeat hungrily as he thought of the opportunity the cloaked figure offered. "Lead the way, my friend," he whispered eagerly.

A cackle emerged from the hood, short and low, but the bard caught it. The figure swept ahead and he followed, past the guests at the inn. One or two of them nodded at him as he passed. He recognized them as the ones who would occasionally tell him what an excellent story he had told, but he could sense their underlying pity for him. The poor, sad bard, abandoned by the beautiful mother of his child. The poor, lonely bard, trying to raise a daughter on his own. He could see the pity behind the kind words, see the guests lean toward each other, whisper, and shake their heads. He felt a wave of unreasonable anger - a surge of red flame licked at the back of his throat. He moved forward, propelled by the force of his anger and depression.

The cloaked figure was already outside. He felt himself swept along in the wake of the dark cloak, toward the door of the inn.

As the bard stepped out of the door, he felt the energy surging through him shift. The eagerness and red flush of rage that had propelled him so quickly through the door drained away into the mist that floated about his feet. He felt heavy, his mind slow. He pushed on after the figure, motivated by the last remaining coal of courage he had found in the inn. They continued on, past a huddle of scantily clad beggars on the street and toward the edge of town.

The bard had to know the story, learn the trick that the stranger had alluded to. His deep exhaustion increased as he got farther and farther from the comforting lights of the inn, but he continued to press after the figure, pulled by the temptation of a new story. He would occasionally lose sight of the figure in the shadows and a bolt of fear would lurch through him, forcing him to lift his reluctant feet more quickly, hastening after the shadow.

Finally, after what seemed like a vast expanse of time and space, the cloaked figure stopped. They had left the welcoming light of houses far behind and were at the edge of the forest. Nothing looked familiar to the bard, but he was washed with a sense of relief that they had finally stopped.

"Sit," the figure commanded, not turning around to face the bard.

The bard gladly plopped to the ground, the mist enveloping his lower half as he folded his legs. He looked expectantly to the cloaked figure.

"Now," the figure started. Its tonal fluttering hummed

with power. "The part of the story that you have heard is true, but there is more to the prophecy at the end. It says that though the heroes will try to rise, they will face trials unlike any other. They will be pitted against family and friend. The dark king will send many creatures to stop them, making sure that they will never defeat him. And as from darkness came the light, from the light will come darkness." Even though the story the creature had told was short, the bard was entranced by the raspy voice that always seemed to be just a notch away from his hearing.

"Excellent," whispered the bard, this new information giving him a flash of energy. "I could put it to rhyme and mesh it with the rest of the story." He stopped. The figure had turned to face him and his eyes glowed with a fire that put him on edge. He felt fear trickle through his numbed limbs as he remembered the second part of the figure's deal. "What is it? Wh... what is the trick?"

"A trick, yes. But you offered me something in return, right?"

"What would you like?"

The figure's eyes narrowed into fiery slits. "The answer to one question."

The silence grew as the figure waited for a response. Hesitantly, the bard replied, “What question?”

The figure’s eyes gleamed and a chuckling purr emanated from his hood. “What, my friend, is your name?” He hissed the last word, letting it flow through the night like a snake through grass.

The bard hesitated for a moment. He felt compelled as if by some external force to tell the shadowy figure his name. Yet the task seemed ominous, and he resisted as long as he could, pushing the name farther and farther into the depths of his mind, but it was no use.

“Logan,” he finally released the word, the syllables coming out as mere squeaks, a faint remnant of his rich voice that had filled the inn a short while before.

Logan felt calm and free for a moment, then the force was on him again, greater than before. “Thank you, Logan,” said the figure, and then broke into smokey laughter. It reached up with shadowy hands. Slowly, it pulled back the hood of its cape, unbuttoning the golden wing-shaped brooch. As it did so, the rest of the cape fell, revealing a humanoid creature. However, unlike a man, the dark being was made up of a smoky, shadowy substance.

Logan was overwhelmed by the smell of rot and

death that now washed over his being, coming from the shadow itself. "Listen, mortal," said the beast, its voice growing in strength. "Listen to the screams of your people."

Logan listened and was horrified to hear the screams of men, women, and children. As he stared, mouth agape, at the shadow creature, he thought he saw shapes flickering in and out of existence within the shadow itself. He peered closer, then gasped and pushed himself backward, his eyes wide with terror that sliced through his trance-like torpor. He thought he saw the faint outlines of screaming people. He scuttled backward, tripping and falling flat against the ground, paralyzed with fear. The people were somehow trapped in this creature. He looked at the cloak lying on the ground near the being and realized that what he thought was dye was actually the blood of these innocent people.

His terror had shocked him into alertness, but too late. He stared helplessly at the creature and saw a hand reach out toward him. He tried to get up and run, but he was held captive. *I wish I had seen her one last time.* The words in his head were like the last gasp of a drowning man, his final free thought. The arm clawed at his chest, and he felt himself being absorbed into the mass of shadows and smoke. He felt his blood drain from his body, over the misty ground, and into the cloak. His mind slowly merged with a new awareness as the creature's consciousness poured through him. Logan was immersed, part of the mass of trapped souls.

The creature sighed contentedly. “It’s been too long since the last soul I ate. Now I have to find Corbin - he could be a nuisance to my master.” His eyes narrowed at the thought of Corbin. “You won’t get away this time. Not this time.” A cold determination filled him and his red eyes burned for a moment before he wrapped himself in the cape and turned away from the corpse. He moved quickly through the forest: a dark hound picking up the scent of a fresh quarry.

I:

A Stranger in the Storm

Roan sat bolt upright in his bed; his body drenched in a cold sweat. *Just another nightmare,* he thought.

He lived in the forest outside of the town where he had grown up, too afraid of what lay there to go back. His nightmare was the same as always: his old home burning, the death of his parents, and the loss of his old life. For a moment, he allowed himself to revisit the familiar nightmare, embracing the pain that came with it.

As he drifted back into the nightmare, his old memories flooded in and took control of his mind. That night, he had woken up to the stench of burning timber, the light of fire illuminating his house, and the distant screams of onlookers outside. At first, he had been afraid of the burning wood and smoky air, but then something strange happened.

The fire spoke to him.

Roan shook his head, the true memory overtaking the dream. Spoke was the wrong word. It had been more like the heat had pressed into his mind and communicated with him in broad signals and complex imagery. The flames that blazed in front of him comforted him. They revealed images of hearth fires and families dancing happily around bonfires, each image accompanied by a warm and comfortable heat. Roan's fear had melted away, leaving him with a pleasant feeling that masked the danger of the actual fire consuming his house. In this way, the blaze had coaxed him through the house, always sharing happy imagery and calming him. Down the stairs they went, boy and fire, hand in hand. The fire led him out of the door and told him to stay put. He obeyed; his mind saturated with cozy images. He didn't spare a thought for his parents until it was too late.

No, he corrected himself. He *couldn't* spare a thought for his parents. The fire had overtaken his mind. It had left him no choice.

Then fire grew around the house, tongues of flame leaped, sprouting like budding vines. He heard a scream, a scream that would stay with him for the rest of his life. It was his mother's. Her scream penetrated the fire's trance. He ran toward the house, only to be pushed back by the very fire that had moments ago been so comforting to him. The heat of the blaze was too fierce for the young boy to withstand. Roan had been forced to stay away from the house. He fell to his knees, crying. A group of people gathered behind him. They watched the spectacle but, like Roan, could do nothing. Some went to comfort the boy while others rushed for water to stop the advance of the fire, but all of them knew it was too late. They marveled that the young boy had escaped the inferno.

The villagers managed to douse any flames that tried to crawl away from the epicenter, leaving the rest of the town undamaged, but none could get close enough to put out the flames on Roan's house. A pillar of fire rose from the house and the onlookers gasped in unison as the swirling flower of flame engulfed the wooden cottage, blossoming until the house was hidden from view. The tears flowed like rivers from Roan's eyes then; his life was being destroyed in front of him, and he could do nothing.

The night wore on and slowly the rest of the village went back to minding their own business as the flower of fire wilted and died. Roan stayed put, refusing any offer of kindness from the rest of the villagers while he waited, tears still pouring out as he stared at the fire. After what seemed like an eternity, the last of the giant flames were extinguished, leaving behind coals and licks of flames on the few wood beams that remained.

At the center appeared to be two bodies, burned beyond recognition. However, Roan knew who they were instantly: a boy can always find his mother. He rushed toward the figures, tears streaming down his face and staining his cheeks. He slowed as he approached their corpses, his mind too paralyzed to fully comprehend anything. Reaching out fearfully with one shaky hand, he touched his father's arm only to have it crumble to ashes. He screamed in horror and watched as the once proud and noble man's body disintegrated into nothing. He saw flakes start to fall off his mother and cried out, his voice tearing out of a deep, primal source and ripping through his throat. He couldn't stop himself. He rushed in for one last embrace as his mother fell apart just like his father.

He wept and grasped in vain at the ashes that floated to the ground. His cries brought the villagers back out from their houses. They slowly gathered around the boy as he clutched at handfuls of ashes. The men took off their hats and looked down at the ground, ashamed that they couldn't have done more to save their friends. Women broke down in tears and hid their children from the broken boy on the ground.

None of this registered with Roan as he continued to stare at the last remnants of his life, a river of tears continuously cascading down his face. A hand touched his shoulder, but he shook it off and started to run. People yelled after him to stop, but he didn't listen. He just ran through the town and over the fields surrounding it until he reached the edge of the forest. He stopped for a moment, fearful of the massive trees, before staggering into the heart of the woods. His old life was gone; he had no reason to fear the deep forest.

That night, Roan didn't stop until he lurched into a small glade with a tree in the center. Something about this place made him halt. His feelings overwhelmed him. He fell to the ground and curled into a ball at the base of the tree. Even though the ground was hard and cold, images of the fire haunted his mind and cocooned him in a warmth that seemed to ward off the chill.

The rest of the night and the next day he lay there, his sobs trickling out through the forest and calling all types of animals out of the trees. They stood quietly and looked at the sad lump of a boy on the ground. His body lay in a heap beneath the tree, but his mind had left it and wandered in a dark, lonely place full of shadows. Such a creature was best left alone, the forest animals knew. They stepped carefully away from the boy: such meat was too strange to be eaten, the sweet meadow grass too sullied by his smoky scent and the salty pain of his tears to be palatable. The animals of the deep forest sensed the abnormal within him and left him undisturbed.

As the sun began to set the day after the fire, Roan managed to drag himself far enough out of his shock and sorrow to realize he needed to find water, food, and real warmth if he wanted to survive. He picked himself up, walked numbly around the clearing in search of berries, and heard the faint trickling of a creek. He followed the sound until he found a stream. He sat at the edge, the reliable flow of the water comforting the aches deep inside him.

Hours passed and he managed to push his body back to the tree. He put off what he knew had to come for as long as he could, gathering a few berries and absentmindedly eating them, his mind too broken and numb from the previous night's events to be able to focus on the most rudimentary actions of survival. After he had combed the bushes free of all signs of food, he went to work on the inevitable task of survival: fire.

He began to gather wood and pile it on the grass, keeping his mind far away from the thought of heat or fire as long as he could. Finally, he sat before a pile of sticks and logs. He sighed and gave in. He let his mind wander gently toward the thought of fire.

He danced around the idea of a hot and blazing flame, focusing on warm campfires and sitting at the hearth back at home. At the thought of home, anger and pain flickered back into his mind and he felt his whole body grow hot as if he had a fever. His hands started to shake and he felt a burning sensation rising inside him. Something that was part of him and yet strangely separate told him to push out the heat, push it out before it burned him. He reached out, surprisingly calm despite the rising heat inside his body, and pushed the fiery feeling out of himself, through his hands.

He felt a surge of heat that pulsed against a barrier, a gate deep inside of him. He felt the gate open and the heat rush through. It coursed through his body, his skin turning light blue as the flames surged under it to his hands. The blue light reached his hands, ripped them open, and flooded through his flesh. He screamed in agony. A blast of blue fire leaped out of his hands and licked at the wood, eating it and burning away the surrounding grass.

As the flow of fire ceased, Roan fell onto his back, his hands clenched, tight fists. He wavered in and out of reality as his body cooled and searing pain enveloped his hands. He managed to stay conscious just long enough to raise his hands and see two diamond-shaped burns on the palms. He looked over at the fire and smiled. "I did it," he breathed to the silent forest.

The pain in his hands dissipated and he slept where he lay. His sleep was peaceful, unfettered by the pain of his experience. It was as if the fire had cleansed him, allowing his mind and heart to heal.

After that day, he slowly learned how to control his newfound power and eventually built himself a house in the tree, cutting off his old life as best he could. He worked for months on end to set up a new life, hiding from those who came searching for a way to bring him back to that painful place. Eventually, the villagers accepted his isolation, saw that he was surviving on his own, and understood that he would only show up when he wanted to.

Roan sighed. Despite his self-imposed isolation and

wariness, the memories lingered. His attempts to avoid the tragedy of his past could not stop the memories that still haunted his dreams.

He groaned softly, and slowly lifted himself out of his bed. *So many what-ifs and whys. I wish I could go back. But it's pointless to try to change things now,* he thought sadly. He looked outside and saw the pale glow of the sun rising to the east. He forced himself to shrug and focused on feeling grateful to have slept the whole night for a change. He felt rested. He turned away from the window and looked around the small room. *Still dark,* he thought. *Might as well light the lamp.* He had found that recovering from the nightmares required determination and attention to small tasks. How many times had the little tasks of his life saved him from despair? Too many times to count.

He picked up the lamp from his bedside, then looked at his hand, thinking once again of the first night he had used his power. A white diamond stared back at him, its edges jagged and broken from multiple failed attempts at starting fires. He winced as he remembered accidentally burning himself time and time again before he turned his attention back to the lamp. He opened the gate inside himself and let a tiny trickle of fire rush through his body, the now familiar blue glow moving up his arm into his palm. He touched the glowing blue diamond on his hand to the wick and the lamp flared to life, illuminating his house and his new life's work.

Around the room lay memories that made up who Roan was now. In one corner of the room was a roughly hewn table that held a clay pot and hand-carved cutlery, along with a few other pots and bowls. Next to the table hung a lute. He chuckled and let his hand slide down the neck as he passed by. *I'll be back for you soon enough.* He looked away from the instrument and at the far wall where a broken and charred slab of clay hung, a memento that he had decided to keep from his first year of learning how to work with fire.

The day he had made the slab, he had let too much power out and put another jagged scar on his hands. He had grown from then, learning more about the power and becoming accustomed to the forest, springs and creeks, and the plants and animals. He had dedicated his life to building a new home and honing his newfound abilities, keeping the memories of that painful night suppressed by exhaustion. Even when his work with fire led to burns and scars, he still pushed on, partly because he wanted to prove to himself that he could control the thing that had destroyed his life and partly to keep his mind from wandering back into that depressed state it had been in for those first few days. Not only had his fire powers grown stronger, but his mind and body had been toned and hammered into strong tools that Roan could rely on no matter what.

Eventually, he had run out of things to do for his survival and so he started to create something that resembled more of a home. At first, he simply worked on creating dishes and silverware that he could be proud of and that would give his house a cozy and personalized feel. Then he began to add etchings and carvings onto the already built furniture. He created ornate artwork on his bed and table, and painstakingly sketched and etched maps into the walls of the house. This had kept him occupied for a few years, and now his house finally felt like home. Still, his mind wandered when he wasn't busy and he searched frantically for something new to occupy his time.

One day when he was journeying near the town, he had seen it. A bard was wandering through the streets with a lute strapped to his back. Roan saw the lute and immediately took a mental note of what it looked like before hurrying back to his house and sketching out a blueprint to work from. After the blueprint was designed, much of his time was spent making and remaking models, each with its own unique issues. Eventually, he had a finished product and spent many of his days simply sitting under his house and picking out songs and patterns, his mind wandering as he played the soft and crooning melodies.

A silly grin came over Roan's face as he remembered making foolish songs about fair maidens and drunken sailors. He chuckled to himself and continued on toward the clay oven in the far corner of the house. He knelt and followed a line of artwork that wound around the door, his hand eventually coming to rest on the latch. He opened the door and threw in a few pieces of wood before willing the gate inside himself open just enough to let out a small flame. He didn't flinch as the fire burst through his scarred skin, the heat instantly opening and resealing the scar. The wood was soon enveloped in flame and Roan closed the door. He picked up a pot from the ground nearby, one of the few things made of metal in his house, and set it on the stove. He filled the pot with ingredients for a stew, going through the familiar motions, humming a soft and sweet melody as he worked.

The fire well-stoked and the stew starting to bubble, he walked back to his bed and picked up his lute. He tuned each of the strings, a comfortable feeling that managed to soothe any remaining pain from his nightmare. Before starting to play, he looked at his most prized possession: a broken shard of a mirror he had found one day in the woods. In his reflection, he was lean and well built, his hands running up and down the frets confidently and casually. His hair was dark brown, almost black. He had won the clothes he wore in a bet with a trader and he noted that they were now well-worn, even ragged. In his reflection, everything about him seemed completely normal. Everything except his eyes: pitch black, not dark brown or blue, but pure black through and through. If this wasn't spectacular enough, on closer inspection, tiny golden flecks were spattered around his eyes. They gleamed and glowed with a life of their own, dancing in and out of the pitch-black as he started to sing.

Roan stared at himself in the mirror. He watched each of the sparks of gold blink in and out of existence as he let his voice stray from a major chord progression to a minor and finally into something resembling a pentatonic scale. At first, he had lived alone in the woods out of desperation, with no desire to return to the town and the memories that it held. But the power of the fire had marked him. Now, he could not return to his old life, even if he wanted to. The townsfolk felt pity for him now: the poor lonely boy who had watched his parents burn. If they saw his gold-flecked eyes, saw his power, they would no longer pity him; they would fear him. Their fear would lead to suspicion and hate. They would eventually turn against him. He had seen it happen before, with people in the town who were much less outlandish than he had become. One old woman had been exiled to the edge of town and treated with disdain just because she knew more about herbs and minerals than anyone else. A boy with black and golden eyes who could control fire? He wouldn't have a chance. At times he longed for human company, but one look in the shard of mirror brought him back to reality. It was best that he stayed where he was and keep everyone at a distance. Pity was harmless; fear would only lead to more tragedy.

He looked away from the mirror and closed his eyes, his mind deep in the music that flowed so smoothly out of his fingers. He let his voice die down and started to solo on the lute. He must have stayed like that for half an hour, the music soothed and healed the wound that opened in his mind after his nightmare memory and helped him accept the strangeness that the mirror reflected back to him. He sighed deeply as the memory faded into the corner it inhabited in his mind. The music ran wild. His hand flew up and down the neck, each note struck with perfect timing and pressure. The music he played came from his soul and was touched with the power of fire. If they could have heard him, not even the most skilled of artists, writers, musicians, or bards could begin to describe the sound that emanated from the young man's hands.

Outside, the sun hid behind dark clouds that flew in from the north. The combination of deep forest shade and the overcast sky made the interior of Roan's home nearly dark. The dim flame of his lamp flicked and danced along with the music. The flickering light and music created a sense of timelessness.

Something outside made the rhythmic dancing of the flame stutter and falter, an out-of-place sound that broke the trance-like state Roan had gone into. He paused and listened intently for the source of the noise. The faint sound of shuffling feet and the distant thud of a walking stick reached his ears. He frowned. *Who could be out here? Especially in this weather?* He silently got up and rested the lute in its nook in the wall. Cautiously, he walked over to the trapdoor and peered through a slat out into the clearing.

From the crack, Roan could see the white wiry hair of an ancient man who stood below him. He noted the tanned and weathered skin from many days under the sun. The man's wool clothes, though well-made, were torn and shabby, indicating previous prosperity and current poverty. He carried a curious black staff that appeared to be carved with strange symbols. Roan's eyes lingered on the staff. Its dark exterior and finely-etched symbols seemed familiar to him. Roan shook his head and the feeling drifted away. If he knew what it was a moment ago, he couldn't remember anymore.

The man paced beneath the trapdoor. Roan saw that he walked with a slight limp on his left side and his face was turned down to the ground, almost as if he was following something. The old man carried himself proudly, but Roan felt something was off about the man. He couldn't identify anything external indicating the sense of oddness he felt. As a matter of fact, all of the man's body language hinted at confidence and forthrightness, so Roan shrugged off the feeling.

He popped open the trapdoor and called out, "What

are you doing out on such a gloomy day?"

The stranger looked up, startled, and peered at Roan between the tree branches. "You've no idea what a happy sight you are to me," he said. Ancient wrinkles appeared across his face as he smiled. "I'm not out here by choice. I was supposed to arrive in Copper Town yesterday, but..." He shrugged and his gaze wandered around the woods for a moment before returning sheepishly to Roan. "I'm lost."

Roan chuckled. "Well, I tell you what, Copper Town's a few hours' journey from here and I can feel a storm coming soon, so why don't you rest here for a while?'

A flush of relief spread across the old man's face. "How kind of you. These old bones are in desperate need of a rest, if I do say so myself."

Roan nodded and threw down a rope ladder before hopping out of the tree himself. "One thing first, could you help me grab a few logs? I don't want to have to walk all the way to the shack during a storm."

"I can help you grab them, but I'm not sure how useful I'll be when it comes to taking them up that ladder." The stranger glanced uncertainly at the thin rope ladder.

"I wouldn't be a very good host if I asked my guest to do something he wasn't comfortable with. Just bring a few to the bottom of the ladder and I can handle it from there. The shack is just over here, follow me." Roan turned and headed toward the wood shack, the old man's distinct footsteps close behind.

The old man cleared his throat. "If you don't mind my asking, what's a young man like yourself doing out here in the middle of nowhere?"

Roan shrugged. "Things happen."

They were silent for a moment as Roan forced back any thoughts of his old home. Then he slapped himself on the forehead. "I'm a terrible host, aren't I? I haven't even properly introduced myself." He turned to the old man smiled and reached out a hand. "I'm Roan."

The old man smiled back at him and took his hand, shaking it vigorously. "The name's Corbin."

"Good to meet you, Corbin. And what are you doing out in the woods besides getting lost? If you don't mind me asking, of course."

Corbin sighed. "I guess that's a good question. Hand me a few of those logs and I'll sum it up as we work."

Roan obliged and passed Corbin several pieces of wood, grabbing an armload for himself.

"To start out, I have no wife or family to speak of, so in my retirement, I decided to become a traveling bard for fun - you know, travel around, see new places, meet new people. I just finished in Galleon and heard about a shortcut through the woods to Copper Town. But my eyes aren't as good as they used to be and I missed a landmark the other day. Then I ended up here." He shrugged as the two trudged back to the tree, "Probably should have just stuck to the road."

"Galleon. That's a long way from here." A thread of doubt trickled through Roan.

Corbin nodded. "About two weeks, I'd say. I ran out of rations just yesterday."

Roan pushed the finger of doubt aside. The man seemed honest. Living out in the woods alone had made him overly suspicious. "Well, then it's a good thing you found me. Drop your load right there and head inside. I've got stew on the stove that's just about ready." Roan pointed to a spot near the ladder and Corbin dropped his few pieces of wood there. "If you want, I can carry your staff for you."

"Thank you, but I think I can handle bringing it up with me." Corbin strapped the staff to his back before carefully making his way up the ladder. He moved with surprising ease, considering his ancient appearance.

Roan raised his eyebrows in surprise. *He's hiding something.* Suddenly Roan knew it was the truth. His odd suspicions about the man had been pointing to it all along. The man himself did not have bad intentions, but he was hiding something. *Why? What is he hiding?* Roan's mind raced as he calmly balanced a few pieces of wood in one arm and nimbly climbed the ladder. He popped in and saw Corbin looking around approvingly. "What do you think?" Roan asked as he threw the logs in a corner and walked over to the stove.

"I'm impressed. Did you do this all by yourself?"

Roan smiled proudly as he ladled out two bowls of the brothy stew. "Sure did. Took a long time, but I'm happy with it."

"Mhm," Corbin responded and Roan turned around to see him admiring the lute. "Do you play?" asked the old man.

Roan shrugged, careful not to spill any of the stew. "A little. I'm not all that good. I've never had anyone to train me. Here's your stew."

Corbin turned and graciously accepted the proffered bowl, "Thank you." He smelled the steam and sighed. "A musician and a cook, good thing you live out here otherwise the ladies would be all over you." Corbin grinned at Roan who blushed and rubbed the nape of his neck, too embarrassed to come up with a response. "Go on, let's hear you play."

"I'm really not that good, it would probably ruin your appetite." Roan's normally confident personality was hidden behind the veil of embarrassment Corbin's request had managed to pull over him.

Corbin shook his head. "I've heard the worst in the business and they haven't done anything to me. Besides, if you really are bad then I can give you a few pointers. You said you've never had anyone to train you - here's your chance, if you need it."

Corbin smiled, amiable and friendly, unlike the grin from earlier. Roan felt the wave embarrassment slowly pass and he sighed. "If you insist."

He set down his bowl and picked up the lute; his fingers strayed over the neck until they found a shape they were satisfied with. Roan took a deep breath and started to play. He closed his eyes and let his mind drift back to the perfect calm it had found before Corbin disturbed him. He rarely had the opportunity to play in front of people and it took him longer to find the flow of music deep within himself, but once he found it, all fear fell away. He started to hum, softly at first, but soon it grew into a full-fledged song. What he sang of he wasn't sure, but he felt a heat slowly stir and dance throughout his body.

Slowly but surely, the heat grew in Roan. It made him play faster and faster until his hands raced along the lute in a fevered dance, the melody fast and full of emotion. He felt hot salty tears begin to roll down his face but he didn't stop, couldn't stop, until the song was done. He opened his eyes and saw Corbin watching him intently. In the corner of his vision, something flickered and he turned to see the candle dancing in rhythm with his fevered song. Looking down at the frets, he felt the gate deep inside him open and the familiar heat raced through him. However, this was different than ever before. Instead of trying to get out, the heat pushed him to new limits. The music was unnaturally beautiful and it burst out at a burning speed, each note blending seamlessly and blurring into the next.

He closed his eyes and let the song run wild, his voice filled with a power and depth he had never felt before. His body sat calmly, but his mind was wild and on fire until he felt a cool and calming pressure on his shoulder.

He opened his eyes and saw Corbin standing in front of him. Roan looked into the man's eyes and felt the heat that had flowed through him begin to ebb away. The room darkened and he realized that a blue glow had been coming out of his arms. Corbin continued to stare into his eyes. The gate deep inside Roan eased shut and his playing slowed to a halt, his voice raspy and full of pain.

Corbin took his hand off of Roan's shoulder then let a smile flow over his face. "Sorry to stop you, but I think your stew might be getting cold."

"Thank you," Roan croaked. He shook his head and set down the lute, his hands cold and numb. He grabbed the warm bowl of stew and started to eat.

"I've never heard anyone play like that before. Who'd you learn from?" Corbin asked, the open smile still on his face.

Roan shook his head. "I told you, I didn't learn from anyone. Kinda just figured it out over time." He looked into Corbin's eyes and saw something flash across them.

Is he worried about something? Does he not believe me? Is he afraid to tell me how bad I sounded? The flicker of emotion disappeared before Roan could figure out what it was.

A boom shook the house and Corbin snapped his

head toward the window, just in time to see another flash of lightning fill the sky. "What a bother," he frowned. "How far did you say Copper Town was from here?"

Roan shook his head again, "It's about two hours east, but you can't seriously be thinking of traveling in a storm." As he finished, the rain started to pound against the roof.

Corbin sighed. "I don't have anywhere to stay, so I guess I don't have a choice."

"You can stay here." Roan was surprised at how fast the answer had come out. "I don't often get the chance to have guests here."

Corbin smiled fondly at the boy. "I don't imagine you do." He looked around at the cozy interior of the house. "Living all the way out here in the middle of nowhere, it's almost as if you don't want many guests." He gave Roan a shrewd look and Roan found himself adjusting his gaze toward a knothole overhead. "It's very thoughtful of you to invite me to stay, but I couldn't do that to you."

"I insist," Roan responded quickly. There was something about Corbin that made him fiercely curious and he knew his desire to keep the old man close showed. “At least stay here until the storm clears up,” he shrugged, trying to sound indifferent. Roan looked at the old man, his eyes filled with determination, confidence, and a touch of challenge.

Corbin’s frown slowly started to fade into a grin and he laughed. “Well, I doubt that I would have any chance of convincing you otherwise. Alright. I’ll stay, but only till the storm passes.”

Roan grinned back. “Good.” He looked at the lute. “You said you could show me a few things. Go ahead. Play something.”

Corbin smiled. “If you insist, but it won’t be anything compared to what you just did. That was a masterpiece.”

Roan chuckled as the feeling slowly returned to his body. “It sure wasn’t a masterpiece, but it was alright, I guess.” He handed Corbin the lute. “Besides, I played for you so you might as well play for me. Isn’t that a fair exchange?”

“Fair enough. In some places, it’s called singing for your supper.” Corbin took the lute and thought for a moment before he started to play. His voice was gruff and he played the notes hard and sharp, but there was a charm to his playing.

Roan sat back and watched the old man play, the storm outside beating with futile vehemence against the cabin. Within the shelter, the two men found themselves exchanging stories and songs, the lapses between their conversation and music-filled seamlessly with the fire's happy crackling.

II:

The Stranger's Story

Eventually, the storm started to fade away and Roan glanced at the fire. "I need to go grab a few more pieces of wood."

Corbin looked up from the lute and over at the window. "Storm is almost gone. I might as well get going."

Roan made a gesture of rejection. "Wait until it completely dies out. I wouldn't want to have it start up again with you stuck in the woods."

Corbin smiled. "If you say so. But if I stay here much longer, I think I might become a permanent part of the house."

Roan laughed as he opened the trapdoor. "Don't get your hopes set on it." He threw down the ladder and carefully slid to the ground. His feet were met with the wet, mushy grass and he grimaced. *Worst part of a storm, without a doubt.* He walked thoughtfully toward the woodshed, his mind still filled with a fluttering energy from his fiery performance. A light mist drifted around him and the sky above was filled with wispy clouds. The trees stood still in the calm of the storm and regained some of their composure as they waited for the inevitable return of the gale that had been buffeting them. Something about the momentary peace made Roan change directions.

He turned from the shed and walked toward the stream, his mind clouded by a haze much like the one that misted on his skin. The ground sucked at his feet and the dew on the grass stained his shoes, but Roan paid them no heed as he continued to tramp on. *What could he be hiding?* Roan was thinking of Corbin. Something wasn't right about the mysterious man. *I like him and he doesn't seem to have any bad intentions, but something about him is just... off. It's almost as if he knows something, something that's too painful to talk about. But what could it be?* Roan kept thinking about it as he stopped near the edge of the stream and stared at its rippling surface. He thought back to the flash of emotion that had crossed the old man's face when he had stopped playing. It had only been there for a fraction of a second, but Roan had seen it. Corbin had looked… sad. That was definitely it, but why?

Roan shook his head, *It's probably nothing. Besides, he'll be gone by tomorrow.* He looked more closely at the water and saw a broken reflection of himself. His image was distorted by the drops of water that dripped from the branches, his body both connected and unconnected at the same time. *I have an amazing life, but even so, I'm still just as broken as I was when I was a kid.* Corbin's presence had awakened the old feelings of closeness and family that he had missed for so long. It felt good to be with another human and share moments of connection. He felt something hard and cold melt inside of him.

He smiled and turned away from the broken and distorted image of himself, his feet following the same path that he had taken to get here. His footprints through the wet grass were dark and clearly defined against the silvery moistness. The clouds in the sky started to move more swiftly and the trees braced themselves for another onslaught. Roan started to run back to the shack, his worn shoes squelching on the muddy ground. He paused at the shed and grabbed a few pieces of wood before hurrying back toward the tree. As he did so, his mind raced with the memory of his parents that he had sealed away for so long.

A bright blue light filled the sky, followed by a blast of thunder and Roan stopped dead in his tracks. The flash of lightning opened a hidden door in his mind, emotions flooding out like water out of a busted dam. The feeling from that terrible night began to overwhelm him again; it froze him in place and forced him to relive the painful memories over and over again. The pain was multiplied with each replay and tears began to stream down his face; they burned with love, hate, sorrow, and an undying anger. He felt a cry building inside him, but he could not let it go. Instead, the scream continued to build inside of him until it writhed throughout his whole body, including the gate that held his power. He felt the cry begin to beat against the gate, begging for the strength to overcome this never-ending nightmare.

He held it back as long as he could, falling to his knees and baring his teeth in agony as he felt the pressure continue to mount. His vision grew hazy and the world around him began to swim. Then, something broke. The lock that held the gate closed split open and all of the built-up power rushed out in a fiery explosion. Roan's whole body was enveloped in blue light and the heat rushed through his arms, each blast a vibrant blue light that slashed through the grey day. Roan screamed and he felt the heat rise through his throat. This power was unlike any he had ever felt before. He closed his eyes. Then the fire escaped. It exploded out of his hands and from his throat, each fragment of flame combined into one giant fiery ball that threatened to consume everything in its path. The last bit of heat and power flowed out of Roan's body and he collapsed to the ground in a heap.

He looked up at the giant ball of fire and saw it take shape: a giant bird flying in a circle before crying out in rage and pain and heading straight for his home. Roan reached out with one hand and tried to stop it.

"No." He whispered the word hopelessly before his head dropped to the ground and the world started to fade to black. The last thing that Roan saw was a figure standing in front of the fiery creature, hands out as if he could stop it. Then everything went black.

As Roan fell into the shadowy realm of unconsciousness, the figure who stood in front of the fiery bird grimaced and braced himself. He held out his staff and reached out with his mind toward the creature. He felt the immense pain from which the beast originated and flinched. *What could have happened to that boy to create something so painful?* Corbin flicked his hand and the creature suddenly stopped, its screams muffled by the invisible barrier he had created. He swiped downwards with his staff and the barrier started to shrink. The creature screamed and pushed against its prison, but to no avail. Within a few seconds, the only thing that remained of the creature was a wisp of flame and soon enough even that was gone.

Corbin let his staff rest on the ground and wrapped himself in his cape, transforming from the proud and powerful mage to the old bard in an instant. He walked over to the charred grass and caught a glimpse of something shiny. He bent down and picked up a small rock, its surface swirled through with multiple hues of red. Corbin shook his head and looked at Roan's crumpled body. "If I had known you were that powerful, I would have said something sooner." He slid the stone into a hidden pocket in his cape and walked over to the boy. He felt Roan's forehead. It was ice cold. Corbin shivered. *So, the rumors are true, He's back.* With that thought, Corbin hurriedly gathered the boy into his arms and rushed him into the house.

Corbin put Roan on the bed and rested his hands on the boy's head. He closed his eyes and frowned. "Just hold on for a moment, Roan. I'll get you back in no time." Corbin opened his eyes, cracks that glowed light blue filled them and a white glow emanated from his hands. "You're the last hope we've got," he growled, his face grim. "I can't let my doubt end that." With those words, the glow filled the whole house and thunder roared outside. The wind whistled and the sky grew dark; the only place that had any light left was the house.

Roan jerked awake. He looked around, but his eyes could not penetrate the pitch-black blanket that surrounded him.

"Hello?" His voice echoed in the darkness and he was filled with fear.

He gulped and got up.

All he could see was darkness, but he started to walk, if only to calm his nerves. He moved carefully, not sure where he was headed, but he wouldn't stop. He pressed onward through the darkness and shivered. *Where am I? And why is it getting colder?* Whatever was happening, Roan continued to move forward and the cold grew stronger.

Then he saw something in the darkness, something so deprived of any source of light that it stood out in the shadows as a darker shadow. Roan crept toward the dark spot, his teeth chattered in the cold, and he felt the terror building inside him, but his determination was as solid as a stone pillar.

His movements became sluggish and his breath misted as he drew closer to the thing, but he still pushed forward, propelled by an unidentifiable force. Soon he was within a few feet of the thing and he could see its outline more clearly. It was a human-shaped shadow that dripped oily drops of darkness; the air around it shimmered with an intense cold.

"Hello?" Roan spoke again, but his voice came out in a whisper. His tongue felt swollen and slow, his brain was sluggish and his body felt frozen in place. The shadow seemed to flicker slightly and Roan's eyes widened. For a moment, the sense of terror that emanated from the shadow was pushed aside by pure, bright curiosity. "What are you?"

The shadow flickered again and Roan gasped. The face in front of him was his own. "What are you?" a voice emerged from the shadow. Roan's voice. The shadow stretched its jaw and rubbed its arms before looking at Roan and letting out a low cackle. "What are you?" it repeated. "I'm you. Take a good look."

Roan couldn't speak as the figure continued to stretch in front of him. *How... How is it possible? No, it can't be possible, this is just a dream.*

"I assure you, it's no dream, Roan," the figure spoke without looking up. Roan could hear his voice, familiar yet strangely altered. "And before you ask, I can hear your thoughts. You and I are two halves of the same coin."

Roan struggled to think clearly, to push away the sense of terror, and replace it with a logical explanation. He was too dumbfounded by the thing in front of him to do anything. The figure looked behind Roan and sighed, "Oh, what a bother, looks like you've got someone on the other side to get you."

Roan managed to get a look over his shoulder and saw a dim grey light filtering through the dark shadows. "Go on, I won't stop you."

Roan took the advice without a second thought and ran toward the light. The figure laughed as Roan ran and shouted after him, "We'll meet again, I'm sure. And next time you won't have someone to help you."

Roan jolted awake for the third time that day and looked around, his eyes crazed. He sighed in relief as he saw the familiar walls of his house and let his head fall back onto his pillow.

"Good. You're awake." Corbin's voice came from the other side of the house and Roan looked over at him. The old man was sitting in a chair and looked tired and worried. "We've got some things to talk about." Roan looked more closely at the man. He seemed… older.

"What do you mean?" Roan asked cautiously, still not sure if what had just happened was some sort of dream or something real.

Corbin raised an eyebrow. "You still haven't figured it out? How about I give you a little help." He closed his eyes and took a deep breath, holding it for a moment then realizing it. He opened his eyes. Roan felt more than saw an invisible veil drop from the man.

He's not hiding anymore, Roan thought, then took a sharp breath. Corbin's eyes were lined with cracks of blue lightning and a soft white glow surrounded his arms.

"Now you get it." The light faded as Corbin spoke. "Go ahead and ask your questions. I'm sure you've got a lot of them, so let's take them one at a time."

"Who are you?" Roan asked, the words spilling out of his mouth faster than he had meant for them to. "Was that a dream? What happened outside? Why is this happening now?"

Corbin gestured for him to slow down. "One at a time, one at a time." Despite the situation, a smile managed to creep across his face. "You remind me of someone I knew a long, long time ago. First off, I'm like you only much, much older."

"What do you mean like me?"

Corbin shook his head. "Don't play dumb, Roan. We both can access powers that normal people can't, powers that the common folk knows as magic - powers that not even the oldest and wisest fully understand." He stared at Roan. "Do you know what I'm talking about or do you want more of a history lesson?"

Roan shook his head. "No, but why didn't you say something sooner?"

Corbin sighed. "That's a long story."

"Tell me."

"I don't know if that's the best idea, but…" Corbin

grabbed his beard thoughtfully, "...but it might be the best way to explain things. Are you sure you want to hear it?"

Roan nodded, too unsure of his voice to answer properly.

"Fine." Corbin nodded to himself. "How to start, how to start. It all began eons ago...

When the world was first made, the ancient gods filled it with the power to create life. Deep inside its crust, they released rivers of power. These rivers led to the creation of life. From the tallest trees to the smallest mouse, every living being came from the power the ancient gods released.

At first, all creatures had access to these deep veins of power and the world was full of fantastic and mystical things, but it couldn't last forever. Over time, the gods became dormant. Eventually, the only one left to watch over the world was the moon. She realized that without the other gods the power would ultimately diminish into nothing, so she closed off the places where the magic bubbled to the surface.

There were a few races that held strong ties to the

power and could still access it, even though it was sealed away. Even within these races, the ability to use magic was not something that all could do. The skill was passed down through generations; certain bloodlines could channel the power through their own will.

As time passed, a place for all young mages to train and hone their abilities was created, a place to the north marked by a circle of standing stones. There, many went to discover new ways to learn how to control their power and keep it in balance with nature. But it couldn't last forever.

The greed of the creatures of this world eventually won; their lust for power drove them to find ways to cheat the system and break the balance. It was during this time that both the world's greatest hero and its most evil foe were born. Both of them were sent to the college of magic and trained in the ways to control their power, both at the top of their class. Through the college, they met and formed a bond of friendship. Together their power was nigh on unstoppable. Their names were Corbin and Railin.

As they aged and exhausted the knowledge of even the most learned mages of the college, Railin grew bored of his position and searched in secret for ways to reach new levels of power. These secret channels of power had been prohibited because of their extreme danger and the threat they posed to the balance of power.

Meanwhile, Corbin pursued different arts. He learned to be an expert swordsman and a great bard. The satisfaction of these pursuits tempered his desire for a deeper understanding of the power of the ancient gods.

Railin's lust for power seemed insatiable. Railin could not understand Corbin's complacency; Corbin distrusted Railin's aggressive and risky search for ever more power.

As the years wore on, the friendship between the two waxed and waned, but always it remained true at its core. Even though the two had chosen different paths, they remained connected and shared a deep affection for each other.

Railin finally discovered something profound in his research. He was eager to share it with Corbin. He quickly rushed to his friend and told him that he had found a way to infinite power, power beyond anything in this world. Corbin dismissed it as a fantasy, but Railin insisted that what he had found was true.

What did he find, you ask?

Railin had found a way to contact one of the old

gods, The God of Darkness. He went by many names: The Dark One, The Forbidden, The Black Beast, and so on. The most well-known name was The Shadow King.

The Shadow King had been sealed away by the other gods when they created the world because he had only been interested in covering it with shadows and darkness. He had been the most powerful of the ancient gods and they had only managed to seal him away with luck and cunning from the great goddess of the moon. Together, they had lured him into a realm full of darkness and shadows, closing any way for him to get back. However, over the years he had managed to find the weakest point in the barrier and had influenced men into creating a way to release him.

Railin had discovered the ritual that would release the dark lord. Nothing could stop him from fulfilling his hunt for power. He told Corbin where he planned to go and what he intended to do before leaving. Try as he might, Corbin could not dissuade Railin from his chosen path.

Corbin had scoffed at the idea at first, but as time wore on and he saw no sign of Railin, he set off to find his friend. It was too late. By the time Corbin reached the spot where the Railin promised the ritual would take place, Railin had just finished the last spell. Corbin saw his friend swallowed in a wave of darkness. The power of the transformation cast him into the nearby forest. That blast had saved his life, but when Corbin awoke from his fall and rushed back to the college, he found it in ruins.

The Shadow King had been set loose on the world and his reign had only started. Corbin saw the cloud of shadows spread over the land and was consumed by an unreasonable rage. He did the only thing he could think of and started a rebellion. The rebellion worked in secret, driving the minions of the Shadow King from the land one by one. Corbin exerted all of his knowledge of the power of the ancient gods in his attempt to defeat the threat that his friend had brought into their world.

Many brave men and women died for his cause, but in the end, they managed to reach the Shadow King's castle. After suffering heavy casualties, Corbin ordered the last of his army to retreat and took on the remaining Shadow King's warriors before he met the dark lord face to face.

They fought long and hard. Both were powerful, but the Shadow King wasn't a mortal. Corbin realized that he stood no chance against this great enemy and threw all of his remaining strength into creating a seal to imprison the Shadow King and save his people for the time being.

He wove a spell that held the Shadow King in his own dark realm long enough for new heroes to arise and gain the strength necessary to defeat him. Corbin also tied his own life to their course, offering it as an energy source to hold the monster back. When he died, the Shadow King would fully awaken from his slumber and the world would be tossed into darkness once again unless the heroes could defeat the king.

It was a risky path, but Corbin knew it was the only chance they had to save the world.

Roan looked at Corbin, still entranced by the story for a minute before closing his mouth and starting to process things. "So, you're telling me that you're the same Corbin from the story?"

The old man nodded, not looking up.

"And I'm one of the heroes?"

Again, Corbin nodded.

"So, the Shadow King must be coming back."

"Yes," Corbin replied softly, as if he was afraid.

Roan shook his head. "This morning I wouldn't have believed you, but now I'm not so sure. What was that dream?"

"It wasn't a dream. You visited the Shadow Realm."

"Why?"

"Long ago, the gods decided that anyone who tried to use too much power would have to visit the Shadow Realm. It is a place where mortals repay their debts of power, and it maintains the balance in the world."

Roan nodded slowly. "When I was there, I saw something."

Corbin looked up, curious. "What did you see?"

"I saw a creature made of shadows that looked exactly like me. He knew my name and spoke as if he knew everything about me. As if he was me."

Corbin was quiet for some time. "I'm not sure what it was, but I'm sure that it's some sort of trick the Shadow King has made. A trick to create doubt, an obstacle to block you. He knows how to master the weaknesses of his enemies, to use them against themselves. Railin..." Corbin's voice drifted to silence and he looked down at his hands again. Roan saw a drop fall from his eyes.

"He was like your family, wasn't he? Railin, I mean." Roan spoke softly and kindly and Corbin nodded, his face still turned down.

Roan grimaced as he pushed himself out of bed and walked over to the old man. "I know how it feels to watch those you care about disappear while you sit there unable to do anything." He sat next to Corbin and thought back to his family. "I suppose that's the reason I lost control today, I couldn't keep it bottled up anymore." They both sat there in introspective silence, the only noise the storm raging outside.

Finally, Corbin looked up, his face red, and stared at the opposing wall. "I'm sorry about your family. They must have meant a lot to you."

Roan nodded. "They did, but it's no use thinking about it now. Nothing can change the past."

"True, but we can change what will happen in the future."

"What do you mean?"

Corbin rose from the chair and turned to look at Roan. "We can stop anyone else from feeling like that. You are one of the ones who can defeat the Shadow King, I'm sure of it. I can help train you to become stronger, maybe even strong enough to save the world, with a little luck. Maybe more than a little. What do you say?" Corbin held out his hand and his eyes glinted with steely determination and the grin of someone who loves a good challenge.

Roan looked at the hand for a moment then up at Corbin's determined gaze and set his face in a hard grin. "Let's do it."

He reached out and shook Corbin's hand. Outside, lightning struck and thunder rolled throughout the land.

III:

The Girl and the Wolf

Rain gusted down in torrents and shook a small house in the woods; it left the house's very foundations beaten and worn. It buffeted the trees and they groaned as they tried to ride out the storm, the undergrowth huddled underneath the branches as it tried to escape the worst of the gale.

Inside the house, a young girl paced back and forth nervously as she waited for the storm to move on. She had fair skin and light brown hair; her eyes glittered green and she wore tomboy clothes. She muttered to herself and chewed at her nails as she looked at the surrounding trees in between lightning strikes. The forest stood its ground and did its best to protect both the animals and plants that roamed underneath its canopy, including the girl in the house, Lyria.

Lyria looked fitfully at the fire as the wind pummeled it, the flames twitching and dimming as the storm grew stronger. She kneaded her hands together and stared at the flames, putting together a prayer as she did so. *Oh, Goddess of the Moon, watch over the fire and please, please, please don't let it go out. I can't stand to be in the dark when the wind knocks on the door like that.*

Another boom of thunder shook the house, followed by a blast of wind. "Please don't go out!" Lyria implored, her voice barely a whisper over the wind that attacked the house. The fire flickered again as the chill wind shook the house. It was dying. The last of the flames licked dully at the wood and slowly grew dim as wet air crept down the chimney.

"NO!" cried Lyria as the wind battered the house once more and the fire blinked out.

The house was left in darkness, the last of the embers quickly quenched by the mist-filled air that rushed into the hearth. Lyria shook, partly from cold and partly from fear, her only defense from both stripped away. She felt a tear begin to roll down her cheek and quickly wiped it away, not wanting the darkness to see her fright. *My only chance now is to be brave - I have to find a way to beat the darkness.* As she finished her thought, a bolt of lightning flashed down from the sky and Lyria leaped back in fear. For a moment, shadows loomed out at her from all around the room and then they disappeared, swallowed by the absolute darkness that filled the house. Outside, thunder rolled across the forest and Lyria gulped; her fear increased exponentially from the lightning strike.

She felt her mind go numb as fear began to cut its way deep into her. She forced herself to move, to try and find a way to defeat the bodiless darkness. She felt her way toward the hearth and reached blindly for the mantle. The room was lit again in a flash of light and Lyria gritted her teeth before making a panicked move in the direction of the mantle.

Gotcha! She grabbed onto the ledge and grasped at the invisible objects on top. Thunder rattled the house and her teeth ground against each other, but she still pursued her objective. She came across many objects in her search for light: old deer antlers, a deck of cards, multiple spider webs, and at least one rock from the collection of her younger days. *What was I thinking when I picked up these stupid rocks?* she asked herself as she fumbled across the third one in a row. *Well, I guess*

I never thought they'd get in my way when a storm blew out the fire and the whole world turned dark.

Finally, her hand struck the thing she had been searching for: a metal tinderbox. She quickly grasped the box and pulled it close to her chest. She dropped to the floor and carefully unboxed the tinder, flint, and steel, her hands a shaky mess as she did so. *I wish that Da was here, then the dark wouldn't be so scary.* Lyria pulled away from the thought and focused on making some sort of light source. She set the tinder on the ground and did her best to fluff it up. She struck the flint and steel. The first result she got was a sharp pain in her knuckles. "AHHH!" she yelled and almost dropped the flint as she practically threw her hand to her mouth where she proceeded to nurse the wound for a few seconds.

After another few rounds of lightning and thunder, Lyria felt that her finger had healed enough to have a try at the flint and steel again. She very carefully went through multiple practice runs, trying to improve her aim in the darkness. Another flash of lightning filled the house with light, startling her and causing her to drop the flint. She scrabbled about with her fingers on the rough floorboards, located the flint, and went back to work. At last, she took a deep breath and did her best to calm her nerves before she glared into the dark and struck the flint and steel together firmly. A shower of sparks greeted her and she whimpered in glee, the shower falling easily into the tinder. A glowing ember appeared and Lyria coaxed it gently into a flame.

I have to find something to light. As the idea came to her, the panic from before returned and she looked around frantically. The dim light from the small flame revealed a candle standing on the table nearby. Lyria sprinted to the table and grabbed the candle, nearly slipping as she raced back to the flame.

She fell to her knees near the flame and quickly pushed the wick of the candle into the small ember. Her features relaxed as the fire spread easily to the wick. She sighed and set the candle down on the ground. The tinder flared brightly for a second, then exhausted its fuel and went out. *Just in time.*

Lyria looked away from the ashy remains of the tinder and around the partially illuminated house. She felt her fear slowly fade as the warm light of the candle created a small circle of light, able to fight back the darkness that had seemed so threatening before. At the edge of the light, shadows danced back and forth, but they always stayed just far enough away that Lyria felt safe.

The storm raged on outside and the night grew darker and more frightening, but nothing could touch Lyria. She sat and ate an apple she had found on the mantle. Lightning struck again and again, still as close as it had been hours ago. *I wonder how much longer this storm will go on. I hope Da didn't get caught in it.* She shivered at the thought of her dad stuck in the terrible weather outside.

Another bolt of lightning struck and something creaked momentarily before it was muffled by the thunder. Lyria looked around nervously for the source of the noise and saw a distinct shadow slip through the door, quickly blending into the rest of the dark room. Suddenly, Lyria's candle seemed less comforting.

She turned in circles, her eyes searching the darkness for any sign of movement. Time passed slowly. She gulped, not wanting to accept the inevitable fact that if she wanted any sort of comfort, she would have to look for the creature. The candle had already burned to half its size. *It's now or never.* Lyria took the candle and began to search the house. She moved from corner to corner, her gut writhing in terror as she moved onward. The light of the flame licked the walls as she passed by and she saw a familiar painting hanging on the wall. Despite the desperate situation, she couldn't help but pause and glance at the painting.

It was a family picture, sketched by one of her father's close friends. Her father was tall and proud while her mother stood shyly in the background, a warm smile on her face. Lyria was in between them; her head reached her father's stomach and her mousy brown hair fell to her shoulders. Her face was full of fiery determination - as many short people's faces are, and she smiled defiantly. *I haven't changed much since then,* Lyria thought to herself and let a smile flit across her face. Her smile quickly changed to a frown as she thought of her father, *I hope he gets back safely from barding in Galleon.* She sent a quick prayer to the goddess before she returned to the job at hand. Her stomach churned once again as she approached the second to last corner hidden in shadows.

The light filtered through the darkness and revealed nothing in the corner. Lyria was both relieved and terrified at the same time. *That means whatever it is must be in the last corner.* As she thought it, another bolt of electricity sent out a flash of light that lit up the house and revealed a huge shadow standing in the corner. Lyria gulped and swallowed her fear. *I am not afraid, I am brave. I am not afraid, I am brave. I am...* She repeated the same lines over and over as she walked slowly to her certain doom. The edge of the candle's light flicked closer and closer to the place Lyria had seen the shadow and her heartbeat quickened. She closed her eyes for a second and made a prayer to the goddess of the moon, her feet moving slowly forward. When she opened her eyes again, she screamed.

The scream split the night. Even the rain seemed to stop pounding on the roof as the cry echoed through the darkness. In front of Lyria stood a massive wolf, two glowing orbs shimmered from its face in hues of green as they reflected the fire. They seemed to hold deep wisdom and intelligence greater than she had seen in any other animal. It was almost as though the wolf knew something that she didn't. Those eyes made her even more afraid than she already was.

The beast's head was level with Lyria's shoulder and his body easily filled the large corner of the house. Along with the already enormous body, the wolf's tail stretched far behind it into the shadows and its mouth looked large enough to comfortably fit Lyria's entire head inside. Its coat was a ruddy brown, patched with lighter maroon splotches. To call it frightening would be an insult: it was a combination of beauty and terror.

Lyria couldn't move as the wolf continued to stare at her, its deadly gaze a trap that held her in place. She gulped as she waited for the end to come, but nothing happened. The wolf didn't charge at her and bite off her head. It didn't try to attack her or even take any aggressive action at all. Instead, it only cocked its head to the side slightly and seemed to be trying to make a decision. *What is it doing?* Lyria's mind had started to thaw out of the terror that held her frozen in place. *Why is it letting me live?*

An interesting question. The thought startled Lyria, as it wasn't something she had come up with on her own. *I suppose you'll find that out soon enough.*

What is happening? Who is in my head? Lyria thought frantically as her eyes flitted around the room for some source of these insane thoughts.

That would be me. The wolf grinned and Lyria fought against her fear as she saw its massive teeth.

"Calm down, you have to be brave, Lyria," she whispered out loud to herself as she thought about the situation. *Who could he be talking about?*

You humans really are as dense as they say, aren't

you? Who is the only other creature in the room? Realization dawned and Lyria looked at the wolf her curiosity outweighing her fear. *There you go,* the wolf grinned again

"You mean you're the big, scary, terrifying wolf in my house?" She knew the answer already, but couldn't bring herself to believe it.

The wolf snorted. *No, I'm the horse that fell down the chimney. Of course I'm the wolf, and my name is Ferox.*

"Ok, then, if you're the wolf, prove it."

How?

"Lift your right paw."

The wolf growled. *This is unnecessary. You already know that what I've told you is true.* Lyria didn't respond and the wolf sighed. *Fine, I'll do it.* It lifted its right paw and stared at Lyria. *Happy now?*

Lyria had been prepared for the movement, but she was still stunned. "Yep."

You seem surprised.

"Yep."

Ferox yawned and settled onto the floor. *This is gonna be a long night.*

"Yep."

Is that all you can say?

"Yep."

Ferox sighed. *Well, I guess now's as good a time as ever to tell you why I'm here.* He looked lazily at Lyria. *It all started with a prophecy. Long ago, eons before the days of your father's father, an evil shadow of a king ruled the land…* Ferox proceeded to recite the rest of the prophecy while Lyria sat in stunned silence, the information not yet absorbing into her mind. *And so the darkness left this land for a time. Do you understand?*

Lyria slowly shook her head. "I don't think I do."

Ferox looked at her, his jaw fell open and his tongue rolled out. *One of mind. Doesn't ring any bells?*

Deep inside Lyria's mind, something started to stir, but she still couldn't make heads or tails of what the wolf had said. "Nope, I can't think of anything that sounds like that."

You mean you've never noticed that you aren't like other people?

"Well, I haven't been around many people. Mostly just my Da and my Ma when she was around." She tilted her head thoughtfully. "Although I guess that having a conversation with a wild animal isn't exactly normal, is it?"

It most definitely is not. There are few humans left that could hear me the way you do. Ferox stretched on the floor. *And I'm sure you've had other odd experiences that would come to mind if you would stop to think about them.*

He was right. Lyria thought back to when she was a kid and had felt the pain of trees as they were cut down, her ability to always know how others felt even if she didn't know them, and times with her Da when she had felt like she knew exactly what he was going to say before he said it. In fact, that happened so frequently that it was a sort of joke between the two of them. "I guess you're right, but I still don't see what the prophecy has to do with me."

Ferox snorted. *One of mind. You are one of the five that are meant to stop the Shadow King.*

Finally, the words penetrated Lyria's frozen brain and her eyes widened.

"No way." The words were barely audible as Lyria looked down at her hands in disbelief. "No way," she said louder this time. "I mean, why would it be me? There are plenty of people who would be better for the job. Da, he would be the right choice. Not me, I'm just a kid." She felt a new emotion in her mind and quickly looked up at

Ferox to see his head downcast and his features melancholy and ashamed. “What?”

It’s… It’s your father. We tried to reach him first, to warn him about what was to come, but… we were too late.

Lyria felt her body go cold and she looked at the wolf, hoping against hope that it wasn’t what she thought it was. “What do you mean too late?”

Ferox refused to look at her as he spoke. *When we found him, he was already gone, taken by the Shadow King. I’m sorry. There was nothing we could do.*

Lyria went numb for a moment, then felt rage building inside her. “No. NO! You’re lying! Da can’t be gone! You’re wrong!” She fell to her knees and clutched at her head, barely holding in the tears that threatened to spring forth. “You’re wrong,” she whispered, but deep down she knew the truth.

Lyria, I--

She interrupted Ferox by throwing a command toward him, so sharply that she could sense the echoes of it in his mind: *SHOW ME.*

Ferox whined, backed away, and pawed uselessly at his muzzle.

Show me or I’ll tear it from you. SHOW ME!

Ferox relented and opened his mind to her icy presence.

Lyria ripped wildly through memories as she searched for anything about her dad. She tore apart childhood memories and left behind stories of hunting with the pack. She recklessly carved a path straight through Ferox's mind in the hunt for her father - then she saw it. A picture of her father was in one corner of the room full of Ferox's life. She pushed her way to it, tears streaming down her face as she approached. She reached out and touched the memory and was teleported away from the room full of thoughts.

Everything was different here. She didn't inhabit her body or her thoughts. Instead, she had become Ferox. She felt graceful as her body moved from side to side and smelled a thousand new smells, her senses almost overwhelmed as she struggled to adapt to this new perspective. Her body moved without her control and the world blurred with new colors and smells. She felt very far away from herself, as if Lyria was a faint memory unrelated to her. She sensed the danger of losing herself in this new realm. *I have to stay focused.*

Pay attention. I'm here to look for Lyria's Da - my Da. She forced herself to take a closer look at her surroundings.

She was at the edge of the forest, the dim lights of a town just barely visible. In front of her was a small clearing filled with shadows and swirling fog, but there was something else. With her newly heightened senses, she smelled something dark and foul. Her hair stood on end and she growled. Something at the edge of the clearing shifted and she saw a dark figure slip quietly into the shadows and disappear.

Lyria felt the foul presence and smell she had sensed moments ago fade away and she cautiously made her way into the clearing. Fog obscured much of her view, but a faint whiff of something unfamiliar stood in the air. Death. She slowly searched the clearing until she found the source of the smell: a dried-up corpse. She walked toward it and her heart dropped. It was her father. Even in his mummified state, she recognized his face. *Da... Da, Da I-I...* Lyria felt the memory slip away and the burst of energy that had coursed through her fade back into the unknown place it had come from. She slid quietly out of Ferox's mind and back into her own body, her mind shattered by what she had seen.

Time passed around Lyria. She had curled into a ball and hid her mind from anything that could hurt her. Ferox tried to nuzzle and coax her out of the stunned state into which she had fallen, but she had managed to shut her mind off from him, so he eventually retreated and left her to figure it out on her own.

He's gone, he's really gone. I don't even know what to do. What is my world without him? The storm continued to beat relentlessly against the house and thunder boomed through the forest, but nothing could penetrate the shell around Lyria.

After an hour had passed, Ferox tried again. *Lyria? Can you hear me?* Lyria refused to respond. *I know it must be hard, but we have to go. You are more important than you could ever imagine - without you, everyone will suffer the same fate as your father.* Lyria shifted and Ferox pressed his advantage. *Do you think that he would want you to stay here and mourn him while you could save countless others? What do you think he would want?*

Lyria shifted again and whispered, "No. He'd want me to keep moving. To do my best to help others, to honor his memory not with sorrow but with joy and adventure." She looked at Ferox, her face stained with tears. "Besides, I'm not the only one who lost someone I care about."

Ferox cocked his head cautiously. Lyria smiled kindly and reached out to pat his head. "I know about your family. Your mother and father killed by a dark shadow, and your sister stolen by traders. What right do I have to stay here and complain when you've gone through so much and you're more determined than ever to push on?"

How do you know? Ferox was so baffled and stunned, the thought was barely able to form in his mind.

"I saw them when I was in your head."

Ferox stared incredulously at the girl, his composure broken for a moment. Then he growled and shook his head. *That was very rude. You shouldn't look at others' memories without their permission.*

Lyria made a face. "Sorry, but that's the first time I've done anything like that. How was I supposed to know?"

Ferox snorted. *Fine, but just be glad that I'm forgiving, otherwise you'd be dead.* He paused and looked closely at Lyria.

She noticed the odd stare. "What is it?"

Something is different about you, but I don't quite know what it is. He looked again then understanding filled his face. *It's your eyes. They're different.*

"How so?"

They have... sparks in them, little blue flecks floating down like falling leaves.

"Really?" Lyria looked around the room for something in which to catch her reflection and saw the small silver hand mirror her mother had left. She stood up and hurried over to the mirror, her mind buzzing with curiosity as she stared at her reflection in the dim light. Sure enough, small blue leaf-like sparks floated lazily around her green eyes. "Wow," she whispered to herself. "It's pretty. What is it?"

I'm not sure, but I know someone who can tell you the answer to that and more.

Lyria flipped around and looked excitedly at Ferox, "Who?"

I don't know his name, but he is the king of the forest and one of the oldest beings on the earth. He was the one who told me who and what you are. I am supposed to take you back to him.

Lyria felt the melancholy that filled her heart fade away, gradually replaced by curiosity. Impulsively, she said, “Let’s go.”

Ferox nodded and paused, listening intently. *There’s a break in the storm, let’s go while we can.* The wolf quickly turned and headed out of the door, Lyria close behind him.

As they stepped out of the front door, Lyria paused and looked back into her old home one last time. She felt a tear roll gently down her face before she turned away and followed Ferox into the forest, her body tingling with excitement at the idea of an adventure.

IV:

Orphans Lost in a Storm

Whap, a heavy boot landed hard against James' side and he wheezed as the boot's owner spoke. "You just don't get it, do you? Whenever you stand up to Freda, it's not just you that gets punished, it's all of us." The voice belonged to Marvin, an older boy at the orphanage where James lived.

James coughed and gulped for air before he managed to wheeze out a response. "I have… to stand… up to her… because if I don't--"

"Let me guess, 'who will?'" another boy from the group that surrounded James said. "Well, the answer is no one. If we leave her alone, then she leaves us alone, simple as that."

"I won't let her break me," said James firmly before collapsing in a fit of coughing.

"Ugh," groaned Marvin. "Are you gonna go into

another of those damned speeches about pride and honor? Well, let me stop you right here. It might not seem like it, but we're doing you a favor right now. Get him, boys." With that, the majority of the group proceeded to kick and beat James; they left him bloody and bruised before they walked away.

James groaned and winced as he breathed. He picked himself up off the cobblestone sidewalk and limped back toward the orphanage. This was his third beating in a week. He wasn't well-liked by the other kids. He saw his reflection in a puddle on the side of the street and couldn't help but chuckle. His face was bruised and cut and his eye was swollen, but his head of fiery red hair still fought back. It stuck out jaggedly from his scalp as if in defiance at being attached to such a grimy boy. *You and me both,* James thought as he let his gaze drift away from the reflection, his eyes glittering their deep hazel brown.

A small creature ran squeaking from the shadows and leaped onto James' arm, crawling up to his shoulder, following the same path it always did. James managed a half-hearted smile. "Glad to see that you still want to be my friend, Henry." The mouse settled down on his shoulder and sat there like a bird. James pet the creature before he turned back to the journey home. He winced as he took a breath. “They got me good this time, Henry. Must’ve broken a few ribs.” Henry chittered a reprimand back at him and James smiled.

“I don’t know why you keep that thing around.” The voice came from the dark of an alleyway.

“Well, at least he does his best to help me. He doesn’t hide in the shadows ‘till the fight’s over.” James looked sternly at his friend before he sighed. “But I’m glad you’re here now, Kael.”

“I’m sorry, James,” said Kael and looked at his feet, hands behind his back. “You know that I’m not like you. I would’ve broke the first time that Marvin even looked at me the way he looks at you.”

“I don’t want to hear it. All that matters is that you show up just in time to carry me home after my beatings.” James coughed and clutched at his side as the effects of the beating manifested themselves. “Could you help me back? It's getting late and I don’t think that having Freda whip some sense into me would go well in combination with this afternoon’s event.” Kael smiled then quietly walked over and put James’ arm around his shoulder. Together they limped through the city, similar in appearance save for Kael’s black hair and James’ fiery locks.

They passed throngs of people making the last rounds of the trading booths, barely noticed by anyone. They would only get the occasional disgusted or annoyed look from a particularly snobby rich child who would turn and strut away after they had seen the boys. James looked at Kael and grinned. "I know your face is scary, but not that scary."

Kael laughed. "You're one to talk. You look like you just got in a fight with an alley rat." He cocked his head and considered what he had said. "Well, I guess that's kinda true."

They both chuckled before turning back to the task at hand. Years of sneaking through the marketplace made it easy enough for them to slip through the crowded streets. Little if any attention was paid to them as they traveled to the edge of the market place and toward the orphanage. The people of Arrdell were used to urchins like James and Kael walking around and paid them little heed.

As they continued, James' thoughts wandered away from the present and back to the good old days. He remembered times before he had come to the orphanage, times when he had been happier, times before men had gone through the city collecting all of the kids they could find as a "service to the people." All of the do-gooders were just in it for the money. A rich merchant had become fed up with portions of his product being stolen daily and had hired thugs to catch those responsible. The men had worn black suits and carried cudgels. "To help the uncooperative understand," they said. James shook his head slowly and let his memory drift farther back, away from any thought of his capture.

He thought back to his time on the street, living day to day with no one to depend on except for himself and Henry. The mouse had been with him longer than anything else in his life. One of the beggars he had known told him once that he had never seen an animal as attached to someone as Henry was to James. Henry had been the first friend James had found after he ran away from the foster home he had been in, a terrible family that believed children were only good for work. He had been crying in an alleyway, hungry, tired, and sick of life when he heard something squeaking. He opened his eyes and saw a mouse crouched timidly in front of him. "Hi there," he had said. "What's your name?" The mouse had squeaked out a reply and James smiled. "Come here, little guy," he said as he wiped tears from his face. The mouse moved forward and James smiled. "I'm gonna call you Henry."

From that day forward, the two had been inseparable. They were partners in crime, each able to get more than enough to eat as they raided trading stands and food carts. Henry would distract the merchant and James would snatch apples by the dozen, baskets of bread, and pocketfuls of hard candy. The world was their playground and they loved every minute of it, backstreet kings through and through. Not only were they successful when they looked for food, but also when they searched for valuables. Many rich men and women had lost jewelry and pocket change back in those days, and with this newfound source of income, James and Henry created their home. They found an abandoned house and set up camp on the roof, creating a beautiful patchwork home that kept them warm and dry in the winter.

Then the men had come.

James shivered as he remembered the time. *It's all their fault. If they hadn't taken us away, then we would still be happy.* He remembered the men in suits had barged into the house and onto the roof, his roof, and proceed to drag James down into the street.

"Shut up, brat," one of them said. "We're doing this for your own good. Don't you want a nice warm place to stay with a happy and reliable caretaker?" The rest of the men had laughed and cuffed James if he tried to respond, the reality of his situation all too painfully obvious.

That day, he had been taken to Madame Freda's Home for Lost Children.

James let out a dry chuckle at how naive he had been. Now he truly understood and appreciated how much three years could change a person. Kael looked over at him with questioning eyes. James grinned at him and said, "You remember when they dragged me here, all that time ago?"

"Yeah..." responded Kael cautiously. "What about it?"

"Oh, I was just thinking about how you looked at me back then, almost like I was some sort of animal." Kael smiled nervously and James patted his shoulder. "Well, you weren't wrong. A lot has happened since then and when I look back, I can't help but think about what I could have done differently."

"I think that's something that we all do," said Kael thoughtfully. "Even if it's pointless to think about changing the past, we all do it for some reason or another. For example, just today I was thinking about how smart it would have been to skip dinner last night." He smiled shyly and let his hair fall in front of his face.

James grinned and nodded. "You're right. I think if I'd have skipped that terrible meal, I'd have felt less hungry today." Kael chuckled and James let his joke take a home run. "To tell you the truth, I think the dirt is better for you than that mystery slop." James laughed at his own joke and winced, clutching his side as he did so.

"Careful, you don't want your terrible sense of humor to kill you before Freda does." Kael grinned and playfully cuffed at James' ear. "Besides, I don't know what Henry would do if you died from a coughing fit."

"He'd probably go crazy," said James as he punched back. The two laughed and fell into companionable silence as they approached the ominous orphanage. The closer they drew, the more distant Kael became. James noticed his friend withdraw and felt the silence gather around them. He sighed quietly to himself. *This place is killing both of us,* he thought sadly as he watched the part of Kael that he liked slowly disappear behind barriers. "One day I'm getting both of us out of here, I swear," James said, his tone serious and sure. Henry squeaked from James' shoulder as he cried in outrage at the thought of being left behind. "Of course you'll come with - it would probably be impossible to leave you. You'd find some sort of way to get to me." The mouse nuzzled James' face fondly and squeaked happily.

A little bit of the real Kael showed again as a small grin flashed across his face. "If you ever figure out a way that we can both get out of here and still live to tell the tale, let me know."

Before James could say anything, the boys were interrupted by a scratchy, high-pitched screech that almost passed for a voice.

"Where have you been?"

It was Freda.

The two boys snapped to attention, not eager to receive any extra punishment for being inattentive. Freda's face was so wrinkled that it was difficult to tell if she was smiling or frowning. In fact, she never smiled, so it was safe to assume that her grimace was a frown. She wore a dress with an old and tattered checker pattern, barely able to hide the sinewy and boney body beneath it.

"We finished our work for the day and went out for an afternoon stroll, ma'am," Kael offered. He looked at the floor and his voice fell into a submissive tone.

"Finished your work... Well then, I guess you never thought to report it to me, did you? I had so much more for each of you to do." Freda glared at both of them. Then she chose her target. "Kael, you will get five lashes for your foolishness."

"No, ma'am," said James politely. He stepped forward and did his best to hold himself upright as he spoke. "It's not his fault. I told him that you wouldn't mind it if we left for an hour or two. If you're going to punish one of us, you might as well punish the right person."

"What are you doing?" hissed Kael out of the side of his mouth at James. "You've already been beat up once tonight."

"I'm being a good friend."

After she thought about it for a minute, Freda finally came to a decision. "You know what, I am in a good mood today. Since you were honest with me, I'll let you go without a whipping this time."

Both of the boys were stunned and could only manage a meager "Thank you, Madame." They had never heard of Freda being in a good mood and looked dubiously at each other. They walked off toward the bedroom, the sun covered by a line of dark, moist, intimidating clouds behind them. They continued on in silence, awed at the mercy they had just received. They passed the kitchen and mess hall before they walked up a flight of stairs and reached the sleeping level. The room was abuzz with conversation as the boys got ready to sleep. The day's activities finally caught up with James and Kael and they plopped like rocks onto the bed they shared.

"Did you hear?" asked a boy sitting next to James. "Freda just scored a little extra money by making a deal with a slaver passing through. She's gonna sell him two kids."

James looked at Kael in utter terror. He knew Freda never let kids go without punishment.

"You don't think…" said Kael, his face suddenly ashen.

"I think we need to find a way out - tonight," said James quietly. He looked toward the one window in the bedroom and thought for a moment. A clap of thunder shook the house and an idea came to his mind. "I have a plan, but you're not gonna like it."

At dinner that night, the boys stole as much food as

they could, each discreet in his own actions and aware of what a lack of food would mean in the long run. They went to bed with the rest of the boys as the full force of the storm hit. Rain pounded on the window and wind dashed itself against the house; it was perfect for what James had planned.

As the night wore on, James felt his tension grow. His need for sleep was replaced with bursts of adrenaline and nerves. *What if they catch us? What if it doesn't work? What if...? What if...?* He did his best to shake off the thoughts as the time approached. Finally, when he heard what he thought was the clock striking midnight, he rose silently from his bed and looked over to see Kael do the same. In the dark, they stuffed their pockets with scraps of food and wrapped their blankets around their thin bodies.

The boys looked at each other and nodded before they made their careful way toward the window. Henry rode silently in James' front pocket as they prepared for escape.

James carefully unlatched the window and slid it open a crack; a cold gust of air and rain rushed in, and he shivered. Both of the boys hurried out of the window and onto the slippery edge beyond. Quietly, they shut the window as best they could behind them. James motioned for Kael to follow him up to the slate tiled roof, his heart racing as he was buffeted by gusts of wind. Kael followed close behind, carefully placing each of his feet on the slippery slate. James led the way to a drain pipe. His teeth chattered as the rain penetrated through his clothes and the cold made its way deep into his bones.

Even with the fear, James couldn't help but feel a sort of excitement rush through his body. He had always loved storms and even the terror of falling to his death couldn't take away that love.

They reached the drain and James turned back to see how Kael was holding up. Kael reached his side and gave a shaky thumbs up. "I'll go first," Kael yelled through the wind.

James nodded. He had to squint to see his friend's blurry image in the heavy rain. Kael slowly lowered himself over the edge and James lost all sight of him. All he could do was hope that Kael made it down safely as the storm intensified and threatened to blow him off the roof. He waited for a few seconds before he started to crawl over the edge. He gripped the slippery wood and slate as he lowered himself and grabbed onto the metal pipe with all his strength. The metal was cold and slimy;

James shivered as he started his terrifying descent.

The storm buffeted him as he slowly inched his way down the pipe, each gust a death threat. As he neared the halfway point, a series of gusts threatened to knock him to the ground. He held on for dear life, his hands white as they clutched desperately at the metal pipe. *Don't break* was all he could think as he felt the metal bend and groan beneath his hand.

The barrage of wind let up soon enough and he continued his slow descent, each of his breaths shallow and full of fear. After what felt like hours, he finally felt the ground beneath his feet. James leaped swiftly off the slick metal and made a prayer to the moon as he checked to see if Henry was still safe. The mouse's squeak was barely audible in the rest of the thunderstorm and James patted Henry's head.

"What now?" Kael yelled over the storm. James turned to look at the blurry figure.

"We should head out of town. They'll be looking for us."

Kael motioned his agreement and the two pushed their way through the muddy streets toward the edge of the town. Lightning flashed nearby and thunder echoed, but despite the chaos, James didn't feel afraid. He felt alive. Every muscle in his body was primed and ready for action, his mind was fully active and he felt the adrenaline pumping through his veins. *I've never felt this good! I wonder how Kael is doing.* James turned to look at his friend and saw a flash of teeth as Kael grinned back at him. James smiled and looked up at the sky. Lightning flashed across the sky in a dance with the gusts of wind and rain, the thunder a constant beat in the background.

Finally, they reached the outskirts of town. James paused to look up at the sky, mesmerized by the controlled chaos above him. A meadow opened before them, bordered on one side by the last of the houses. Kael moved along the edge of the meadow, his shoulders hunched into the storm. Before James could follow him, a rush of memories filled his mind: beatings from Freda and the other orphans, the men invading his home, watching Kael endure constant abuse.

I won't be that helpless ever again, he vowed to himself. He lifted his head toward the rumbling sky. Rain pelted his face. Lightning flashed and he felt a new, bright power course through his veins. Without thinking, he found his arms outstretched to either side. He felt a tingling sensation all over his body and heard the crackle of electricity jump around him. The power rushed under his skin, and a deep instinct told him to release the power, to let all his pain and frustration disappear in an instant. He opened his eyes and pushed the power through every pore. He screamed in joy and pain as a booming thunder engulfed his mind and, for an instant, the world was gone.

In that instant, he understood the path they must take. After the release of energy, he quickly rushed past Kael and yelled over the sound of the storm. "We have to follow the river downstream. Come on!"

They had reached the edge of the town when James had stopped. Kael looked back and wondered what he was doing. "Let's keep moving," Kael yelled, but James didn't hear him, didn't seem aware of him at all. Kael walked back toward him to shake him and see if he was alright.

He saw sparks start to form over his friend's body. He stopped midstep, stunned and frightened by the electricity that grew into a cocoon around James' body. James turned toward Kael and opened his eyes. Kael stepped back, stunned by the sheer power that filled

James' eyes. They were fully golden; tiny bolts of lightning leaped from them and charred the ground as the ball of electricity intensified. James' red hair stood on end and he seemed to rise a few inches above the ground, the air crackling with power. Kael took another step back. *What's happening?* His mind reeled with the image of his friend electrified before him.

The world exploded in light. Kael barely managed to cover his face in time to avoid most of the light, but he felt the rush of lightning as it exploded from James into the sky.

Then it was all gone. Kael opened his eyes and looked at his friend. He appeared normal. Well, almost normal. A strange light flickered from his eyes. Kael strained to see what was different through the rain and thought he could make out glowing yellow streaks in James' normally greyish green eyes.

"We have to follow the river downstream. Come on!" James yelled over the storm as he pushed past Kael and headed away from the city.

I'm sure he'll tell me whatever that was when we have time, but for now, I don't have much choice but to follow him, Kael thought. He looked back at the town that had caused him so much pain and shivered at the thought of staying there forever. He flipped his gaze back to James and jogged to catch up with him. The storm seemed almost childish compared to what he had just seen his friend do and Kael pushed easily through the gusts of wind and sleet.

What did I just do? The question burned in James' mind as he hurried down the road. *Whatever it was, I know I have to head south. Someone is there, someone who can tell me everything.* He glanced behind him and was happy to see Kael following close behind. *How am I going to explain anything to him when I don't even know what happened?* Kael had always been there for him, someone to understand and share everything. *Not this. We won't be able to share this.* James could not let his mind dwell on what had just happened or what it meant. He turned back to the road. His only hope was to go south until he found someone or something that could explain what he had experienced.

James glanced back one last time and saw the outskirts of Arrdell. He smiled as they faded from view. This was a new chapter of his life, and he was ready to leave the terrible memories of the past somewhere he would likely never see them again.

"It's exciting isn't it, Henry?"

The mouse squeaked a reply and James chuckled before he stepped forward with new confidence

V:

The Broken Dam

Aran uncurled from the fetal position he had assumed when the storm first hit and stretched before he took the time to take in his surroundings. He looked around and saw that, by some miracle, the house had survived the storm. *Huh, thought that tempest would be enough to knock this old place to the ground,* he thought, surprised at the old house's durability. He walked cautiously toward the window, afraid of what he might find outside. Cobwebs infested the room, an accurate representation of the rest of the dull and dreary abode that spoke volumes of his wealth, or lack thereof. His father was his only company; his mother had died many years ago.

Aran peered through the foggy glass and saw the thing he'd been afraid of. *Great, he survived that.* His father sat slumped on the ground and held his head with one hand, a bottle of whiskey firmly clutched in the other. Aran shook his head sorrowfully as he looked down on the broken man. *One more week,* he thought. *One more week until I can leave and have my own life.* After his mother had passed, Aran's father had told him that he had to make it through at least his eighteenth summer before he could leave. "I can't have you running about without any idea how to take care of yourself," his father had said and tousled his hair. "Besides, I still need your help on the farm." That had been before the drinking. The man outside now wasn't his father, not really. That man had been destroyed by the loss of his wife, Hera, and had quickly gone from a proud man to a drunk, from a good father to someone Aran couldn't even bear to face.

Hera had died five summers ago and Aran felt an aching pain in his chest every time he thought about his amazing mother. She had always been sweet and kind to him, and with her by his side, his father had been kind and caring. Those had been the good times when his father wasn't a crippled drunk who couldn't let go of something that was impossible to get back. No matter how well-behaved Aran was, if his father had a bottle in his hand then a beating was soon to follow and Aran had accepted it. He knew that his father only hurt him because he was still in pain, and Aran didn't know what else to do, so he took the beatings without complaint. His back was a mass of scars, each one burned into his skin with a little bit of the hate and frustration that his father felt, a permanent reminder of the monster he had become. Aran looked out the window and saw his father stumble to his feet. He felt his heart drop and came to terms with the fact that today his face and back would be bloody and bruised, again.

Aran sighed and dutifully walked toward the ladder that led onto the second floor of his house. *This may be where I sleep and live, but it isn't my home. It hasn't been for a long time.* Aran clenched his fist then let the anger die out as he reached the ladder. His hair was a mess, and he knew that his father would yell at him for being a slob, but he didn't care. What was the point? If he fixed it, his father would find some other reason to yell at him. The anger was not rational and consumed his father like a disease. Aran was determined that he would not succumb to the poison of anger. He would not become like his father. He grabbed the ladder and swung himself onto the top rung. His bare feet felt every groove, notch and worn spot in the wood. He climbed down slowly as he tried to postpone the moment that he knew was coming. He took some solace in the knowledge that he would not meet his father's rage with rage of his own.

His eyes wandered as he reached the bottom of the ladder, crooked paintings and broken chairs scattered throughout the hallway that led to the stairs filled his gaze and he shook his head. *It looks like no one's lived here for years,* he thought quietly to himself. *I suppose that's truer than I like to admit.* He let his gaze wander a little longer until his eyes fell on one of the few clean items in the hallway. A broken mirror hung at an odd angle from the wall, its surface split into a thousand pieces that gave back a fractured version of reality. He looked in and saw a broken reflection of himself and couldn't help but chuckle darkly at the shattered face staring back at him. It was an adept representation of his life, broken and cracked beyond repair, a tiny fraction of what it had been. His eyes were drawn to one of the only reflections that wasn't completely shattered. The last remnants of the strong and unafraid farm boy he had once been stared back at him and he felt a ball of guilt for falling this far form in the pit of his stomach. He clenched his teeth and was about to turn away when he noticed that something looked different.

He looked closer and saw rivers of blue flowing through his normally brown pupils. *Not this again,* Aran thought as he stared at the distinct oddity. He wasn't exactly sure what it meant, but he knew it had to do with his power. He concentrated and closed his eyes as he told his mind to block the leak in the dam he had built around the dangerous power that flowed deep inside him. He searched for all the cracks and patched them carefully and the feeling of control slowly returned. He finished patching the holes and opened his eyes. He examined them and sighed when he didn't see any specs of blue in them.

Satisfied that his eyes were back to normal, Aran pulled himself away from the mirror and continued toward the stairs. He brushed his hand against the wall as he went and felt the timberwork of the house and the memories that it held. So many happy: the multitude of times he had played hide and seek with his parents, wrestled with his father as his mother watched and smiled, or the stories his mother had told him as he tried to fall asleep after a nightmare. He remembered how his mother had cared for him when he was sick, how his father came in and wished him well.

Then his mind turned to darker things. He saw his mother as she ran in front of the plow horse and tried to calm the beast. He saw it rear up, harness lines askew, and saw his mother trip and fall to the ground; the terrified look in her eyes was permanently stuck in his mind.

Tears started to stream down his face as the memories began to flow. He moved his hand from the wall to the railing and he felt the tears run faster down his grief-stricken face. He saw his father rush across the field to save Hera, just too late, and heard her screams as the horse's hoofs fell on her. The startled horse had bolted forward and trampled his mother. Whatever life was left in her after the hoofs battered her was quickly extinguished as the plow the horse pulled sliced cleanly through her body.

The whole gruesome scene replayed again and again through Aran's mind as he sat down on the steps and covered his face with his palms. He closed his eyes and tried to block out the pain, the tears streaming unstoppably down his face. He tried to think of other things, but to no avail. The images continued to play on repeat, a hellish nightmare he couldn't escape. The only thing he could do was run, and run he did. He sprinted out of the oppressive, musty, and dark house into the damp, dewy grass and sunshine outside.

Aran fell to his knees and gasped as the terrible memory faded from his mind. He felt the sun warm his body and he let himself relax, the rest of the world forgotten for a brief second.

"What ye running from, sonny?" Aran slowly turned around and saw that the slurred words were in fact coming from his father. The temporary peace that he had felt was stripped and a dull sense of duty and fear fell over him as he looked at the man's glazed-over eyes. "'Cause looks to me like you might have broke another of your mother's paintings." His father grinned menacingly as if he was challenging Aran to respond.

"No, I... I jus-*Aaarrrgghhhh.*" The cry was drawn from his throat as he felt a familiar burning sensation across his back. His father had pulled out a supple branch and attacked before Aran knew what was happening.

"Oh, I think yer did, I think ye broke it and doesn't want to tell me," the man yelled angrily. His voice had become more slurred and he struck again. The stick slammed unmercifully onto Aran's back and he couldn't help but yell in pain. The old man continued with a barrage of attacks. In between, he sipped aggressively at the bottle of whiskey. "I think that ye wanted her dead. Yer the one she was tryna save. It's yer fault." He was practically screaming now, his voice almost unrecognizable through the alcohol. The stick came down again and again, but Aran managed to keep his pride and refused to scream. He felt the welts form on his back, the burning sensation was all too familiar to him. He felt his determination not to fight against his father begin to falter. The urge to retaliate washed over him.

"No… I… didn't!" He yelled, his voice filled with pain. "I didn't want her dead! I loved her!" His father could beat him and whip him all he liked, but Aran wouldn't let him blame Hera's death on him. He felt the carefully patched dam inside start to crack as anger filled his body, each painful welt another crack in the dam. The stick continued to rain blows and he gritted his teeth, trying to find the still, cool place.

Instead, something inside broke. *That's it,* he thought, his mind clouded with hatred for the man who had tormented him almost half of his life. He felt the anger inside and he slipped toward it, like tumbling down a muddy slope. He yelled in rage and pain and the dam inside broke apart. It started slowly, but soon enough the power hidden behind it burst free and coursed through his body. He knew he couldn't hold all the anger and pain inside, so he pushed it out. He felt the power rush through his arms and saw a dark blue light emanate from them momentarily before it burst out of his hand. Aran screamed in pain but wouldn't let that sway him from his goal.

The rivers of blue glowed brightly in his eyes, more beautiful and terrifying than the dark blue of the deepest sea. Aran's father was too drunk to notice that anything had changed until it was too late. The stick fell again, but this time it didn't come up easily. He looked down and saw Aran staring back at him, the stick caught in his hand. "What do ye think yer doing? I'm not done with you yet. Now be a good little boy and s--*Arrrrgh!*" He fell to his knees as something struck his back. The old man turned his booze laden eyes up to his son and saw the terrifying light that blazed from them, an animalistic rage that even the dullest of creatures would recognize.

Aran looked pitilessly at the broken drunk in front of him and swung his arm. A whip-shaped arc of water smacked into his father's soft back. The slapping sound filled him with a thrill of control and he attacked again. "How does it feel, *Father?*" he asked savagely and spat out the last word like it was a rotten apple. "Go on, tell me!" His father screamed in agony and Aran bared his teeth in savage satisfaction and continued the beating. A fine mist formed around the two as whip after whip of water struck his father's back, not even the substantial amount of liquor enough to dull the sharp pain that Aran was able to inflict. "How do you think it felt when the man I called a father left? How do you think it felt when he was replaced with someone who felt no shame in beating a young boy? Someone who couldn't live without a bottle of whiskey? How do think it would feel if you felt this pain for years on end with no chance of escape? How do you think that would feel?"

Aran yelled wordlessly, an inhuman sound that came from the very heart of his being. He struck again and again, revenge the only thing that filled his mind as he continued the beating. He struck and struck again as blood began to well slowly out of the welts on the old man's back. Aran couldn't bring himself to stop, the built-up anger and pain a never-ending supply of energy. At last he stopped for a moment, his breath short and his eyes wild he stared at the broken body before him. The animalistic elation that had filled him moments before began to dissipate and he was filled with horror as he realized what he had done. "I- I didn't mean to. I- I- I." Aran covered his face with his hands as the guilt of what he had just done washed over him. "Forgive me."

Aran fell to his knees and felt the last traces of the power that had coursed so vigorously in him moments before disappear back to where it had come from. *What have I done?* He snapped his head back to attention as he heard his father cough.

"So ye Aren't a coward after all." Aran looked at his father's face and was sickened to see a manic grin plastered on his face. "But ye shoud've finished the job. I won't be so kind when I get my hands on you again."

Aran was too stunned to say anything and was suddenly filled with the need to get away from the man. He pushed himself to his feet and started to run, his heart racing as he fled from everything he knew.

"Run all you like, but yer just as much of a monster as I am," his father called out, then broke into laughter.

Aran closed his mind to the thought and pushed onward. *I'm nothing like him,* he told himself, although he fully knew it was a lie. All of his self-control had been nothing but a thin veil pulled over the same vile rage that he hated to see in his father. He had been fooling himself, but the truth was clear now.

His feet pounded over the fields and plants he had so carefully cultivated that summer, carrying him toward the river. He felt a pull from the water and he had no choice but to run toward it. He stumbled and almost fell as the terrain changed from smooth and flat farmlands to small hills and valleys, still he pressed on. He was afraid of what might happen if he turned back, afraid of what he would see, and what he would do. Trees started to fly by as he drew closer to the river. He clenched his fists and felt the warm sensation of blood. He glanced down to see long cuts on each of his palms. *Must've been where the water came from*, he thought then turned his attention back to running. The cuts would heal, but if he stayed here… he wasn't sure what would happen to his mind.

Then he saw the river in front of him and he slowed to a halt at its bank. His mind calmed as he stared into the dark blue depths of the river and he breathed deeply. He knew he had to leave, but he didn't know where to go. "Mother, please help me," he whispered, then felt a tug at his mind. He looked around, felt the same tug, followed it to the edge of the river, then deeper into the flowing water. As the water reached his waist, the tug became stronger and he quickened his pace until he was up to his neck in the water. Still, he felt the tug, so he took a deep breath and submerged himself in the cold water.

He searched the water for something that could have been pulling him in. *Close your eyes.* Aran recoiled as the voice entered his mind; something about it was familiar. *Go ahead, you can trust me.* Without many other options, Aran decided to listen to the voice and closed his eyes. The world went dark and he instantly felt calmed. The water dulled sounds and enveloped him, almost like a hug, as he felt his heartbeat began to slow down. *Not so bad is it?*

Aran shook his head. *It's amazing. But who are you?*

A bubbly laugh filled his ears. *You know me. I've always been with you, even if you can't always see me.*

Aran felt a shock run through his body as he recognized the voice. *Mother?*

The same bubbly laugh filled his mind. *That's right. I'm the mother you remember, a fragment of me still lives on in this world. Now I don't have much time to talk, so I'm afraid we have to cut the reunion short. You must follow the river downstream; look for a man named Corbin. He'll explain everything to you and from there the rest is up to you.*

Wait! Don't leave yet, I miss you. Aran felt salty tears mixing with the cool water as he tried to understand what was happening. *At least let me know if I'll see you again.*

The flow of the river caressed his face and Aran could imagine his mother's sweet face in front of him. *Don't miss me, sweetheart. I'm always with you, even if you can't tell. Now, go on, you've got a destiny to fulfill.* Aran felt the presence slip away and realized his lungs were burning for air. He surfaced and looked around frantically for some way to get back to his mother, but deep inside he knew that she was gone. Eventually, he waded out of the water and looked at his palms. Two watery scars ran down his palms and he shivered at the memory brought with them. He let his hands drop and looked at the river. His mind turned to what his mother had told him.

"I guess there's only one thing to do now," Aran sighed and looked at the bank, his mind too full of new things to do anything but the most basic tasks. He searched for the secret spot where the small, shoddily built raft he had found was hidden and dragged it out.

He looked it over, hands on his hips. "This'll have to do. I just hope I don't have to go far." He turned back to the water and peered down the river, into the future. A small bit of excitement made its way into the back of his thoughts as he pushed the raft into the current. Before he hopped onto the vessel, he glanced back toward his old house one last time and couldn't help but wonder what would happen to his father. *He'll be fine. The bastard would die from drinking too much before he let anything I do hurt him.* With that thought, Aran hopped on his raft and started the journey into the unknown.

VI:

Herbs and Dwarves

The grass flowed seamlessly around Brianna as she searched for the herbs that she had been sent to gather. The breeze sang sweetly and the meadow swayed and waved in the wind like the ocean on a stormy day. Brianna felt perfectly at peace - the breeze flew past her and the ground gave her a sense of solidness and purpose. Her hair, a silky mess of chestnut locks, flared in the air and whipped in the wind. The strands flew behind her and changed shades to dark amber in the early morning light. She looked downward, through the dancing grass, for any sign of the telfern that she was supposed to be gathering.

She followed the miniature hills and valleys that splayed out across the meadow, constantly scanning for a trace of the elusive plant. The wind continued to dash around her playfully. It tugged at her long flowing hair. Subconsciously, she reached behind her head and twisted the rebellious hair into a loose bun so that it wouldn't whip her face. *That's better,* she thought and went back to searching for the small fern. *Good thing I decided not to wear a dress - I'd be soaked if I had.* The grass was still moist from the previous night's storm and her worn pants were already damp. Her plain white shirt was barely touched by the wet blades. She carefully parted the grass as her journey through the sea of wet plants continued. Then she saw something in the mossy ground below.

Kneeling, she looked more closely at the plant. "Gotcha," she said as she identified the telltale signs of telfern. She reached into the tool belt looped over her shoulder and pulled out a small trowel from one of the pockets, her movements smooth and routine. She proceeded to quickly dig up the root of the plant, careful to disrupt as little soil as possible. This was her way of thanking the world for its help in finding the plant. Her hands were calloused from years of working the earth, but they still appeared elegant and graceful. They worked with exact precision as she uprooted the plant and brought it closer to her face for further inspection.

That's a nice specimen. If I find a few more like this, I should be able to head back soon. She let her gaze wander from the plant to the earth then up to the sunrise. She smiled softly. The beautiful colors in the west brought back good memories: times when she had wandered the world with her parents and learned all sorts of interesting things, the days when she had experimented freely with various alchemical formulas, many of which had been failures. Brianna let out a small laugh as she thought about the explosions she had made. *Miss Bretta was ready to throw me out that night.* The memories continued to flow as Brianna rose to her feet and walked onward, the search for more telfern still in full swing.

Good memories continued to pour through her mind, but eventually the happy times began to run dry and she turned to sad and painful memories. The smile slipped from Brianna's face as she saw her parents fight and her dad turn to leave, saw her mother's sullen and melancholy face as she told Brianna that her daddy would be gone for a while.

"How long, Mama?"

Her mother had smiled sadly, hugged Brianna close, and whispered, "Soon, sweetie, he'll be back before you know it." But "soon" passed, and before she knew it, Brianna and her mother had left their old home. They had gone from town to town as her mother ran from the sadness of her old life and carried Brianna along with her. There is only so far you can run before the past catches up with you. For Brianna's mother, that time came all too soon.

It had been just over seven summers ago when the incident had happened, but whenever she thought of it, Brianna was transported back to being a helpless child too naive to do anything. They had stopped in Erindale and were staying with some of her mother's friends. There had been laughter and games and the adults were drinking. It all seemed very ordinary. However, something felt slightly off when they had first come into town. Brianna couldn't put her finger on what the disturbance was, but when she looked at her mother, she could tell something strange was going to happen. "What's wrong, Mama?" she had asked.

Her mother looked at her and smiled, "Nothing, sweetie. Everything is fine." Thinking back to it now, Brianna could tell that the smile was forced and hadn't ever reached her mother's eyes. Her mother's face was a hollow husk of what it once had been, but she had been too young to realize what was wrong. She had shrugged off the feeling and went on to enjoy herself as her mother plummeted to new depths of depression. Late that night, as Brianna lay in bed, her mother walked in and whispered in her ear, "I'm sorry, but just remember that I will always love you." Brianna had yawned and hugged her mother before she fell back into a deep sleep.

The next day, her mother had been gone.

Brianna blocked out the rest of the memory. She wasn't ready to deal with it yet, even after all this time. She closed off her mind and hummed a song as she continued her search. *I'm just glad the Pandelors took me in. If they hadn't, then I don't know what I would have done.* She shook her head and cleared out any thoughts of her past. Nothing she could do would change it now, so what was the point in looking back?

The sun continued its slow journey into the sky and Brianna found a few more telferns as she walked deeper into the sea of grass. The familiar movement soothed and calmed her. Soon enough, the pain that had filled her was gone, tucked away in some secret part of her mind. The warm day brought the smile back to her face and she hummed old folk songs as she worked.

The sun was a good distance above the horizon as

Brianna stooped down to pick another fern and when she rose, its bright rays lit up her features. She looked older than she was. Her face carried a sad knowledge about the world and was soft, welcoming, and filled with determination. Her hair had come loose from its messy bun and flowed down around her shoulders again. It danced and flitted playfully around Brianna's face in the wind, but she didn't see any point in trying to restrain it, so she simply batted it away. She was taller than most women and had a stronger build than all the housewives in Erindale, but the first thing people noticed without fail was her eyes. They were light blue and hard as ice, but if you looked closer, you could see brown flecks scattered throughout them. There weren't many people left that knew what the odd flecks represented, and Brianna was careful to hide her special skills.

As she continued through the grass, she remembered the first time she had discovered her powers and glanced down at the freckles that speckled the back of her hands. Images flashed in front of her eyes and she shivered as she saw that moment replayed in slow motion. Her eyes had glowed and power had rushed out through her arms. It had arced into the ground, creating jagged, jutting formations in the rocks below. She remembered falling back. Her vision had grown dark as the world around her transformed. When she awoke, the earth around her had been upturned and contorted into hideous, nightmarish shapes. That night she had run back home and her dreams had been filled with the rock creatures she had created. She had been terrified of trying to access the power again, but in the end, curiosity won out over fear and she decided that she would become a master of whatever strange power she had been gifted.

As she grew older, she had practiced her power in secret. In her spare time, she had searched for hints as to what the power was, where it originated. One day, a trader came through Erindale and happened to be carrying a book titled *The Brief History of Magic and Myricals*. Brianna had immediately bargained with the trader until he agreed to sell the book to her for a reasonable price. Although the book had very little information that helped her answer her questions, it nevertheless helped her understand that she couldn't push her limits.

If she went beyond her limits, something terrible would happen. The book never specified what that something was, but it always alluded to the strӕntae, creatures Brianna knew of from myth, and their master.

I'm glad it's all just myths and children's stories, but something inside Brianna still quaked in fear whenever she thought of the dark creatures. She shivered even in the hot day and turned her thoughts away from the book.

By now Brianna was proficient and could create weapons and structures that almost matched the images she created in her mind. *But why me? Why did I get these powers?*The familiar questions nagged at her as she waded through the grass, her thoughts far away from the task at hand. *If only that book had more history and fewer warnings, I might have some idea of why I was picked, and what I should do with it.* She felt her foot bump against something and glanced down into the grass to see what it was. A rope ran taught across the path she had been traversing and she knelt curiously to examine it.

"Now!!" yelled someone near Brianna as she knelt down.

Her head whipped around and she tried to jump back from the rope, but it was too late. As she was distracted with the rope, two small figures had snuck up behind her and caught her in a net while she tried to get away from danger. She struggled against the ropes, but the figures held her tight.

"Grimsvor, get over here and help us tie her up. She's a feisty one," said one of the figures holding Brianna.

"I'm coming, I'm coming. A bit hard to get around in this grass." The grass near Brianna rustled and a small man with a red beard popped out.

A dwarf! thought Brianna.

"Ah, there you are, Gravrek. Erik, get over here!" Brianna heard more rustling and another dwarf popped out of the grass. This one had a dark brown beard.

"I'm here, I'm here. Now, let's get her tied up," said the new dwarf.

Grimsvor grinned. "And that's why I like you, Erik. Straight to the point."

"Wait! What are you doing?" stammered Brianna as the dwarves took out rope and began to wrap it around her.

Grimsvor grinned and bowed sarcastically. "My apologies, miss, I'm afraid I haven't properly introduced myself. I'm Grimsvor of the Blood Clan. These here good dwarfs are my companions and partners in business. What business? Well, I'm glad you asked because you have an important role to play in it. You see, we run..."

He looked around and made a show of getting closer, then said in a stage whisper, “You see, we run one of the best slave trains this side of the mountains.”

Horror and realization came over Brianna’s face and the two dwarves near Brianna laughed while Grimsvor pulled back, proud of his act.

“Good show, Grimsvor,” said the one called Gravrek. “Now, let’s get her back to the carriage and find a buyer.”

Grimsvor nodded. “Erik, go ahead and grab her feet, but don’t any of you bruise her too badly. I’m sure we’ll find someone who’ll pay a high price for such a pretty girl.”

Again, the two dwarves that held Brianna chuckled, but she noticed that Erik didn’t.

“Please help me,” she appealed to Erik. “I’ve got a family to get back to - they’ll look for me if they see I’m missing.”

He watched her with sorrow in his eyes and shook his head. “No hard feelings. It's just business.”

“You can’t just take me! Dwarves are supposed to be honorable and respectfu--”

She was cut off by a sharp boot from Gravrek. “Shut up. Erik, do you have something to make her stop talking?"

Erik nodded and pulled out an old rag. He moved to gag Brianna but suddenly stopped. His eyes went wide. "Grimsvor, you need to let her go."

Grimsvor turned around with a look of impatience. "What are you talking about? She's our prisoner, and it's not like she could do much to hurt us."

Erik nodded. "Oh, yes, she could. She's got the telran mark."

Gravrek growled, "What are you talking about, Erik? There hasn't been anyone with that mark in years."

"I know, but she has it. Go ahead and look for yourself."

Gravrek peered at Brianna's face and gasped. "That's it, alright." He looked at Grimsvor and shook his head. "Sorry, Grimsvor, but I'm not sticking around to try to fight with a telran. Come on, Tark, I'm not letting my little brother get himself killed."

Brianna felt both of the dwarves holding her let go. She fell onto her back, just barely able to see the two small figures slip into the grass and out of view.

"You two get back here now!" Grimsvor yelled. He turned to Erik and Brianna and spat. "I don't believe you, Erick, but just for safety, why not cut her throat?" With that, he pulled out a knife, and moved in on Brianna, an evil grin twisting his face.

Brianna felt panic threaten to overwhelm her and searched for the hidden gate deep within. She found it and flung the doors open; the power rushed out like an avalanche, and the brown flecks in her eyes glowed intensely.

She felt the power course through her body and forced it out, an energy greater than any she had ever used before. It leaped down her arms and out into the surrounding ground. A rocky spire popped out of the earth and slashed through her bonds. Her hands now free, she pushed herself to her feet and glared at the dwarf in front of her. "You should've let me go when you had the chance." She held out her hand as a stone spear rose from the ground. She grabbed it; energy sparked up and down its shaft.

Grimsvor had stopped in astonishment when he saw the rock spire. Now, he realized his mistake. As he heard Brianna speak, he turned and began to run away, barreling through the tall grass, but it was too late. Brianna tossed the spear after him, blue streaks of power flashing from it as it arced toward the red-bearded dwarf.

Grimsvor turned around at the last second and

managed to avoid the spear stabbing him in the heart. Instead, the stone tip slammed into his shoulder and pinned him to the ground.

Brianna walked over to him. Her eyes flashed with anger as she looked down at him. "Just for safety's sake," she said and a stone dagger flew into her hand. She lifted her arm as she prepared to stab Grimsvor, fully intending to kill him.

As she brought her knife down, she saw the terrified look in his eyes and was brought back to herself. At the last second, she changed the dagger's path and stabbed it into the ground next to Grimsvor. She screamed and felt the rest of the power flow out of her and into the ground. Jagged outcroppings of rock formed while she struggled for control of her body.

The outburst only lasted for a few seconds, but when Brianna was in full control again, the ground around her was shattered and Grimsvor lay in front of her, eyes wide and full of terror. She looked at him with disgust and pulled the spear out of his shoulder. "Get out of here, and if we ever meet again, you won't be walking away." Grimsvor nodded and clutched at his broken shoulder as he retreated

Brianna watched him run, then took a deep breath

and felt exhaustion come over her. She fell to the ground. She spied Erik a few feet away. "You're still here?"

He nodded and started to move toward her. Brianna was too exhausted to try to stop him. "Do you have any water?"

Erik nodded again and pulled out a leather water bottle. "Here you go, have as much as you want." He handed the bottle to Brianna and she nodded her thanks. "I've never seen anything like that," said Erik, fear and awe evident in his voice. "What's your name?"

"Brianna." She gulped water. "How did you know about the mark?"

"A promise to an old friend," said Erik and looked down at his hands for a moment as if lost in thought. "I promised that if I found a person like you, I would deliver that person to him." Erik looked hopefully at Brianna.

She shook her head slowly. She was so tired. "Who? Why?"

"He's an ancient shaman and alchemist who can tell you more about your power--he might even be able to help you control it. He never told me why, but it was the most important thing to him, so it must be for a good reason."

Brianna thought about it for a moment. Her foggy mind reeled. "Fine. It's not like I could explain this to anyone back in town, and I doubt that they would accept my oddity. Let's go." She tried to stand, but her vision became red and hazy. The world swirled around her and she fell to the ground, her eyes misting over. The last thing she saw was Erik leaning over and staring at her, a worried look on his face. Then everything went dark.

VII:

The King of the Forest

"How much farther do we have to go?" asked Lyria, her voice nearly a whine. They had spent the night of the storm beneath the shelter of two massive oaks, and the next two days hiking toward the "center" as Ferox called it.

Not long. His reserve of patience impressed even Lyria, who knew she was acting like a brat. He looked back at her. *Do you see that line of trees ahead? That is the outskirts of the center.*

Lyria peered ahead and saw the trees to which Ferox referred. They towered above her, their limbs crisscrossed to let in only a smattering of light that played across the leafy mess on the ground as the wind shifted the trees. The rest of the forest had felt old to Lyria, but compared to the line of trees in front of her, the previous part of the woodland seemed young. She could tell that this line of trees divided the younger forest from an ancient part of the woods, one that had been untouched for eons.

Lyria started forward as Ferox began to pad toward the timber--his paws made deep imprints in the soft leafy ground that she playfully tried to follow. She hopped from paw print to paw print until she got closer. "Why do you call it the center?"

I call it the center because that is where the King of this forest lives, Ferox replied. He shrugged as though it was a silly question. *It's a place filled with ancient power; it's called the center because it's where the first tree of these woods grew.* The wolf continued forward, his gait increased just enough to put Lyria behind him and let him know that he wouldn't stand for pointless chit-chat about such a serious question.

Lyria grimaced at Fexrox' suddenly serious attitude. She liked him better when he was playful.

She looked back at the trees. She wondered at their age and magnificence. She gazed at the moss that had so intimately woven itself into the nooks and crannies of each tree.

On a whim, she opened her mind and used a bit of her power to reach out for the grove. Her mind stretched toward the first tree. As she touched the great lifeform, she felt its thoughts and was overwhelmed. Its mind was so much different than anything that she knew; ideas flowed from it like lazy rivers of honey. Each thought-stream was filled with more knowledge and understanding than hundreds of years of human history.

The tree took no notice of her. Or, rather, it noticed her, but she was of such extreme insignificance that she warranted no response at all from the great being. It was entirely taken up by the millions of dapples of sunlight and the thousands of combinations of minerals in the earth, the bees that flew around its uppermost branches, and the birds that flitted through it. Why would it need to be concerned with such a tiny thing as Lyria? She started to be sucked into the tree's immense awareness. She felt her mind slow and knew what it was like to be a tree that had stood for millennia. The tree had thousands of different words for sun, millions for water, billions for every type of weather.

Lyria shook herself and closed off the gate that kept her abilities to herself, leaving only a small crack so she could communicate with Ferox. As she pulled herself away, she shivered, frightened by the gargantuan mind of the tree. She stopped staring at the trees and ran after

Ferox.

Trying to speak to the ancients, are we? mused the wolf. *If I've learned anything from my days of talking to trees, it's that the older they grow, the duller they get. Unless you think that having five hundred different words for "rain" is entertaining. Come on, pup, let's hurry to the center, otherwise I'm afraid these trees will catch you like honey catches a fly.* He drew back his lips in a snarl that Lyria was beginning to recognize as a smile. A dry sense of humor played across his mind.

He's laughing at his own joke, thought Lyria. *Even though it wasn't that good.* "Ok, Ferox, whatever you say," said Lyria and let out a slight chuckle.

Well, in that case, why don't you scratch my back? said the wolf playfully, back to his fun-loving self.

Lyria laughed, relieved to pull away from the overwhelming tree-mind. "Go on, you big-headed oaf, lead the way to your King."

Ferox snorted happily and began to jog through the old trees. Lyria had to sprint to keep up with him and they ran through the blissfully silent woods. Animals began to emerge. A squirrel sat on a branch eating nuts, a deer looked up from the grass it was nibbling, and a badger poked his head out of his burrow.

Lyria waved playfully at the badger. To her surprise, he nodded and she heard a voice in her mind. *Good afternoon. We've all been expecting you. Hope you have a nice chat with the King.*

She gaped for a moment, then laughed in delight and ran even faster after Ferox.

This is something straight out of a fairy tale! she thought to herself. Her bubbly laugh filled the quiet woods as she took in her surroundings. Ferox yipped joyfully, bounded ahead, turned around and bounded back over and over again until he was panting. Lyria would've laughed, but she was already gasping for air and it was all she could do to keep moving forward. They passed herds of elk that browsed lazily on the plentiful undergrowth, passed intricate patterns of light formed by the dancing leaves above, and jumped over small creeks and streams. The dense canopy of ancient trees surrounded them at all times.

What do you think? asked Ferox.

It's amazing! I never thought I would see anything like it, Lyria thought, conserving air for the run. *Everything is so big and beautiful!*

Ferox barked in agreement and she felt his mind blush with pride. *Someday I'll show you the whole of the Center. If you want.*

That would be lovely, Ferox.

Good. I hope that day comes soon.

The two came to another line of trees and Ferox burst through a small opening into a large glade, Lyria close behind. Ferox slowed to a halt and his tongue lolled out of his mouth as he panted heavily. Lyria stopped and put her hands on her knees, gulping in the air.

After they had both recovered Ferox said, *This is it, the Center. When we speak to the pack leader and the King of the Forest, you'll have to get rid of your awful manners and be polite.*

"Why, of course, my good fellow. I'll do my best to treat these old blokes politely," Lyria said in an old-timey accent and curtsied.

Ferox growled. *Lyria. I'm serious. They could both kill you in an instant. Be respectful. You know how to do that, don't you?*

Lyria realized that Ferox was serious. She blushed in embarrassment. "Sorry, I'll make sure I'm nice." She nodded sincerely to the wolf and motioned that she was ready.

Ferox met her eyes meaningfully before they walked into the center of the forest. Lyria was stunned by the sheer beauty of the place. There was a lake in the middle, placed perfectly so that a ray of pure sunlight would make it through from the canopy above and strike its surface, unaffected by the thick foliage. On the lake were lilies, their white flowers in full bloom. The water was crystal clear and the air above it shimmered and flickered, a rainbow mist that looked almost like stained glass. The grass around the lake was lush and thick, a verdant and full green. The rest of the clearing was covered in less fertile grass, moss, and ferns, all of which were the same dark green. At the far side of the clearing, Lyria could see the entrance to a cave, but her attention was drawn to the main attraction of the clearing: an enormous tree.

The tree was so massive, it was a wonder that it was still standing. Its trunk was easily twice as wide as Lyria's shack had been and its lowest branches looked like smaller trees sticking out of it, each with its own ecosystem of ferns, moss, and small shrubby plants. Lyria looked up and saw the tree towering far above her, the top obscured behind thick layers of the tree-like branches. *I wonder how far up it goes?* she thought to herself as she continued to stare up in awe. After a few seconds, she was able to tear her eyes away from the unimaginable treetop and looked back at the base of the tree.

Standing proudly on one of the massive roots, she saw a colossal wolf that hadn't been there a few seconds before.

Ah, good, you brought her. I hoped that you, on the other hand, might have gotten lost. The wolf said, his message directed at Ferox. The wolf had a jet-black coat and his voice sounded like a deep mountain stream, old and wise.

You know you couldn't get rid of me that easily, Roku. Ferox bared his teeth in a grin. *But I did find her and brought her here just like you asked. Surely that deserves your gratitude?*

Well, maybe next time I'll find a more efficient way to get rid of you. Roku turned his attention from Ferox and onto Lyria. *As for you, welcome to the Center, Lyria. Now did my young friend Ferox tell you why you're here?*

"He said something about how I was one of the heroes destined to save the world, but…" Lyria looked down, too ashamed to continue.

But what?

"But I don't think I'm the person you're looking for.

I mean, all I can do is hear a few thoughts. It's not like I could do anything to stop someone from being hurt." She shrugged. "Sorry, but you guys got the wrong girl."

Roku looked at Ferox. *Is this true, Ferox?*

Ferox shook his head vigorously. *No. She can do much more than just read minds. When I told her what happened to her father, she invaded my mind and completely immobilized me as she tore through my memories in search of anything related to her father. I do not doubt that she is the chosen one.* Lyria looked over at Ferox, warmed by his touching defense of her developing skills.

It seems that Ferox believes in you, and I'm more inclined to believe him than you. Roku looked at her with a fierce determination in his eyes. *But it doesn't matter what the rest of us think. You have to believe in yourself, otherwise, the world is doomed and--" Roku* was interrupted by a disturbance in the great tree behind him. A tremor ran up and down its trunk, birds flew from its branches, squirrels hugged the branches they were perched on, and thousands upon thousands of leaves fell to the ground. Roku turned and bowed his head to the great tree. *I didn't mean to disturb you.*

Let me speak to the girl, young one, said a voice from

the tree. The voice held a reflection of everything Lyria knew and more, a near-perfect mirror of the world and at the same time the start of an entirely different world.

As you wish. Ferox, come with me. The two wolves quickly exited the clearing and left Lyria alone with the tree.

Ferox. Was he the one who retrieved you?

Lyria, startled at being addressed by the tree, answered quickly. "That's right. He found me and led me here."

Good, I'll have to think of a suitable reward for him. He deserves something after all he's been through. But let's get onto more important matters. I'm afraid that I've forgotten your name already."

Lyria was about to respond when she remembered her father. She bristled with anger.

"Hold on one minute," she said defiantly. "Before I tell you my name, how about I hear something from you? I think that's the least *I* deserve for being dragged out here after Da died." She looked up at the great tree. She needed to understand what had happened and what she was. She felt certain this creature was her best opportunity for finding answers.

A moment passed and nothing happened. Then

Lyria felt bright happiness drift into her mind. It was accompanied by a sound akin to a stream burbling and she couldn't help but smile. *In an eon, I have never heard anyone talk to me that way,* said the tree. Lyria realized that he was chuckling. *It's good to see some still retain independence. You're right, and I'll do more than tell you. I'll show you.* As the tree chuckled one last time, Lyria felt herself swept into a great sea of memories.

She closed her eyes as she struggled to keep her being separate from the vast mind that now enveloped her. When she finally felt comfortable enough to open them, she was no longer in the same place. Instead, she was in a grove that looked very familiar but without any of the trees or water.

"Where am I?" asked Lyria.

You are in my memories, and this is the story of the forest. Now watch.

Lyria saw no other option but to as she was told, so she watched.

She saw the first sprouts appear and watched one grow into a large tree. Nowhere near the same size as the one that lived in the grove now, it was still massive. She saw the tree reach out with tendrils of its mind and encourage the other plants to grow, saw the beginning of a small ring of lesser trees. Slowly, the first tree grew and he always watched over the things he had created and those that inhabited his forest. He watched as animals began to populate the woods and she understood what it was. The tree was the guardian of the forest. Not only that, but it was also the creator and the king of this new world.

"You? You made all this?" whispered Lyria.

Yes, said the tree, his voice transformed from the unimaginably immense identity to a warmer feeling, like a drop of honey on a hot day. *I am the father of this forest; the trees are my children. Would you like to know my name?*

Lyria nodded, too stunned to say anything.

I could tell you a thousand different names I've been given over the years, but I think I'll give you my true name. My name is Trallger, and now I believe that I have earned the right to know your name.

"My name is Lyria. I don't have a story nearly as fantastic as yours, but people keep telling me that I'm supposed to save the world." She shrugged. "Like I mentioned before, I'm not so sure they've got the right person."

Trallger was silent for a moment, deep in

contemplation. *I am no expert on the subject. I don't know much about magic or human history. However, I can tell that there is something special about you. You managed to stay yourself when I took you into my mind. Even in my mind, you are still capable of free will. It seems that you have also convinced young Ferox that you are destined, even if it was by accident. But perhaps the most compelling evidence is that you have more determination than any creature I've seen in the past, so I can't help but think that you may well be the one destined to save the world.*

Lyria sat down and cupped her head in her hands. "Thanks, I guess. I was really hoping that you would have all the answers, but I guess I'll have to keep looking for that."

You can never find all the answers, Lyria. The best you can do is make sure you believe in yourself. That is the strongest power in the world. As for someone who could tell you for sure if you are destined to save the world, I can help you with that but let's get back to the real world first so the others can hear.

Lyria felt her stomach flip and she closed her eyes as she was returned to her own body again. *I don't think I'll ever get used to that.*

She opened her eyes and was happy to find herself back in the clearing. The great tree stood as tall and proud as ever in front of her. "What now, Trallger?"

First, let me get the others. Ferox! Roku! Come here. You should hear this.

The two wolves trotted into the clearing from the ring of trees and Ferox looked at Lyria. *Are you ok? You look different.*

"Yeah, I'm fine," said Lyria as she shook out her arms. "I was just talking to your king, something I only need to experience once." She looked over at Ferox. "Thanks for standing up for me back there. I don't know if you're right, but I'll do my best to live up to your expectations."

It was nothing.

Lyria smiled inwardly as she felt Ferox's mind gush happiness at her gratitude.

Roku nudged Ferox. *Pay attention, Ferox, the king is waiting on you.*

Ferox whimpered and turned toward Trallger, his tail between his legs. The trickling chuckle came again. *Don't worry, wolf, I am not offended. I've waited much longer for much simpler things. Now, let's get on to the real discussion.* Trallger focused again on Lyria and said,

The man we spoke of is currently near Copper Town. You can start off on your journey now, or you can spend a night here.

"I'd love to stay here!" said Lyria. "This place is much more comfortable than where I've spent the past few nights."

Good. I'm sure we can arrange that. There is one more thing. Ferox.

The wolf straightened and listened intently.

Will you be Lyria's escort on her adventure?

If you would be all right with it, then I would love to accompany her. Ferrox looked over and grinned at Lyria.

Then that's settled. Ferox, you and Lyria will set out tomorrow morning at first light. Now, Roku, go get these two set up with dinner and a sleeping spot. I have a forest to manage.

Just like that, the massive mind dispersed into the surrounding forest.

Roku turned to Ferox and Lyria. *I suppose that this might finally get you off my back for a bit, Ferox.* The huge jet-black wolf grinned and then went about his job. *Come with me and I'll have food prepared for you in no time.*

Lyria walked behind the wolf. She gasped as they moved to the other side of the tree. Before them was a beautiful sight. Trallger's trunk had been hiding an awesome structure. It was a group of maples that had grown into the shape of a hut. Its walls were leafy and nearly transparent, but they would do for a warm summer night. The maples wove together into an epic structure that seemed to have come straight from Lyria's dreams.

Roku turned to her and grinned in that wolfish way. *Do you like it?*

"I love it," said Lyria, "Thank you so much, Roku, and thank you, King of the Forest."

It's perfect for a night, but it's not quite as fantastic as the places we've been staying the last few nights, Ferox butted in playfully.

"At least I'll be able to sleep on something soft," said Lyria as she glared at the wolf. "Besides, I'm sure we'll have plenty more nights roughing it on our way to Copper Town."

As I was saying, interrupted Roku, *your dinner is inside. Oh, and don't mind the bees--they won't hurt you.*

"Thank you," said Lyria as Roku slipped toward the

cave. "Come on, Ferox, let's go have some food."

They walked into the house and saw a table laid out with a magnificent feast. Plates were heaping with apples, pears, and all kinds of fruit, stacks of assorted berries, and various other vegetables scattered across the table. The main course of the meal was in a large pot and when Lyria ladled out a bowl for herself, she was happy to find that it was a mushroom stew that tasted divine. The bees Roku had mentioned flitted in and out, gathering nectar from the flowers that splattered the ground. On the ground was a bowl filled with fried eggs, raw meat, and toasted nuts. Ferox dug into this with passion and refused to stop until his hunger was sated.

After the main course, the trees reached into the small room and removed the platters. They startled Lyria at first but made sure to calm her with gentle conversations. The young trees were much more enjoyable to talk with than the ancient wooden pillars that composed most of the forest. The food was replaced with golden honey bars brought in by the bees. They were sweet and savory; all in all, it was the best meal Lyria had enjoyed in a long time.

After dinner, she and Ferox stayed up and talked, but between their full stomachs and the events of the day, they both grew tired quickly. The light in the room had faded and Lyria saw that a mossy bed had been laid out on one side of the room. She lay down on it, sinking into the soft, warm moss. Ferox flopped next to her. In moments, they were both asleep, their minds merging with the peaceful forest night.

VIII:

A Fateful Meeting

James' feet pounded across the dry ground, his legs a fiery mess of pain as he sprinted away from the terror close behind him. "Hurry, Kael!!" he yelled over his shoulder. Thunder rolled across the barren landscape and drowned out any response from Kael. James risked a look behind him and saw Kael close on his heels. Behind him was a dark mass of clouds. The clouds were not those of a storm; they moved too fast and purposefully for that. The edge of the dark wisps of clouds raced forward with malicious intent, and James felt goosebumps form on his skin, shivers running down his spine as thunder boomed again.

Lightning struck the ground near Kael, a dark spike of energy unlike anything else James had seen before. He yelled into the roaring cacophony that enveloped him as he saw Kael stumble and fall to the ground. James stopped, turned, and ran back toward his friend. His feet flew across the ground, the wind whipped past his face as he pushed his body to new limits in an attempt to rescue his friend. But it wasn't enough. Moments before James could reach Kael, another bolt of dark lightning flashed from the heavens and enveloped the figure on the ground.

James saw the electricity arc through Kael's body, burning his once fair skin to pitch black. Then the bolt of energy was gone. Kael pushed himself to his knees, his mouth open in an inaudible scream as the energy coursed through his body and into the ground, the black skin slowly spreading over his body. The last thing James saw before the charred skin completely consumed his friend was his eyes. They looked fearfully and angrily at James, accusing and full of a hatred James had never seen from his friend. *Why did you let them do this to me? You could have stopped them,* they seemed to say before the life drained from Kael's face and all that was left was his blackened corpse.

It's all my fault… it's my fault! He's gone and it's my fault. What's wrong with me? James thought as he saw the life slip from Kael's eyes. He rushed forward even though he knew it was hopeless and cradled what remained of Kael's body in his arms. He held it close and let the tears stream down his face. "I'm sorry… I'm sorry!!" The dark storm rushed toward James, but he paid it little heed as he cradled Kael's dead body. The shadows fell over him and slowly consumed him, his thoughts full of desolate despair and regret as he sobbed.

"James!" yelled Kael. "James Wake up!"

James blearily looked up to see Kael standing above him, the same worried look from the other day on his face. "Kael?"

"Good, you're awake. Sorry I yelled at you, you were rolling on the floor and screaming." He trembled as he spoke, his eyes wide with terror.

"Thanks, Kael," said James. "It was just a bad dream." James looked around and saw the edges of daylight creep through the entrance of the cave and create a strange glow as they trickled through the thick fog that lay outside. "Let's get moving, we've still got a long way to go. At least that's what it feels like."

Kael nodded. He could tell that James wasn't going to tell him anything else and James was relieved that his friend didn't question him. He sighed inwardly. *I've got so much to explain to him, but I don't know how. Hopefully I figure it out soon.* With that thought circling in his mind, James set out on the road, Kael close behind him.

The world materialized around Aran as he slowly blinked awake, yawned, and grimaced as he stretched, his back sore and cramped from uncomfortable nights on the shoddily built raft. It had only been two days since he had crawled onto the boat, exhausted from his fight with his father. He had fallen into a deep sleep. Hours later, he finally jerked awake and had been surprised to find the boat hadn't run aground. *So, it wasn't a nightmare after all,* he had thought. *I guess this means that I'm important to someone.* The boat continued down the river, not straying far from the center of the current at any time. The voyage gave Aran plenty of time to come to terms with what had happened and tuck the experience away deep inside his mind.

The raft followed close behind the dark clouds of the storm that had started his journey, the occasional sound of thunder or flash of lightning reached Aran and brought him out of his trance. After the first day of travel, the storm had flown far ahead and left Aran to fend for himself. When his stomach first growled, he had been scared about not having enough food, but no sooner had the thought crossed his mind then a fish threw itself onto the raft. *Well... I guess that means I don't die here,* he thought before steering the raft to shore to make a warm meal for himself. The next day had been much the same. Traffic on the road had been nonexistent after the storm, and Aran watched the bank in search of some sort of marker to tell him where he was.

I'll have to talk to the next person I see and try to find out where I am. The raft coasted smoothly down the river while Aran sat cross-legged, the thick morning fog that spilled over the water wrapped around him like a blanket. As he closed his eyes and let the fog comfort him, Aran thought back to his father's last words. A shudder ran through him and he clenched his fists in fear and anger. *What does he know? How would he know anything about who I am? He turned his back on me and left me to fend for myself. Why do I even care?* Aran realized he was shaking with rage and tried to calm down by breathing deeply. Slowly, the memories and anger that accompanied them drifted back into the hidden mind-crevice from which they had come.

Aran sighed as he felt the last of the intense emotions trickle away. He turned his mind to what he was doing now. *I hope you're right, Mom. I hope that this Corbin guy can give me some answers.* Aran looked downstream and clenched his fists, not in anger or fear, but with determination to find out why he had been cursed with these powers. All he ever wanted was to grow up as a normal kid with a normal family and live a normal life, far away from any kind of adventure or unknown situation. Those dreams had been stripped away the moment his mom had died, the chance at being normal stolen away from him by forces beyond his control. *What did I do I deserve this punishment?*

A lonely tear rolled down Aran's cheek as he contemplated his life, the droplet of salty water nearly hidden by dense fog. He quickly rubbed away the tear, then laughed softly at himself. There was no one to see him cry. As he took a deep, steadying breath, Aran's mind cleared. He pushed away all of the unnecessary thoughts and, with each breath, blew away the bad memories like leaves floating down a stream. It took a long time before he felt like he could look around again, the leaves piling into a dark corner of his mind, a place where he dared not look. With the thoughts and memories swept safely out of the way, Aran looked up and glimpsed something through the mist.

He strained his eyes and tried to get a better view of the bank. *I'm sure I saw something.* A slight breeze blew away some of the fog and revealed two ragged figures trudging down the road, both unaware of Aran's presence. He paused and went completely silent. He needed to know where he was, but he didn't feel like dealing with any brigands or bandits roaming the road in search of easy prey after the storm. *What's the worst that could happen?* he wondered. After a moment's hesitation, he decided to get closer and see if he could find out anything else about the travelers before making contact.

Slowly and cautiously, Aran maneuvered the boat through the fog toward the shore. He lay down on the thick wooden planks and proceeded to listen and watch the two figures as they made their way down the road. Over the gentle sound of water lapping against his raft, he heard one figure say, "How much farther?"

"I'm not sure, but it feels like we are getting closer. I'll let you know as soon as I get a clearer sense of what I'm looking for." The voice was young, but that of a confident individual who, even if he seemed to be unsure of where he was going, managed to keep his composure and some semblance of leadership.

A grunt of acknowledgment came from the first speaker. After a moment of silence, the first one spoke again. "I wish the fog would clear up. It's damp and cold."

"Me too, but I guess we'll just have to..." The voices faded into the distance and left Aran with a thoughtful expression painted on his face. He sat on the raft for another long moment before he decided to go after the two and see if he could get some directions. They seemed to be too young and naive for bandits or brigands. Besides, he was sure he could take two kids in a fight. *He seems to have the same feeling I do... I wonder if... No, it couldn't be.* Aran shook the idea from his mind before he grabbed the oar and started to paddle toward the shore, any noise he might have made covered by the thick air around him. He heard a soft thud as the raft glided into the sandy bank. He hopped off onto the sandy shore, securing the raft on the beach.

The breeze steadily grew and pushed the mist until it was nearly gone; only a few wisps remained to shroud the sun from view. Aran nimbly climbed the bank to the dusty dirt road. He paused and listened for the two boys' footsteps. A frown fell across his face when he heard nothing but the birds chattering in the morning mist. *Where could they have gone?* he wondered as he crept along the side of the path and searched for any trace of the two figures. He peered at the dimly illuminated road and managed to make out a pair of footprints. *They can't be far from here. I'll just have to-* his thoughts were interrupted by a high-pitched squeak near his foot. His eyes darted down and he saw a small mouse staring up at him with dark, beady eyes.

"What's up, little fella?" Aran asked, his heart softened by the tiny creature. "You haven't see-oof." He was cut short as a makeshift club whistled through the air and hit his head with a loud smack that made him crumple to his knees.

"What should we do with him?"

Aran groggily opened his eyes and saw two figures standing in front of him, or rather he saw the lower halves of two figures. He could only make out their feet from his crumpled position, and as he tried to raise his head for a better view, a splitting pain echoed through his skull. He groaned and reached up to massage his temples, but was surprised to find his hands bound behind him.

"Hey," he croaked out as he grimaced from the splitting headache.

"He's waking up. What should we do?" The voice sounded frightened and unsure.

"I'll handle it, you just let me do the talking." Aran felt a steely note ring through the voice. This speaker wasn't afraid or unsure of what he was doing. "Who are you?" The tough-sounding voice was directed toward him, demanding an answer.

"Who's asking?" Aran managed to wheeze. He winced as the pain continued to crash around his brain. He tried to raise his head again and see the figures face but to no avail. *Damnit, I guess I'm at their mercy.*

The figure paused for a moment before answering and Aran thought he caught a slight sense of uncertainty in his voice. "You don't have much room to be asking questions. Now, tell me who you are and why were you following us."

"I'm trying to… find someone and I was gonna ask if you two had seen him."

Aran heard the figure take a breath then whisper to the other figure, "Do you think?"

"No, it couldn't be."

"Maybe, but that line sounds all too familiar."

"You might be right." There was another pause before the figure turned back to Aran and spoke. "Who are you looking for?"

Aran saw his chance to gain some leverage. "I'll tell you, but first you'll have to untie me and help me up."

The two whispered hurriedly between themselves, so hushed that Aran couldn't hear them speak. "Fine, we'll untie you, but don't try anything funny."

Aran chuckled. "I wouldn't dream of it." He saw one pair of shoes move out of his line of sight, then felt the rope binding his hands slip away. He rolled his fingers as the blood slowly made its way back to them. "Do you mind giving me a hand up?" He didn't receive an answer and sighed. *Should've guessed as much.* He slowly and painfully lifted himself to a sitting position.

"Go ahead and answer the question now."

Aran looked at his captors and saw that they were no more than boys, each in their early teens. One of them had brown hair and looked shyly down at his feet while the other, the leader, Aran assumed, had fiery red hair and a glint of steel in his eyes.

"How old are you two?"

The redhead stared him down and answered,

unblinking, “Doesn't matter. Now, answer the question before I have to hurt you.”

Normally, Aran would laugh at the threat, but something about the boy’s stance and stare warned him not to. “Fine. I’m looking for someone named Corbin.”

A light of recognition filled the boy’s eyes, which he quickly tried to mask.

“You know him?” Aran pressed.

“I’ve never heard of him.” The redhead tried to control his expression, but his composure had been broken, and Aran could tell he was just as curious as he was ready to fight.

“Right. Well, in that case, may I ask what two young boys are doing traveling the road alone?”

The question knocked the redhead farther off the platform of nonchalance he tried to maintain and he blustered, “None of your business.”

“Well then, I suppose I’ll be on my way. You don’t seem to have any need of me, nor I you.” Aran turned around to walk away but was stopped by a shout from the boy.

“Wait! Why are you looking for Corbin?”

Aran jumped triumphantly inside his mind at the small victory before he turned back with full control of his body. "Why does it matter? You said yourself that you don't know him."

The redhead blushed feverishly as he accepted defeat. "I don't… but, at the same time, I think I know who you're talking about." His eyes dropped to his feet and Aran noticed the mouse perched on the boy's shoulder. "I know it doesn't make any sense, but I know I've got to find him or something terrible will happen."

"I understand what you mean." The boy looked up as Aran spoke.

"You do?"

Aran nodded. "It's like something pulling you from deep inside your soul, something you can't resist."

"I… I guess so. Never thought of it like that." The boy looked at Aran curiously for a moment, and as he did so, his companion inhaled sharply.

"James, look at his eyes."

I forgot about him, thought Aran as he noticed the brown-haired boy who had been examining him carefully this whole time.

"What are you talking abo-oh." A look of shock and realization fell onto James' face as he saw the cracks running throughout Aran's eyes. "They're like mine," he said, almost in awe.

Aran did a mental double-take and his mind worked overtime to keep his body from jerking back. *Like mine, he couldn't mean that…* But he already knew the truth. He could see the jagged stripes of yellow lighting streaking through James' eyes and felt a sense of relief and disbelief wash over him.

"You have it too, don't you? The power, I mean."

"I guess you could say that." The two looked at each other as they tried to come to terms with this discovery.

"What does it mean?" chimed in the voice of the bewildered brown-haired boy.

"I'm not sure," said James, "but I think we can trust each other. Right, stranger?"

Aran knew he had to speak and shook himself out of his mental fog enough to reply. "Yeah. I think we can." He held out his hand. "My name's Aran."

"Aran, it's nice to meet you. I'm James and this is Kael." James pointed at the shy boy who smiled sheepishly and waved. A sharp squeak came from James' shoulder. "Oh, and the little guy's name is Henry."

"It's nice to meet you," said Aran, still more bewildered than anything. *What could this mean?* He thought back to his conversation with the mirage of his mother and remembered what she had said.

You've got a destiny to fulfill.

Could this be what she meant? He was brought back to the present as he heard one of the boys' cough. "Sorry, I got lost in my thoughts. Did you say something?"

James glanced at Kael before he looked at Aran and nodded, the confidence slowly creeping back into his body. "We were wondering if you wanted to travel together until we find this Corbin guy. After all, it almost seems like we were destined to meet. And, I'd like to talk to someone who also has this gift." He looked eagerly at Aran, his eyes filled with curiosity and wonder.

He's brave, I'll give him that much. Aran looked at Kael and found the boy's eyes nestled safely behind a wall of long, messy, brown hair. *And that one knows how to hide what he's thinking.* Aran looked back to James and nodded. "I think traveling together would be a good idea."

James pumped his fist in the air and Aran couldn't help but smile at the boy's eagerness and sense of adventure.

"I've got a makeshift raft that will be faster than walking if you want to use it."

"You've got a raft?!" exclaimed James. "Then what are we waiting for? Let's find Corbin!" He bounded down the rocky bank, mumbling excitedly to the mouse, "Henry, we're going on a boat! This is really gonna be an adventure!"

Aran smiled fondly after the boy, then caught Kael's suspicious eye on him again. *He's a smart kid to be afraid of strangers. Still, I hope we can become friends.* "Let's get going, Kael," said Aran. "Let's find Corbin." With that, he turned and walked away, Kael following his trail a few moments later.

Kael stared warily after Aran as he walked down the slope after James. His mind was ablaze with questions that he didn't dare ask for fear of what the answer might be, but he knew one thing. He didn't trust Aran whatsoever. *He's hiding something. I can tell.* Kael felt a slight breeze slip past him coming from the north and shivered as the chill crept down his spine. Something was coming, and he wasn't sure if he wanted to find out what. Aran was almost out of view and Kael sighed, *I guess I have to follow now. James, I hope you haven't gotten yourself wrapped up in something even you can't handle.* Kael took a step forward and felt the breeze blow past him, stronger this time, and he shivered again. *This*

may have been a meeting decided by fate, but what kind of fate I'm not sure yet.

IX:

Wind in the Night

A crisp, cool, brisk breeze whistled through the otherwise undisturbed night. It caressed the tops of trees and softly blew on the heads of sleeping birds. It tickled the grass and left waves of laughter to flow through meadows in its wake. It blew gently across the top of the river who responded with a ripple of satisfaction. The wind continued to fly aimlessly through its midnight kingdom, the secret paths illuminated by the full moon's smile. The wind smiled back at the moon, happy to be able to explore freely in the dark without fear of things that hide in the shadows. At least that's what he thought.

As the wind explored valleys and dales, he saw a shadow flicker across a field. A cold chill ran down his length, it caused parts of the straight flowing breeze to curl into small eddies and fold over themselves. On a normal night, the wind would avoid anything that looked as suspicious as the shadow that flitted around below it, but tonight he was unafraid. The moonlight acted like beer, giving the wind a crazy, dangerous, and foolish courage. He slowly floated toward the flickering shadow below, taking his time and looking happily at the beautiful night. The moon's gleam tinted the thin layer of mist on the ground with a shimmering, silvery light that spread across the valley and filled it with an ethereal liquid. The treetops and meadows blended together as the wind looked down from his height, the ghostly liquid in the valley painting a beautiful picture. Slowly, he submerged, the light slipping through his airy body and giving him the wonderful sensation of gradually being lowered into a warm bath.

The wind twirled lazily and touched the tops of the trees; he giggled like a child as they swayed to and fro at his touch. *They're dancing!* he thought, happy to let the moonbeams cloud his normally sharp mind. He gusted gently through the forest and let his mind wander far away from the original purpose of floating down into the moonlit valley. As his mind wandered, so did his body. He lost his normal strongly defined edges and let his body spread through the forest, like a river spreading out into a marsh. He curled around trees and bushes, floated easily above the divots and holes in the ground, and relaxed for the first time in years. He let his mind float freely and was completely submerged in the euphoria-inducing moonlight. A small part of his mind tried to remind him why he had come down, that there was danger afoot, and that he couldn't stay long, but the rest of his clouded mind pushed the warning voice into a dusty corner and simply enjoyed the feeling.

The wind lay on the ground for a long while, his mind so foggy from the moonbeams that he couldn't tell if he had been there for minutes or hours. Eventually, the wind felt something odd at the very edge of his consciousness. At first, he only shivered and drew that part of himself inward. Almost immediately he settled back into the dreamy state that he had been in, gently letting the warm breeze that he had become smoothly brush past the greenery. After a few moments, he felt something again, a cold, dark feeling that started to rouse his numbed mind. Grumbling, the wind began to reluctantly pull himself back together, sighing sadly as the wonderfully warm, lazy feeling slowly slipped away. With leisure, the wind pulled himself into a partially defined breeze, then a warm eddy of air, and finally into a series of repeating gusts, shaking the trees and shrubbery lightly.

As his body coalesced, the wind felt his mind assembling itself. He wondered why he had stopped in the valley, knowing that it was unlike him to stop anywhere for long without a purpose. He shifted through his memory in search of an answer but came up empty-handed. Something was out of place in his consciousness, so he investigated. At the very edge of his mind, he found a thought. It was covered in a film of dust and the wind carefully brushed it off, coaxing the thought back into being. The thought yawned and looked at the wind blearily for a moment, then its eyes grew from peas to melons. The wind was taken aback. "What is it?" The thought didn't say anything; instead, it simply flew into the wind's newest ideas. The wind turned from gusts to puffs, then back to gusts as he remembered the reason he had come to the glade.

Hurriedly, the wind rose to the treetops and made sure that he fit in with the rest of the environment, becoming a warm breeze that dusted the tops of the trees. He felt a cold, wrathful evil walk under him and shivered. Cautiously, the wind peaked down at the thing. It looked like a man at first, but upon closer scrutiny, the wind saw that its outline was dim and smoky, like a shadow. He also saw that the thing didn't walk. It floated over the ground, sticking to the darker parts of the moonlit forest. Warily, the wind followed the creature through the woods, dropping down a little from the tops of the trees. As he did so, the wind felt the air around him become cooler, no matter how much he tried to warm it.

Suddenly, the figure stopped and turned around, carefully examining his surroundings. *Surely it can't tell that I'm here,* thought the wind. The figure slowly looked upwards, and the wind felt the air grow colder. A pair of red dots appeared from behind the edge of the figure's hood and the wind felt as though they were boring into him. The wind stilled, his equivalent to holding his breath. All of a sudden, the wind felt the air around him turn to ice, freezing him in place. Caught off guard, he struggled to break free but found that he could barely make a breeze. Stunned by the sheer power in the feat, the wind whispered, "What are you?"

The figure below chuckled. "At least you know not to ask who I am." Its voice was harsh, like smoke from burned and rotten corpses of the dead and dying. "Although I believe that you are old enough to know what I am." The wind stayed silent, stunned by the fact that the creature could hear and understand him. "No response? I would've expected more from the North Wind." The red dots stared up at the wind, their intense gaze making him feel like his skin was crawling, a very unusual feeling for him. "Well, since I won't be getting a response out of you, I see no harm in answering your question. After all, there are very few people left who can even speak your language. I am the King's left hand, the shadow in the flame, the smoke from the dead, and the light turned dark…" The creature paused then, waiting for a reaction, but the wind didn't recognize any of the names. The red eyes blazed for a moment. "Has it really been that long? Long enough that even the wind has forgotten ME?!"

The figure grew as it bellowed in rage, the edges of its shadow reaching out around it. "Maybe you will remember my true name, and my master," it hissed angrily. "I am Railin, the first of the Shadow King's warriors. I am the one who summoned him to this world. I am the reason that puny college is now just a mass of rubble at the bottom of the ocean. Do you remember me now?" The wind felt another sensation that was strange to him: fear. He remembered that name. He remembered a time when the Shadow King had ruled the kingdom.

He remembered the great strætae, telran gone to the dark side. The wind had been there the day the college had fallen. He remembered that it had taken one strætae to tear down the great walls of the college and defeat all inside, including the archmage. The wind remembered all of this and was afraid.

The figure laughed in satisfaction as the wind pushed against his strength harder than before. "So, you do remember me. Good. I have a task for you." It stopped to make sure the wind was listening. After a moment of struggling, the wind gave in and listened to what the creature said. "Spread your fear, take it with you, because my master has awoken. All should be afraid." With that, the creature let go of the wind and let it fly away. The wind would do as it was told, if not because it wanted to, then because it was in its nature. The wind couldn't help but spread its feelings to the surrounding environment. The figure laughed again then turned back to its path, following the river toward Copper Town.

X:

Talking to a Shadow

Brianna jerked awake, her head spinning as the shrouds of sleep slowly fell away. She looked around, blinked, rubbed her eyes, and wondered what kind of sick joke someone was playing on her. She was surrounded by nothing. To her right and left lay pools of swirling shadow. Behind her was an invisible wall that wouldn't budge no matter how hard she pushed on it, but in front of her lay the strangest thing. A distinctly out of place shape slumped against the ground, almost like a pile of rags. It wouldn't have stood out normally, but with the surrounding black nothingness, the odd figure caught her eye.

Cautiously, she crept toward the shape, not wanting to disturb anything in the darkness. As she neared, she began to see the shape moving; a broken up and down motion that almost resembled breathing. Brianna began to shiver as her legs moved stiffly toward the shape, the air around turned icy and the ground sucked the warmth from her feet. Her breath misted and froze in front of her, leaving the frosty particles to fall to the ground. Brianna would have never noticed the almost silent noise the tiny ice droplets made as they hit the floor, but in this hollow, dark place it sounded like glass shattering. Each time she heard the sound, Brianna would flinch and, even though she was certain she was the only living being around, glance around to see if anything else had heard.

Subconsciously, she started to hold her breath, trying to keep the sound to a minimum and only taking the occasional sip of the frozen air. The closer she got to the figure, the shakier its breathing became. Eventually, Brianna heard a dull rattling sound and looked around startled, thinking that there was something hidden in the dark. She stood still, hardly daring to breathe as she concentrated on what little area of her surroundings she could make out before she realized that the sound was coming from the shadowy form on the floor. Relieved that it was the one thing that had become normal to her in this bizarre place, she let out her pent-up breath in a long sigh. However, her sigh was quickly cut off as she heard her icy breath hit the floor. Slowly and carefully, she proceeded forward.

Brianna was within a few feet of the shadowy lump when her teeth started to chatter against each other in the cold. Even though she wore warm leather shoes, her feet were completely numb and she had to repeatedly look down to make sure that they were still there. Her fingers were icicles, a thin layer of frost forming over them, and her clothes were stiff from the frigid air, any moisture in them frozen solid. Her cheeks were pink from the biting cold and her lips were blue, but she still pressed onward. *If I stop now, I won't be able to start again. I can't die in this forsaken place.*

The swirling, formless shadows started to close in around her from the dark nothingness and she felt her muscles screaming as they began to cramp from the life-sucking cold. *Just a little farther,* she thought and gritted her teeth to stop the incessant chattering. At last, she was about an arm's length away and cautiously reached out to touch the thing. Her instincts yelled at her to stop as she heard the wheezing intensify, but she refused to listen. *Too late to stop now,* she thought and touched the pile of shadows.

She was surprised and horrified to find that her hand

didn't slip straight through it. Instead, she saw a thin greasy layer of shadows surround her fingers. The shadows stained her skin black. A few centimeters beneath, she felt a thin membrane. A searing pain shot through her fingers as the freezing cold moved into her hand and sent a cold so great that her numbed hands felt like they were burning. She let out a sharp cry of pain and quickly pulled her arm back, afraid of what might happen next.

The lump paused its breathing for a moment. Then it did an odd thing for a pile of shadows to do: it moved. Not in the same jerky and mechanical way it had moments ago, but in a way that almost resembled a dance. It twisted and turned, a snake slithering in the grass until it had unfolded to about Brianna's height. *It can't be.* Brianna had heard stories about them before, but she always assumed they were myths. The stræntae. *I'm just having a bad dream,* she tried to convince herself, but the biting cold was too real.

She wrapped her arms around herself, trying to keep any warmth left in her body. The shadowy thing finally stopped its unnerving movement and Brianna let out a frosty breath. She only now realized that she had been holding it and immediately felt a throbbing at the base of her skull, the lack of oxygen combined with the cold more than enough to give her an immediate headache. Her eyes narrowed as she tried to avoid the throbbing in her head. *I'm dreaming. It's all just a nightmare -- it isn't real.* She stared at the shadow, waiting for something to happen, still shivering from the cold. After a long moment, the greasy layer of darkness began to part.

The hole in the film of shadows widened, unveiling a pale gray face that looked eerily familiar. A thin coat of oily darkness covered the face, like a dusting of ash from an erupted volcano. The face gave the creature the appearance of peaceful and comfortable sleep, but the illusion was ruined as more and more features were revealed by the receding black nothingness. A large nose and stubby ears were shown, followed by hair that changed from being a dark black to grey, red, and all other colors until finally deciding to stop on a light brown, almost chestnut color. *It can't be,* thought Brianna as her mind, numb from the cold, started to unthaw and slowly realize why the face looked so familiar. Still, she couldn't quite come to terms with what she saw before her until the creature's eyes fluttered slowly open. They were a hard, icy blue, speckled with brown splotches and spots. Brianna gasped in astonishment as the truth finally broke through the icy shroud that surrounded her mind: *It's me.*

Brianna stepped back in shock and felt like she was moving in slow motion through the cold air. The eyes followed her with a blank but cold expression. Even though the face bore an uncanny physical resemblance to Brianna's, there were variations in the way it was put together. The eyes were set in a cruel and angry manner, the mouth slightly tilted in a gruesome grin, and a glint of greed and hunger that ran through the pupils. Brianna tried to turn around and run away, but she was held in place by the thing's stare and the cold. The rest of the thing's body emerged from the shadows and the rosy color of life flowed into its cheeks. The thing dropped to its knees then looked up at Brianna and grinned maliciously.

That was enough to shock her out of the trance she had been in and to turn around and sprint away. Only there was nowhere to run. She saw the hopelessness of her situation as the shadowy valley of darkness around her started to close in. It cornered her against an invisible wall and she banged pointlessly against the wall. "HELP!!" she screamed in fear, knowing that no one could hear her. She glanced behind her and saw her look-alike gliding gracefully across the floor toward her.

Brianna looked into her face and was caught once again by her eyes. They were cold and ruthless, filled with a desire to hurt and punish all. She smiled at Brianna with gleaming white teeth, teeth that reflected all light and made Brianna cringe away in disgust at the unnatural sight. The clone smiled, a cat who knew that its prey couldn't escape and was ready to play with it. It was a smug, cold, hungry smile.

"What do you think you're doing?" asked the figure. Brianna almost leaped out of her skin as she heard her voice come out of the creature's mouth. "Nowhere to run, no one to save you, nothing to do but wait. Wait until the cold kills you."

A spark of rebellion flared in Brianna's soul at the comment. "Letting the… co--ol-d dddo… yo-ur wooork foor you?"

The thing laughed. "Look at that, you still have some fight left in you. How cute. I never thought that someone as soft-hearted and weak as you would be able to even stand, let alone resist me in this realm." She smiled the same predatory smile at Brianna again. "I don't see any harm in telling you what's about to happen. Besides, it'll be fun for me to give you the exact details of how you'll die."

The clone lazily walked over to the invisible wall and, like a cat playing with its food, slid down next to Brianna. She patted the ground invitingly. "Come on, I don't bite." She smiled cruelly at the last phrase. Brianna shook her quivering head, trying to retain any freedom she could. A frown momentarily passed over the clone's face, but she shook it off and just shrugged. "Have it your way, it's your death after all." The thing looked out toward the shadowland. "Where to start, where to start?"

That's right, just keep on talking. I've gotta figure a way out of here.

"I guess I should start with what I am, unless you somehow already know what that is."

"St-- stræntae," Brianna managed to get out.

Her doppelganger looked over at her, pleased. "Very good. But can you tell me what a stræntae is?" She waited for a response, then returned to looking at the shadowlands in disappointment. "I figured as much. I am the beginning to a new you, a stronger, more powerful, more intelligent, better you. You know of the stræntae's reputation, or at least what it used to be." The stræntae glanced her way and Brianna managed to nod. The strætae smiled hungrily before she continued. "Since you know so much about us, I'll tell you where we really come from. The strætae were, and are, a proud race that seeks mastery of all powers. Your history books mark us as being simple telran, mages, I suppose they are called now, who overused their powers and were taken over by demons and devils. The truth is much more frightening."

The strætae paused and looked at Brianna with that evil grin. "Strætae are not simply the shells of telran turned evil by the powers they control. They aren't even demons that consume the souls of those that try to get too much power. No. They're all of the wizard's weaknesses and failures, worst characteristics and traits, and simple undefinable flaws meshed into one. The reason that the telran turns to a shadow billowing cloud is that there simply isn't enough room in their body to contain the true embodiment of life." Slowly, the duplicate rose from the ground, sliding gracefully to her feet and turning her hungry eyes toward Brianna. "That's where I come in. You see, this realm that we are on is home to all of those emotions that you and many others try to hide. You wouldn't believe me if I told you that there billions more valleys of dark shadow like this one. One for each living creature, but you aren't from here and couldn't see them even if you wanted to. It's a true shame, this is a very beautiful world once you get used to the shadows."

Brianna thought she heard some trace of remorse in the stræntae's voice, but couldn't use the weakness as her teeth chattered uncontrollably and her body shook with cold. The copy faced her and looked at her with the same hungry, gruesome smile. "That's better, shake and squirm like the weakling you are. You'll understand your situation soon enough, but we haven't even gotten to the best part yet. The best part is how you're going to die. You see, when most things die, their soul is split, the emotions and mistakes coming to this plane and the rest going to The Valley of Souls. I don't expect you to know the name, suffice it to say that anything and everything that has ever lived has some part there. But you won't have anything going to the valley. Your essence will be stuck on this plane, the very air is eating away at your courage, trust, kindness, and all the other feelings you think are good. Your soul will be stuck here and your body will become an immortal vessel for me, your stræntae."

Brianna's copy sighed contentedly, looking at her hands and smiling. "The one problem with being a stræntae is that you never know what your host will look like until they arrive in this realm. I have to say, I'm quite pleased with what I got."

Brianna shivered, the only reaction that she could give in the unforgiving cold. "I hardly feel cold," she managed to slip past her chattering teeth.

Her twin frowned, her patience almost at an end. "Well, that won't last..." Brianna couldn't hear the rest of what the copy said because the warm crackling sound of a fire started to fill her ears. The frown on her twin deepened as it drew no reaction from Brianna, then grew into a dark scowl as Brianna smiled. A warmth had started to spread through her limbs; stopping the dreadful shivering of her body and making her feel so blissful that she couldn't have stopped the smile if she wanted to.

The warmth coursed through Brianna; the sensation was so wonderful in comparison to the dreadful cold that she giggled. The stræntae in waiting's scowl turned to a look of bewilderment. The warmth and the once fierce being's now utterly confused face turned Brianna's giggle into a wholehearted laugh, not the halfhearted laugh you give your friend after they tell you something mildly entertaining.

This was a laugh that traveled straight from the pit of Brianna's stomach, the kind of laugh that happens so very rarely, one that springs from being completely at peace with life and you hear a hilarious joke. It was a laugh full of love and truth. The dark Shadow Realm that Brianna had felt so solidly attached to moments before slowly began to fade. The darkness changed from the cold, frightening shadows of the unknown to the warm kindness of sleep. The last thing that Brianna saw before the warm arms of sleep took her was her copy's face. She was screaming in rage and horror as she slowly dissolved into the black shadow from which she had come.

XI:

An Alchemist in the Mountains

A warm fire crackled cheerily in a clay-brick fireplace when Brianna woke. She smiled and closed her eyes, all her troubles and concerns swept away temporarily by the blissful feeling of a warm bed. Something in the back of her mind tried to get her attention, but she swept it aside and mumbled that it could wait ten minutes. Brianna enjoyed the comfortable heat that crawled through her system and let it mask the important questions: *Where am I? What happened? How did I escape?* These questions should have been the first to cross her mind when she woke, but the wonderful heat from the fire and bed compared to the cold she had come from overwhelmed her senses. This, combined with the unbelievable situation in which she found herself, stopped the thoughts from flowing freely through her mind.

Brianna stared at the fire and twisted her hair in delicate swirls. She looked fondly at the flames for a few more moments. She knew that when she let go of the warmth and embraced the world again, a flood of nightmarish memories would flood down on her. "Thank you," she whispered to the fire, so low that no one heard it. The fire flickered in response. Its flaming arms reached slightly out toward her. Brianna smiled, then let her focus slip to the memories fluttering around in the back of her mind. She opened the cage in which she had hidden them, and let them fly freely into her awareness.

First came the memory of the fight with the dwarves. She winced at what she had been forced to do. Next was the image of Erik helping her, standing by her and telling her something important. *What did he say again?* The question was quickly swept away as the tidal wave of memories flooded her brain with the dark imagery of the Shadow Realm. She shivered at the cold, evil void she had inhabited, of the terrifying creature that had spoken to her. *A stræntae. If they are real, then…* Her spine shook with nervous tension at the implications and she felt a dread weight pressing down on her. *I have to warn everyone at home. Everyone needs to know what might be coming, the stræntae are here and that means that their leader isn't far behind.* She remembered vague passages from *The Brief History of Magic and Myracles* about the Shadow King. *If he's real, too, then there is little hope for the world.*

Brianna's thoughts were interrupted by voices nearby. She strained her ears and tried to hear what they were saying.

"... I don't know, Erik."

"I'm sure of it! She has to be one of the five!"

"You might be right, but..."

Brianna held her breath as she pushed her hearing to the limit, but the voices had moved out of range. Carefully, she lifted the edge of the blanket and started to slip out toward the fire. She attempted to roll stealthily out of the bed, but to say that she accomplished this would be an utter lie. In actuality, she managed to fall out of the cot and land headfirst on the floor. She groaned quietly as she slowly rolled to her back, the world a red haze as her head spun. A dull thudding pain was emanating from her nose and spread through her body, turning her head into a painful, throbbing mess.

Brianna tried to push herself to a sitting position, but her arms felt like twigs and she slumped helplessly to the floor. She managed to stop her head from being the main area of impact, but only just. Her head hit the floor with a solid thud and her vision turned a deep red hue. The dull throbbing in her mind became a sharp, shooting pain.

"Help," she called out meekly. *How am I going to get anywhere in this state*? The world continued to spin around her. Her vision still cloudy, she lay on her back and let the shooting headache that had come to occupy all of her mind run its course.

Slowly, the world around Brianna came into focus and she saw a rocky ceiling supported by thick pine logs, the edge of a roughly hewn table, and the dancing shadows made by the fire. A strange odor penetrated her world, not necessarily a bad smell, but one that Brianna wasn't accustomed to. She rolled her eyes around in an attempt to see the rest of her surroundings without moving her head. She saw the underside of a wooden shelf, and could just barely see the top half of a candle resting on the shelf. She saw the fireplace to her right, and to her left was the small cot on which she had been resting. The only other thing that she could see was the edge of a small chair.

Sighing inwardly, Brianna geared herself to sit up again. Slowly and very carefully, she bent her knees. No sharp pain. She raised her hands toward her legs. No red haze around her vision. Finally, she started to raise her head off the ground. The resulting mixture of excruciating pain shooting through her skull and the bright distorted colors that washed into her world put her over the edge. An animalistic scream of pain emanated from her throat, her sensory system completely overloaded. She let her head fall back, the jostle making her world go black for a moment. Her eyes flickered open again; she wouldn't give in to the peacefulness of blacking out.

A small, pudgy, humanoid figure with white hair and a grey beard hustled into her view. He looked at her, extremely worried, an almost comical expression on his round, rosy face. Brianna would have laughed if she hadn't been so overwhelmed by pain.

The little man knelt over her and put a hand to her head, whispering a few words under his breath as he did so. Brianna was amazed to feel the pain fade away and her muscles relax, the world returning to its normal color. Almost as surprising, the man lifted her as though she were a feather and gently set her down in the cot.

"Who are you?" Brianna managed to say as the man wrapped the blankets around her.

Without looking up from his task, he said, "A friend."

He carefully wrapped the blankets around Brianna. "Now sleep," he said in a voice that didn't offer room for negotiation. His words were unnecessary, as Brianna had already slipped back into a deep, restful, and healing sleep.

The world came together in flickering pieces as Brianna opened her eyes for the third time that day, but this time the traumatic events she had experienced were clear in her memory, replaying as they had happened, comprehensible in sequence and content. As the rocky ceiling materialized through several rapid series of blinks, Brianna felt an aching in the back of her head and groaned softly.

Almost before she was done groaning, the shriveled face of the white-haired man appeared above. His rich, earth-colored eyes seemed unusually large for his small face and were surrounded by deep wrinkles of concern.

How old is he? wondered Brianna as she took in more details of his face. Aside from his white hair, the seemingly endless rows of wrinkles showed his age. *He must be centuries, no millennia, old.* She hadn't guessed this based on his white hair or even his wrinkled skin; she didn't even think to base it on his bent back or the rest of his worn appearance. No, Brianna based his age on his eyes. She had learned that much can be discerned about someone through their eyes, and the man's eyes held more stories and history than the king and his courtroom full of men with many years of combined experience.

His eyes were not only a dark, earthy brown as Brianna had thought when she first looked at them, but they were laced with veins of dark blue, a color that reflected the deepest reaches of the ocean. The faint blue was almost hidden by the darker brown that surrounded it, but the old man was only a few inches away from Brianna, so the details appeared clearly before her.

I feel... safe. The thought coalesced in her mind.

"Good," said the man. His voice was a higher pitch than Brianna had expected. "Now, tell me exactly what you were thinking when you decided to roll off your cot and go smacking your head on the floor." He looked at her quizzically. Brianna would've taken him seriously at any other time, but right now her head felt fuzzy and the world was funny, so she couldn't help but grin impishly at his voice.

He sounds so funny. She giggled and shook her head. *Why is everything so fuzzy and weird?*

"What?" asked the man, and leaned away from her. "I thought you were smart, not like the normal drunk or broken boys I'm always fixing up."

"It's just your voice," said Brianna, surprising herself as she spoke aloud. "It sounds like squeaky sand." She giggled and put her hand to her mouth in an attempt to control the light laughter. *What's wrong with me?* she wondered.

The man's disgruntled face slowly turned to a smile and he chuckled to himself as some sort of realization dawned on him. "Of course," he said almost to himself. "Taeroot." He looked at Brianna, his eyes bright with curiosity. "Do you know what Taeroot is?"

"Taeroot…" She thought about it for a moment, then opened her mouth, and words started to spill out. "Taeroot, or shadow root, is an herb found mainly at the edge of the flaming plains and is used as a numbing agent that also helps put people to sleep. It is highly prized by many doctors due to its rarity and powerful healing uses. It-"

"That's enough," the old man interrupted before Brianna could fully get into the memorized rant. "Do you know what happens if you mix it with telfern?" Without pausing to give Brianna enough time to answer, he continued. "If combined with telfern, it can be used as a truth serum that affects the mind in a way similar to alcohol, only more potent and for a shorter time. However, the combination also can coax an injured mind back from a coma."

"You used the two to bring me back from the shadowy place." Brianna felt the odd intoxication diminish even as she spoke.

"You're almost right, but to bring you back from there I had to make something stronger. I added a plant called shriggus root to help bring you back to this realm. Have you ever heard of shriggus root?

"Nope, can't say I have. What is it?"

The old man smiled. "I'm glad you asked. It's a relatively useless plant found high in the eastern mountains. The only known use is building a partial bridge between our realm and the Shadow Realm. Its name also comes from the alchemist who discovered this property, Shriggus Doeain."

The old man swelled with pride as he spoke the last few words and Brianna felt bad as she asked her next question. "Who?"

The man's chest deflated and his smile soured slightly, then he sighed. "I suppose the name wouldn't mean anything to a youngster such as yourself. My golden days were many, many human lifetimes ago, back in a time when we weren't worried about the Shadow King or his many servants. It was a time of discovery and prosperity for all before I became Shriggus, last of the heiren." He looked at Brianna and smiled sorrowfully as he thought back to his past. "I do hope Erik is right about you. Maybe you are one of the five prophesied to save us."

Brianna sat, stunned, letting all the information that the small man, Shriggus, had told her sink in. *He must be thousands of years old. The Shadow King is said to have first started his rule well over 2000 years ago, and he's saying he was alive before that. What does he mean I'm one of the five? What is happening to the world?* Brianna took a long breath as the information settled in her mind. Finally, she asked, "How are you still alive after all this time, and what is a heiren?"

Shriggus chuckled. "Humans never change, do they? Always asking questions that catch you off guard. I suppose that answering the second would also answer the first, so let's start there. The heiren were an ancient race closely related to the elves, dwarves, and humans. An in-between species, if you will. We had the dexterity and determination of a dwarf, the mind and life of an elf, and the free will and creativity of a human. But it came at a cost. We thought of nothing but accumulating knowledge and were absurdly curious, which lead to our eventual downfall at the hands of the strætae." A sorrowful expression crossed Shriguss's face. "Now I'm cursed to be the last one left alive. After I created a passageway to and from the Shadow Realm, the ancient laws of magic that govern this world tied me to its fate. I am cursed to live until the bridge that I have made is at last undone, or the world is overcome and cannot hold me here." He looked at Brianna, "Does that answer your questions?"

Brianna swallowed nervously. "It does, and I can't imagine how it would feel to be the last of my kind."

Shriggus nodded. "I'm afraid you'll find all too many lonely representatives of extinct species across the world, remnants of a time long since passed. Like the patch of Shriggus root. Its range has diminished, and the plant itself has shrunk to half its size. Every time I make the journey to gather it, I see evidence that it is losing the struggle to survive. The world is changing, and many living things will not survive the change. We diminish and disappear."

Brianna let the silence hang in the air, unsure of what to say. The words of the old man ushered in sadness and a sense of loss that seemed to dwarf other emotions in the room.

Erik! The thought flew into her mind and she tried to push herself into a sitting position. She managed to get her arms out of the blankets and raise her head a few inches before Shriggus gently but forcefully pushed her back into the bed. "Where is Erik?" she asked, giving in to the old man's motion and letting her head rest again on the pillow.

"He's sleeping. Last night he watched over you after your fall until I told him that if he didn't go to sleep, I'd turn him into a toad." Shriggus rolled his eyes playfully. "He really has far too much faith in my abilities."

Brianna relaxed. "Good." Then in a softer tone, "He saved me, didn't he?"

"Yes, he most certainly did," Shriggus spoke in a

quiet, serious tone. "If he hadn't brought you to me, then you would have become a strӕntae, slave to the creature you undoubtedly met on the other side."

A tear rolled down Brianna's face. "I didn't mean to hurt them." Shriggus looked up, intrigued, but Brianna didn't notice, too wrapped up in the memory. "I didn't mean to, I swear. I just lost control." Her voice wavered as she saw the stony spear flying toward the dwarf. She saw him turn around at the last second. She felt the spear as an extension of her mind as it pierced the dwarf's body and pinned him to the ground. She saw the horrified look in Erik's eyes and the pained look on Grimsvor's face as the stone spear buried itself into his shoulder. "He had no reason to help me. He had every right to leave me to crumple to the ground, but he still helped me." Tears streamed down her cheeks.

Shriggus reached out a comforting hand and touched her shoulder. "Of course he had a reason to save you. He was traveling with those dwarves for the sole purpose of saving whatever poor creature they captured." Shriggus patted her shoulder. "He never expected that he would find you, but when he did, he knew that he had to save you at any cost."

"Why?" asked Brianna as she tried to wipe away the

tears, “What’s so important about me?”

“Everything, maybe.” Shriggus’s voice was so firm and powerful that Brianna looked up from her mourning. She saw a vision of what the shriveled old man must have looked like in his youth. His eyes were fiery with determination and his mouth set in a hard line. The wrinkles in his face smoothed and the cracks of blue in his eyes changed from being barely visible to glowing like lightning flashing across a stormy, dark sky. Shriggus stared her down, the blue fissures seeming to reach out at her. “You are one of the five. The last of the Telran. The only chance we have for defeating the Shadow King.”

As he continued his speech, Shriggus’s words became less and less directed at Brianna, almost as though he was reciting an ancient verse from some sort of prophecy. “One from the fire that rages in our souls. One from strong and steady water. One that was born to bring order to the chaotic storm of life. One born from the pain that lies deep inside our minds.” He returned his gaze to Brianna as he said the next line, “One with the touch of the earth that courses through her veins.” He paused, emphasizing the phrase before continuing, “These five will be the last hope. They will bring an end to the Shadow King and his kin, cutting all ties between this plane and the Shadow Realm as they do so."

Brianna felt a chill go down her spine, fear tingling through her. A few days ago, she would have thought all of this nonsense of the Shadow King an old wives tale to scare children before bed. However, after her trip to the dark Shadow Realm, she knew that Shriggus must be telling the truth. Still, she couldn't accept it. "There must be some mistake." Her quivering voice revealed that she knew it wasn't. "There has to be someone else. I'm not even able to control my powers yet."

Shriggus shrugged. "Maybe there is, maybe there isn't. Either way, I know that you're the only telran I've seen in the last century whose abilities match those I saw before the last invasion. Whether or not you think you're ready for this doesn't matter. You are the best shot we've got, so you have to try."

Brianna didn't say anything. She felt only dismay, coupled with a certainty that she would disappoint everyone, literally everyone. Her failure would not be small and unimportant. It would be on a massive, earth-shattering scale.

After a moment, Shriggus turned away. "It's your decision, in the end. I can't make it for you. I'll give you some time to think."

He was about to leave when Brianna said, "I know." She spoke in a whisper, barely audible. "I'm just afraid."

Shriggus sighed, sat on the cot, and rested a comforting hand on her shoulder. "I understand that, but this isn't just about you. This is about all the innocent families and creatures who don't have a choice. If you stand up and do your part, then they have a chance to keep on living happily among their kind. But if you don't do anything, then they'll end up dying or being left to live the rest of their days without any hope of freedom, alone and afraid." He clenched his fist as he finished the sentence and Brianna saw a tear roll down his face.

He's the last of his kind, and he doesn't want to doom anyone else with that fate. She felt a sense of duty overcome her. *He can't let anyone suffer the same fate, but he's still giving me the choice. I can't let him down.* She slowly raised herself, wincing as a dull pain echoed at the back of her skull. She reached over and rested a reassuring hand on his, squeezing it gently. Slowly, Shriggus raised his moist, old face and looked hopefully at her. "I know more about being alone than you think," she said with a sad smile running across her face. "I'll do it."

Shriggus returned the smile, sitting back up in his chair and slowly pulling away one hand to dab away the salty tears that glistened around his eyes. "Thank you."

Brianna felt a weight fall on her shoulders and her smile became strained. The weight she felt wasn't from lack of sleep, or from being in the dark and cold shadow plane. It was the weight of knowing that if she failed in her duty everything she knew and cared about would be lost, destroyed by a force too powerful to imagine. It was the weight of life. Brianna didn't realize this, but she knew that the weight was something she was going to have to get used to until either she died or the Shadow King was defeated.

Shriggus saw the strain creep across her face and said, "Lay back down and get some rest. When you wake up, I'll be sure to tell Erik, and there'll be some stew for you." He smiled at Brianna fondly.

"I wouldn't mind a nap," Brianna replied and then yawned. She laughed. "On second thought, I think I could use a long rest."

"I couldn't agree more." Shriggus grinned at her, his eyes showing his joy. Brianna lay back down on her side and Shriggus tucked her in, carefully and efficiently, just like before. After he was done, he sat for a moment before throwing another log on the fire and turning to leave.

"Shriggus," came Brianna's voice, and the old man turned around. She was lying on her side, one hand behind her head and the specks of brown in her eyes glowing dimly. "Thank you." Shriggus nodded and motioned her back to sleep before turning and shuffling silently out of the room.

He worked his way to a table stacked with various herbs and bottled liquids. He sat down on a small three-legged stool and felt the smile slip first from his eyes, then from his lips as he thought of how young the girl was. *How brave, how foolish, how strong*, he thought. *I didn't even ask her what her name was. I guess I am getting old.* He chuckled grimly at the thought. *I'll just have Erik properly introduce us when she wakes again.* He sighed. He understood what the girl had to do. She had no clue what the Shadow King was, but she had accepted the burden willingly. *If I were in her shoes, I would run,* Shriggus thought ruefully. *I would run and hide.*

XII:

A Trip Down Memory Lane

Thud! A fist smacked into Roan's side again and he groaned, feeling another welt beginning to form. Corbin slid back gracefully and planted his feet in a fighting stance before he began to talk.

"Better," he said and grinned at Roan. "You almost lasted a full minute this time."

"Remind me why I agreed to let you do this?" Roan moved his feet hip-width apart and bent his legs slightly. He raised his arms in a defensive position and motioned for Corbin to start again.

"Discipline." Corbin raised his arms to chest level and started to circle Roan. "Without discipline, you have no control, and without control, you won't be able to properly harness your powers." He took a step toward Roan and the fight began.

Roan stayed back. He had learned to be wary of the old man. Corbin took a step closer and a dangerous smile played across his face. Slowly he approached Roan, his feet sliding through the grass and his hands ready. Roan eyed him cautiously. Although Corbin looked old and frail, he could move at lightning speed.

The two circled each other, each searching for an opening in the other's defense. Corbin, as usual, spotted it first. He leaped forward, moving so fast that Roan barely managed to block the blow aimed at his upper right thigh. He wanted to sigh in relief, but Corbin's left hand was already headed toward Roan's now open chest. Roan swiped at the hand and, by some sort of absurd luck, managed to bat it away. Then he launched his own attack. Compared to Corbin's graceful and planned punches, Roan's were slow and clumsy. Corbin didn't move his hand. Instead, he moved back a fraction of a step and let Roan lean farther into the punch than he meant to. Just as Roan realized his mistake, Corbin grabbed his hand and pulled him straight onto the grass.

Roan gasped to regain his breath after the impact. He tried to push himself up but was smashed back to the ground as Corbin stomped a foot on his back. What little air he had gathered was forced out of his lungs. Roan battled against Corbin, but the old man showed no sign of letting up. Reaching up and tapping the old man's leg was the only way to get him to stop the fight, but Roan was tired of giving up and pushed harder. He managed to raise himself slightly off the ground, affording him room to breathe. *I've got it this time. I won't let him beat me again.* Fueled by the thought, Roan pushed harder and gained another inch or so before Corbin pressed down with renewed energy.

"Go ahead and give up, Roan. You don't need to hurt yourself." Corbin's voice didn't sound strained and the nonchalance fueled fury in Roan. He growled, fierce and animalistic. He couldn't bear being defeated by the old man again.

He felt the same hot energy coursing through his body again and channeled it into his arms, pushing against the hard clay beneath him. Slowly, he started to turn the fraction of space between himself and the ground into an inch. Corbin pushed down harder, but Roan refused to let go of his hard-won space.

They remained at a standstill for a moment and Roan was satisfied when he heard the old man's breathing grow slightly ragged, the first sign of weariness that Corbin had shown during any of their fights.

However, his joy was short-lived. Corbin pushed down harder and the slight gap between his chest and the ground slowly disappeared. Corbin's strength amazed Roan. *He's not even trying and he still beats me. How am I supposed to save anyone if I can't even stand up to an old guy?* Roan gritted his teeth in frustration and gave up at last. He let Corbin shove him into the ground then reached up and tapped his mentor's calf. Corbin immediately took his foot off Roan's back, and Roan took long, grateful breaths of the dusty air.

"That was stupid." Corbin's voice was hard.

Roan rolled onto his back and looked up at Corbin. "What am I supposed to do if I have to fight someone who's better than me? Should I just give up?" His voice was equally as hard and carried an edge of rebelliousness. He may have lost the battle, but he couldn't let Corbin tell him to surrender.

Corbin looked with sharp disapproval at Roan. "That's not what I'm saying. You shouldn't give up, but you shouldn't try to win with brute strength, either."

A hot coal of anger lit in Roan's mind and slowly grew into a living ember. All of the confusion, frustration, and weariness overwhelmed his thoughts.

"What should I do? What do you expect me to do?"

"What I expected you to do was think." The hard glint in Corbin's eyes began to lessen. "I wanted you to learn that some battles have to be lost in order to win."

The ember of anger in Roan flared at Corbin's confusing words. "What the hell does that mean?" Roan had risen and was practically yelling now. "I'm not supposed to give up, but sometimes I have to? How does that make any sense?!"

The two stared icily at each other. The air grew so full of tension that the forest around them became still, watching the silent battle of master and student. The anger that Roan felt had grown into a blazing fire, but it was slowly suffocated as Corbin met his gaze with stone-cold strength. The fire started to ebb, gradually at first, but as the staring competition continued, Roan felt all his angry energy drain away, replaced by the ache of bruised and tired muscles. After a long time, Roan finally gave in to the weariness, sighed, and let his gaze fall.

Corbin released his breath and moved toward Roan. "I'm sorry," his voice was gentle and kind now. "We've been training hard for the last few days. You must be tired."

Roan brushed away the comment. "I guess so." He

looked up and a small smile worked its way onto his face. "Maybe I need a break."

Corbin nodded. "Sure. I wouldn't mind a little rest either." A mimic of Roan's weak smile crept across his face. "Besides, I need to get a few things from the town. You can come if you want."

Roan thought about it for a moment, then said, "I'll catch up. I need to be alone for a little bit."

Corbin didn't push for any information, and Roan silently thanked him for the reprieve. He simply nodded and picked up his pack and walking stick before starting the journey toward Copper Town.

What did I get myself into? Roan thought as Corbin exited the clearing.

After Corbin was gone, Roan took a deep breath and headed back to the base of his house. His legs were sore from his bouts with the old man, and his mind was weary from his nightly history lessons. Corbin had told him the long history of the telran, including the great epics of their battles and feats. He had told him stories of the Varlen, a group of telran who had each mastered their respective elements, beings so old that their names had been forgotten and lost in time. He spoke of the outlandish things they had done: raising mountains, creating forests, calming the wildest storms, and changing the flow of rivers. Night after night, Roan had listened intently to these stories, amazed by the very idea of the existence of people with that much power.

Then, the lessons had turned to less interesting topics. Corbin taught Roan about the many different cultures that were spread across the land of Tillinue. Roan had learned about kings and queens, wars and treaties, and dozens of other obscure facts. After each lesson, Corbin would quiz him ruthlessly on all of the history, his normally friendly demeanor replaced with a hard, steely countenance. In these moments he demanded the same fierce clarity and control of the mind that he expected of Roan's body during their bouts of sparring.

Although this training had only been going on for a week, Roan had bags under his eyes and woke with stiff muscles and a bleary mind every morning. However, this weariness came not only from the intensive training or the history lessons, it also came from a place deep in Roan's soul. He carried the weight of responsibility and, although he couldn't place his finger on it at the time, this weight was part of the reason for his exhaustion.

The heaviness of millions of other creatures' souls

rested on him now, each one a small weight adding to the cumulative whole. Each day, he felt the weight grow lighter as he grew stronger, but the awareness of his responsibility combined with the rigorous training left him completely drained.

I don't know if I can do this. He reached the open trap door and pulled himself in, taking a deep breath and smiling at the tranquil scent of pine. He closed his eyes, sat cross-legged, and let all of his pain and weariness seep into the surrounding air.

Time passed without his awareness of it. He cleared his mind and reached a state of calm. The stress and exhaustion of his life finally came to a climax and broke, leaving him relaxed, confident, and at peace. He felt like he was at one with the world.

Unhurried and unworried, he got to his feet and grabbed a new set of clothes to replace his current sweat-soaked ones, then nimbly scaled down the ladder. He set off toward the creek, making almost no noise as he moved effortlessly through the clearing. He could feel the ember of anger smoldering in a hidden part of his mind but chose to leave it alone in favor of the new sense of calm that had swept over him.

He reached the edge of the small stream. He let his

free hand brush against the trunk of a massive maple tree. He smiled faintly at the sound of the burbling and babbling stream. *It's almost as if it's talking.* He proceeded to the bank. He sat for a moment before he decided to enter the familiar stream.

He quickly stripped and lay in the refreshingly cold water, his breath coming in short gasping bursts as he became accustomed to the chill. He felt the water wash away all of the frustration and anger from that morning, cleansing his mind and letting him start anew. The smoldering ember in his mind was eventually quenched and turned back into a plain and unexciting piece of coal, easily stored in the newly refreshed recesses of his mind. His face relaxed and his dark hair floated aimlessly in a small eddy. Rays of sunlight filtered through the thick canopy of leaves above and fell in shifting patterns around him.

I could stay here forever. Roan's mind and body soaked in the cool comfort of the silken liquid. The pain eased, and the exhaustion was replaced with the living, burbling essence of the creek.

The calm of the forest flowed around and through him. The water carried with it the ancient wisdom of roots, earth, rocks, and minerals. It also bore filaments of light and threads of darkness, like joy and sadness. All of its many tiny droplets mixed and melded into a strong stream, creating a sense of wholeness and unity with all things.

After a long while, Roan pulled himself out of the water. *I should probably catch up with Corbin.* He climbed onto the bank and shook off most of the water before he opened the gate within himself a fraction and warmed his body just enough for the rest of the liquid to evaporate. He threw on the new clothes and looked around, a sense of joy and purpose now running wildly through his veins. He laughed heartily before he started to run back to the clearing, skipping and laughing at the rejuvenation he felt. He threw his dirty clothes at the base of the treehouse, then headed after Corbin.

"I wonder what he's gotten himself into," Roan said to himself, jokingly. "I bet he's found someone to talk history to. Maybe he's at the bar talking to the fishermen and merchants." He laughed fondly at the idea of old, respectable Corbin talking about the daily catch with the crusty fisherman. He raced happily through the forest after his mentor.

Roan reached the edge of the forest and slowly pulled apart the last layer of ferns to peek out at his old home. It had been well over two years since his last visit to the town, and he had forgotten how out of place it looked. Copper Town was the second largest town in the region, which by no stretch of the imagination made it a big town. Its layout consisted of a scattering of small, unorganized buildings surrounding a slightly larger tavern called The Drunken Cow.

The strange name came from an incident that had occurred on its opening day, the main character of which had been a cow that had managed to find a cracked barrel of beer. The cow had started to lick the oozing beer and, enjoying the taste, proceeded to empty half the barrel before stumbling away. The cow had then somehow managed to lurch its way to the front of the building where it decided to stay, swaying from leg to leg and burping happily. Needless to say, this brought most of the town to gawk at the awkward animal.

As Roan peered through the thin underbrush, he thought that the town looked even smaller than usual. It was normally filled with traders and farmers from all around this time of year, but today it looked just as dull and empty as ever.

Realization dawned on Roan. *The storm,* he thought. *It must've stopped the traders from making it on time.* Even as he thought this, a wagon creaked into the town, caked in mud and gunk. A flock of people crowded around the merchant, chattering and haggling prices. Roan seized this opportunity and dashed to the edge of the smattering of ramshackle buildings.

He remembered how he had been treated the last time he had come here. People in small towns tend to remember strange events, much like the one that led to Roan's parents' death, and Copper Town wasn't an exception. The townsfolk liked to give him a wide berth as they passed by him. Even Calcifer, the jolly owner of The Drunken Cow, had been short and terse with Roan when he had last come to town.

He stuck to the shadows, carefully making his way through the village toward the tavern. He approached a gap in the buildings and took a deep breath, preparing himself for what filled the hole. A bare patch of ground was surrounded by a thin line of yellowish grass and other weeds. Broken wooden beams and rusted metal chunks scattered the ground haphazardly, the shape of the long-gone building hardly recognizable. At the center of the debris was an odd mound, a pile of blackened wood and charred stone. Here, in the center of the ruin, two white flowers had managed to sprout and now twined around each other.

Roan forced himself to look away and go back to his current goal. He let out his pent-up breath when he reached the shadow of the next building, and he let a single salty tear roll down his cheek before furiously wiping his eyes. *What's gone is gone. No use in crying over something you can't change.* He left the remnants of his old life once again, and went back to searching for his mentor.

The door to The Drunken Cow creaked as it swung open, letting a breath of fresh air penetrate the stench of ale and musty patrons. Calcifer looked up from the counter and saw Roan walk in, careful to keep his features hidden in the shadow of his hood. "Welcome, stranger," Calcifer said, happy for the business. "A fresh supply of bread and cheese just came in, if you're hungry. Or, you can try our signature honey beer."

"How much for the beer?" asked Roan, taking on a gravelly voice and hiding his face from Calcifer.

"That'll be three coppers," Calcifer said as he attempted to get a glimpse of Roan's face.

Out of his pocket, Roan pulled a small pouch full of

the few coins he had managed to cobble together in his years in the woods. He reached in and found three copper pieces. "Here you go," he said in the rough gravelly voice he had adopted. The purse felt much lighter as he slid the coins across the bar.

Calcifer inspected each coin until he was satisfied that they were real and grabbed a mug which he filled with a brown liquid from the nearby keg. "There ya are, sir, one pint of honied beer."

Roan nodded his thanks, then took the mug and walked to a table in the corner. He sipped on the beer and let his eyes adjust to the dim light of the tavern. He found the drink very tasty, the sweet honey complementing the sour beer. *The one downside of living in the forest,* he thought to himself as a warm feeling filled his throat and stomach.

He searched the tavern for any sign of Corbin, his face nearly invisible under the darkness of his cloak. After a few glances around the room, he didn't find anyone that resembled the white-haired man and contented himself to wait. He knew that Corbin would come to the tavern eventually. Corbin had been talking wistfully about the taste of good beer the other night, and Roan doubted that he would miss the opportunity to satisfy his cravings.

While he waited, he listened to a group of younger men at the table next to him talk gossip about rumors and news. “You heard ‘bout that bard o’er in Galleon? Say he was dried up when’n they found em, liken a husk of corn.” The speaker was dark-haired and had a thick layer of dirt covering his face.

“Aye, that’s right. Had the life sucked right outta em.” The speaker made a motion with his hand to emphasize his point.

“That’s crazy talk, though, don’t ya think? How could anything a sucked the life outta a man?” dirt face spoke again.

“I don’t reckon I’ve any clue, but on what I heard he looked all dried out and nasty.” The man paused to take a large swig from his mug. “By all ‘counts, he crumpled when they touched’n.”

“Sounds an awful lot like those old fairy tales ‘bout the Shadow King,” a new voice joined in, from a patron at the end of the bar.

“That’s what I thought! And ya know the oddest part? He had just told a story ‘bout Mr. Shadow King emself.” The man paused to take another drink. “And I have it on good authority that he left the bar with a man no one 'ad seen before, and-"

Dirt-face interrupted, "D'ya actually believe any o' that nonsense? Besides, I take any of your 'good authority' with a grain of salt, no offense."

"Hey now, ya didn't let me finish. And now that y'ave done gone and hurt me feelings, I don't know if I even want to tell ya da rest o' it." The drinking man lifted his mug to his lips and took another long pull.

"Now look what y'ave done, y'ave gone and shut up our best storyteller," the man at the end of the bar chided.

"Don't ya go telling me that ya believe dis nonsense, too?" Dirt face spoke, the disdain in his voice obvious. The conversation then fell into apologies followed by crude insults, followed by more apologies, and Roan stopped listening, bored. He settled his eyes on the door, content to wait for Corbin to arrive.

XIII:

Copper Town

James woke to a soft touch on his shoulder and looked up to see Kael's ever-worried face.

"We're there," Kael whispered.

James looked at his face clearly, sleep still clouding his mind. Kael met his eyes expectantly and James felt obliged to answer, but couldn't think of an apt response.

"Where?" he finally mumbled, his voice was slow and fuzzy. The memories from the past few days were still hidden inside his sleep-clouded mind.

"Not sure, but I think he's here." This voice came from James' right and he turned to see Aran guiding the makeshift raft.

Suddenly his memory came flowing back to him and he bolted up, almost throwing Henry overboard as he did so. The mouse squeaked angrily, but James paid him no heed as they approached the shore.

He felt goosebumps form on his spine as the pulling feeling intensified the closer they got to shore. "I think you're right." He looked for any sign of where they were and managed to make out faint lettering on an old sign propped near the wharf. *Welcome to Copper Town*, he read then said, "Copper Town?"

Aran nodded. "I used to come here with my dad when I was younger."

James thought he heard something change in the older boy's tone and he glanced back, but couldn't see any difference.

I wonder what that was? He shook his head, then looked back at the ramshackle dock they approached. "It's a bit disappointing, don't you think?"

Aran laughed. "That's one way to say it."

"Just be glad we got here without anything happening to us," said Kael. He glanced sideways between Aran and James, his expression hidden as usual.

"He's right," Aran said as he steered the raft toward the edge of the dock. "Normally, the paths to Copper Town are filled with bandits, many of whom wouldn't bat an eye at killing people on passing rafts in the hope that some goods would float ashore. The storm must have kept the paths clear enough for us to make it here unharmed."

"Something else you learned from your travels?" asked James suspiciously.

"Yep, and I've heard plenty of stories of people who didn't make it here in one piece."

James glanced back at Aran again, but couldn't find a trace of anything unusual. The older boy had clearly lived a rough life, but that wasn't enough to judge him as untrustworthy.

"Told you," Kael said, his voice faint and shy.

"Yeah, I guess so." James stretched his back and winced at a sore muscle, "I was just expecting more..."

"I feel the same way, but I guess that not everything in life is as much as we hope it is." Aran smiled in genuine friendship as he spoke. The last day of traveling had brought the three of them into a budding companionship. "We made it, boys."

James and Kael both grinned back, James' grin full and adventurous while Kael's was more reserved and cautious. The dock drew closer and Aran hopped onto the ancient thing, nearly losing his footing on the uneven surface but catching himself gracefully at the last second. He tied down the boat and motioned for the other boys to follow. "Watch your step. This thing is falling apart, literally."

James jumped nimbly onto the platform, the only complaint coming from Henry as he hung on for dear life on James' shoulder. Kael was less graceful but still successful as he jumped shakily onto a bumpy patch of planking. He teetered for a moment, then stabilized as James grabbed his tunic.

"Careful, Kael, no need to go jumping into the river," James smiled and playfully pretended to push his friend into the water.

Kael gasped, then chuckled and punched James in the arm. "I'll keep that in mind." Aran smiled at the two as they turned to face him before they started into town.

The three boys followed an old dirt path toward the town, Aran in the lead followed close behind by James and Henry. Kael brought up the rear, his cautious nature leading him to stay back a few paces. James' eyes were full of excitement as they approached Copper Town. "We're almost there," he whispered to Henry.

The mouse sniffed the air apprehensively, not moved in any way by this information. James smiled and rubbed the little creature's head fondly, receiving a quiet humming noise that was almost akin to a cat's purr. Henry pushed his head into James' finger and closed his eyes contentedly. James left his finger there for a moment, a small stream of memories with the mouse flowing through his mind. He soon let his hand fall back to his side and returned his attention to the quickly approaching town.

The first roof came into view and he looked gleefully back at Kael, his excitement plastered plainly across his face. "We did it! We really made it out of that stupid orphanage!"

Kael smiled. It wasn't his normal protected, shy smile, it was a full, trusting, and happy smile. "We sure did." His voice was still soft, but James could hear a real ring to it. Kael rarely let down his guard and James grinned happily at his friend before he looked back at the town.

What greeted his eyes left him utterly disappointed.

"Not quite what you were expecting?" Aran had been looking down at him, waiting for his reaction to the small town.

"Not really. I thought it would be… bigger." James' eyes had lost their curious shine, replaced with a dull, uninterested glaze.

Aran chuckled. "Don't let the look fool you. When the traders come in full force, the town doubles in size, but there are only a few families who managed to stick around full-time after the mines ran dry years ago."

Kael piped up: "Why do the traders come here, then?"

"Two reasons. First is that it is a convenient location for everyone to get to. And second, the people here are overly superstitious."

"I don't think I get what you mean," James said as a puzzled look came over his face.

Aran patted his head and ruffled his red hair. "It's just business. That's all you need to worry about."

James grinned and shook off Aran's hand. "Whatever you say, Aran." Despite his good-natured words, he felt an odd sensation in the pit of his stomach. *I wonder what's come over him today. It's almost like he's got a mask on.* James looked worriedly after Aran and darted the same worried gaze to Kael who responded with a shrug. *I'll ask him later,* James told himself.

If they found out what I was before, they would never look at me the same, thought Aran as he trudged toward the town, the weight of his past heavy on his shoulders. *A liar and a cheat; I'm both and much worse.*

He risked a quick peek over his shoulder and saw the two boys making easy conversation as they followed him. He sighed, content that they were none the wiser about his secret, terrible past.

Aran looked back at the town and saw the familiar ramshackle cottages just the same as they had been the last time he had been here. He cringed as the thought dragged up his horrible memories, the crowds shouting for a chance to buy his father's goods that they peddled as being "blessed by the gods." *Blessed by the gods my ass. He just wanted to make as much money as he could,* Aran thought bitterly. Still, he couldn't help but feel the weight of the lies fall onto his shoulders as he remembered helping right alongside his father. His father's lies had become his own, and he felt just as guilty as if he had concocted them himself. He had scammed countless people out of their hard-earned money just to escape the potential beating at home. A sour feeling rolled in his stomach and he felt tears welling in his eyes, but he fiercely held them back and pushed on. *The past is in the past. I have to move on and do what I can right now.*

They reached the town, and Aran was surprised to see a substantial crowd gathered in the market square.

He strained his eyes to see what they were gathered around and could just barely make out the top of a makeshift trading cart. “Looks like a few other traders made it through the storm,” he called over his shoulder. He turned to face the other boys. “What do you say we go see if we can get something to eat?”

James nodded vigorously. “That sounds awesome. No offense, but fish is getting old.”

“James!” Kael said and kicked his companion.

A hurt look came across James’ face as he looked at Kael. “What? Are you trying to tell me that you’re not tired of the same meal over and over again?”

“No, but…” Kael looked at Aran apologetically then a look of confusion flew across his face.

Aran was grinning and laughing. “Thanks for defending my honor, Kael, but I get what James is saying. I could use something other than fish too.”

“I told you!” said James and the two began to argue back and forth.

Aran grinned and turned to the town in time to see that they were coming awfully close to the edge of the crowd. He glanced over his shoulder and was surprised to see the two boys slip seamlessly into the crowd while still bickering back and forth. *No better way to see who’s strong. Throw them into the crowd and see if they make it out in one piece.* Aran shivered as his dad's old phrase came into his mind, almost as if the old man was still there, haunting him.

Aran grew tense as the memories of his abusive father floated through his mind. He jerked around as someone grabbed his arm. "What?" he asked, his voice harsh and jagged.

James stepped back, his mouth ajar at the shift in attitude that had overcome Aran's normally jovial behavior. Kael was a step behind James, his face hidden behind his hair as he avoided eye contact.

Aran saw the shocked look on James' face and recoiled internally. Quickly, he composed himself, relaxing his muscles and calming his stormy face. James continued to stare at him, confusion and injury showing plainly on his face.

For a moment, Aran froze. Would they see through his cover? See who he really was? He grasped at a way to counteract his error. "Come on, we need to find Corbin." Without waiting for a response, he turned back around and continued toward the trader. *Gods, I'm a mess.* He racked his brain for a way to explain his rash outburst.

As he searched for answers, the group wove their

way through the tightly packed crowd and to the edge of the trader's cart. It was a small, clever creation with a portion that folded outward into a display table and windows that held shelves of trinkets and other oddments. The trader himself was dark-skinned with curly brown hair. He was grinning from ear to ear, showing his bleached teeth. He wore finely embroidered garments several rings glinted on his fingers.

"Everyone, calm down, there's plenty for all." His voice was thick and gravely, contrasting with his otherwise well-groomed appearance. He looked into the crowd and scanned each of the faces, his shrewd nature clearly evident. His smile widened when he saw the three boys standing in front of him. "Aran, what a pleasant surprise."

"It's good to see you, Talon," Aran replied, smiling broadly in return. "How were the roads?"

Talon shrugged. "Nothing bad enough to stop me from getting here in a timely manner, which is well-appreciated." He motioned to the gaggle of people surrounding the cart.

Aran looked around and grinned outwardly. "I can see that. How long have you been here?" *How much have you stolen already?*

Talon squinted up at the sun a moment, "Just about three hours, I'd say. Why do you ask?" Aran could hear the craftiness sneak into the trader's voice. Nothing was ever what it seemed on the surface when dealing with traders, especially the ones who had been friends with Aran's father.

Aran considered his options, then chose a head-on approach. "I'm looking for someone. A man named Corbin." His father would never have openly admitted what he was truly seeking, always choosing a sly approach, always assuming the worst about the intentions of others. *I may regret it,* Aran thought, *but at least I won't choose deceit as the first line of defense.* He had always like Talon and something inside of him wanted Talon to be different, to be trustworthy and caring.

Talon stroked his chin and thought for a moment. "How about you tell me a little about what's going on with you. It's been a long time since I've seen you."

A pang of anxiety shot through Aran, but he smiled to hide it. Talon could easily sift between truths and lies. *But what would Talon do if he learned what had happened?* Aran shrugged quickly. "You know, the same old same old. We didn't get a great harvest from the crops this year, so I don't think my dad will be making any trips."

Talon raised one eyebrow but made no comment on the state of Aran's father. Instead, he turned his attention to the two boys close to Aran's side. "And who are these two?"

"These are some friends of mine that wanted to come along, see the big world and all that." Aran looked at James and Kael, motioning with his eyes for them not to speak before he turned back to Talon. "So, have you heard anything? About this Corbin guy?"

Talon thought for a moment then shook his head, "Can't say I have, but you might try The Drunken Cow." He pointed at a larger building.

Aran nodded. "Thanks, Talon. It's been good to see you."

He turned around to go, but Talon caught his shoulder. "I know things have been getting worse with him for the last few months, Aran. If you ever need a place to stay you can find me. I can help."

The smile faded from Aran's face. For a moment, he wanted to fall into Talon's arms, unload his story. If anyone would understand, it would be Talon. But could he be trusted? "Thanks, Talon, I'll keep that in mind."

Aran lifted the hand off his shoulder and continued on his way. The trader sighed and looked down for a moment, crestfallen at the sight of the young man walking away.

Behind his back, Aran could hear James ask, "What did you mean if he needs somewhere to stay?" He grimaced and kept walking as if he had not heard.

Aran could not see the sad expression on Talon's face as he answered James. "If you don't know, it's not my place to tell you. Just look after him. He's had a hard life." The smile returned to Talon's face as more of the villagers crowded around him.

What could he mean? thought Aran. *What does he know? Who does he think I am?*

"Come on, James, we gotta go," said Kael. James nodded, his face thoughtful. Kael sighed. He grabbed James' shirt and pulled him through the crowd.

Talon's remark had opened a wound deep inside Aran and he struggled to close it. *If I can't take care of myself, no one can. Maybe it's too late for me. Maybe I've already become too much like Dad.* The thought rolled around in his head, crashing permanently like a waterfall. He closed his eyes for a moment and let a single tear roll down his cheek before he slipped back under his mask. *Gotta keep myself together. I've got to find Corbin.*

Aran looked behind him and smiled at James and Kael as they made their way out of the crowd. "There you are! Sorry about that," he said.

"No worries," Kael responded, taking charge, as James was lost in thought. "Where's that place the trader mentioned?"

"Right here," Aran said and opened a large wooden door. He motioned for Kael and James to enter first. James glanced at Aran with curious, worried eyes as he made his way into the tavern. Aran sighed to himself after they were through. *I'm going to have to explain it soon enough, but not now.* He pushed the thought aside as he closed the door and followed the boys.

The inside of The Drunken Cow was dark and the three boys waited a moment, letting their eyes adjust to the light before making their way to the thick slab of wood that created the bar.

Calcifer was polishing the bar and he smiled at them as they approached. "What brings three young travelers to my humble establishment? Are you looking for our famous honied-mead, or a delicious, hearty beef stew?"

"Actually," said Aran, "we're looking for someone named Corbin. A friend of mine said he might be here."

The innkeeper shook his head. "Sorry, sonny, I don't ask names and I ain't heard nobody talking about anyone named Corbin."

Aran's smile disappeared and he looked grimly at James and Kael. "Oh well," he said, turning his eyes back to the innkeeper. "How much for a bowl of stew?"

"Two coppers a bowl."

Aran searched his pockets and came up empty-handed. He glanced over at James and Kael hopefully. They shook their heads and he sighed. Their luck had gone from bad to worse.

The door swung open, and Aran glanced up to see an old man with white, curly hair walk in. Aran felt something tug at his mind but pushed it aside and looked back to the innkeeper, putting on a show of smiling and shrugging regretfully. "I'm sorry, but we seem to be... lacking the funds at the moment, so we'll be-"

He was interrupted by the old man who walked up to the counter. "Nonsense. I won't have these boys going hungry on my watch." He looked at James and winked. "Besides, I haven't had a drink in a long time and it seems a shame to drink by myself."

The innkeeper smiled. "Well, isn't that nice? I believe they wanted three bowls of stew." He looked at the boys to confirm. "And might I suggest a tankard of our famous honeyed-mead?"

"That sounds perfect. How much do I owe you?" asked the old man.

"It's nine for the stew and five for you, so, thirteen coppers is the total." The innkeeper waggled his eyebrows in delight as the man pulled out a hefty sack and counted out three silver coins.

"How about three silvers, and keep the change."

The man winked at James again as the innkeeper hurriedly accepted his offer. "Go 'head and take a seat," he said, his voice slipping into a country accent. "I'll have the stew out as soon as I can."

The old man grinned and looked at Aran. "Best way to get his kind to stop nagging you is to pay them big up front."

Aran looked at him quizzically. He would prefer to argue over the price for hours rather than waste money overpaying. The old man waited for a response, then chuckled at Aran's obvious confusion.

"Well, I guess that I picked a few mutes. Let's sit

down and get acquainted." He looked around the bar and pointed at a table in the corner that had a young man sitting at it. "I see my friend's already found his way here. Let's go sit with him."

Aran looked at James who looked at Kael and shrugged, following the old man. Kael and Aran fell into step a moment later, pulling up a few extra chairs to the table. The old man smiled. "Now, might I ask who I have the pleasure of feeding tonight?"

James was the first to respond. "My name is James, that's Aran, and this is Kael." He pointed to each of the boys as he spoke. "Me and Kael are from Arrdell, and we came here looking for someone. We met Aran on the way and found out that he's looking for the same guy, so we all decided to travel together. Me and Kael, we esc-ow!" He would've kept talking if Henry hadn't bit his chest sharply from inside his front pocket.

Aran looked incredulously at James. *What is he thinking?* Then he felt the same tugging feeling from earlier and looked at the old man. *It couldn't be...*

The old man looked at James curiously then glanced at the hooded figure, an unspoken message passed between them. After a moment, the old man opened his mouth to speak but closed it as the innkeeper brought out a platter with three large bowls of steaming stew and a pint of beer.

The table was quiet as they waited for the innkeeper to leave before getting back to their discussion. The old man took a large swig out of his mug as the innkeeper waddled away from the table, a thoughtful expression resting on his face. "I guess it's only fair that I introduce myself and my friend here. Roan, take off that hood. I barely recognized you and it's no way to make new acquaintances."

The cloaked man slipped off his hood and the boys were surprised to see a young face looking back at them. Kael noticed it first and gasped, causing Aran and James to glance at him, then quickly look back at Roan. His eyes had splashes of gold in them, eerily similar to the splinters of color that were in their eyes.

Aran was more surprised when he looked back at the old man and saw the same colorful cracks in his eyes. "Who are you?" he asked, although he was sure of the answer now.

The old man grinned and looked at the boys. "My name's Corbin."

XIV:

A Fresh Start

The group was silent for a few minutes, the other patrons' soft mumbling loud and echoey as James, Kael, and Aran took in the information. Roan looked at them curiously as he wondered what type of people they would turn out to be. After all, he was going to have to work with them to complete the prophecy. Corbin smiled broadly at their astonishment, the pleasure he felt at their surprise clear as day. *He sure is one for theatrics,* Roan thought and chuckled to himself.

Corbin glanced at Roan and frowned, as if to say *don't ruin my fun,* then turned his attention back to the three newcomers. "Go ahead and eat your soup," he said, "I'll explain as much as I can, then you can ask questions." They were hesitant at first, but Corbin motioned for them to eat. "I won't say anything until you eat, and Roan can attest to how stubborn I am."

Roan looked at the three boys and shrugged. "You might as well do what he says, he really won't budge until you do." James looked from Kael to Aran then back to Corbin before he nodded and started to eat the soup.

"That's more like it," Corbin said enthusiastically before he took a long swig of his mead, smiled contentedly, and began.

He spoke softly, careful not to let his voice travel too far from the table, yet still able to fill every word with conviction and importance. He spoke of the prophecy, and, although he had already heard it, Roan found himself drawn to the edge of his seat as Corbin filled the short poem with extravagant detail.

Afterward, he told them his story, each phrase filled with emotion and power. He talked until James, Kael, and Aran had finished their food and Roan his glass of mead.

Finally, after what seemed like hours, Corbin took one last swig from his pint and wiped his mouth. "And that brings us to where we are now."

Roan looked carefully at the boys to see how they responded to the news, curious and excited to know his new acquaintances.

James smiled happily, excited to be a hero while Aran looked solemnly down at his almost empty bowl, his face neutral and unsure. Kael's face was mostly hidden behind his hair, but Roan managed to catch him glancing at James worriedly.

"Any questions?" Roan felt the sorrow in Corbin's voice as he spoke and looked over to see a pained expression on the man's face.

He feels responsible, the realization dawned on Roan for the first time, but his thoughts were interrupted by James.

"So, you're gonna train us to be powerful Telran, like the guys from the old stories?"

"I can teach you to control your power, but to reach your true potential, you'll need someone else's help." Corbin spoke kindly, motioning for James to keep it down.

"What are you talking about, 'someone else'?" asked Roan quickly.

Corbin glanced at him and smiled. "Don't worry, I wasn't planning on keeping it hidden from you much longer. She is one of my oldest friends and my original mentor. She knows more about the power than I could ever hope to."

Roan nodded and digested the information. "I guess that's fair enough."

Aran spoke next. "What about the other two? The ones that have powers like us. Do you know where they are?"

"I don't know where they are, but I've received word recently from old friends that they are making their way here."

"I haven't seen you talk to anybody in the past few days," said Roan in surprise and curiosity. "How'd you hear anything from anyone?"

A sly grin spread across Corbin's face. "There are many things that I haven't taught you yet." Roan wanted to continue questioning but knew that Corbin wouldn't tell him anything unless he wanted to.

He really can be so annoying sometimes. Roan looked around at his new companions to see who would speak up next.

Aran was lost in thought again, a joyful smile was plastered on James' face and he looked at the ceiling happily. Kael had yet to speak but had finally brushed his hair away to reveal his young face. Corbin inspected their bowls and seemed to decide that it was time to go. He drained the rest of his drink and motioned for Roan to do the same.

"Aran, I assume that you don't have a place to stay tonight." Aran looked up and shook his head. Corbin nodded. "Well, then, I suggest you come with us."

Roan looked at him, surprise and indignation clear on his face. "Corbin, we don't have room for all of them. I barely have enough room for you as it is."

Corbin brushed the argument away. "Your woodshed has plenty of room in it, especially since you've been too busy to refill it. Besides, I'm sure that having a roof over their heads and some real blankets would feel like heaven compared to sleeping on hard ground."

Roan sighed and grumbled, "I guess you're right," more upset about Corbin offering the shed without his consent than at the thought of having more company.

Aran didn't acknowledge Roan's apparent disgruntlement and nodded his head in agreement with Corbin. "That'd be fantastic! We've been sleeping on a little makeshift raft and it hasn't been the most comfortable." He rubbed his back for emphasis.

Corbin grinned, got up, and made his way to the door. He glanced over his shoulder and saw the rest of the group still sitting at the table. "Well, don't just stand there, let's get going."

James snapped out of his happy trance and raised his bowl to his mouth, hurriedly slurping down its contents. He rushed to the door, followed by Aran who chuckled at the show of excitement. Roan followed suit, his grumbling at the intrusion slowly replaced by curiosity about what was to come. Corbin reached up and tousled his hair as he walked past, chuckling when Roan shot him a mean scowl. Kael was last to the door, slyly walking toward Corbin.

Roan heard the boy faintly ask, "Will James be alright?"

Corbin took a moment to respond, and Roan slowed his pace and glanced over his shoulder. "He means a lot to you, doesn't he?" Corbin asked.

Kael nodded, sincere concern evident on his face.

Corbin sighed. All joy had left his face. "Honestly, I don't know. I know that without him all life as we know it would be at risk. He seems very brave, but I can't tell you that he is going to be ok. Not for sure."

Roan felt a sharp weight fall on his shoulders as the reality of his situation came back to him. He turned his head around and tried to shake off the feeling.

"Thanks for being honest," Roan heard Kael whisper

before he was out of earshot.

I almost forgot what we are doing. He shivered and forced himself to run past the other boys, afraid of letting them see how he felt. "Let's get going. It's a trek out of town and I don't feel like being lost in the woods during the night."

Aran grunted and James gulped at the thought; both hurried closer to Roan.

Good, now we'll get there in no time. Roan glanced over his shoulder and saw Kael and Corbin following close behind, still in a deep discussion. The same shiver ran down his spine as he wondered what their discussion entailed. He shook his head and turned back to guiding the other boys through the forest.

They were silent on the journey to the house, each wrapped in his own thoughts, and soon enough they were there. Roan and Aran reached the clearing first and Roan breathed deeply at the sight of his home. "That's more like it," he said to himself.

Aran looked up from his thoughts and whistled appreciatively. "Pretty nice setup you've got here."

"Thanks," said Roan. "It's not too big, but it's somewhere to sleep and it's my home."

Aran nodded as he continued to survey the rest of

the meadow. "It's beautiful. Did you make it with your folks?"

Roan tensed. "My parents died when I was young. I had to fend for myself since then."

Aran looked at him and Roan saw pity and understanding in his eyes. "Me too. I know how you feel." The two remained silent for a few seconds, a bond of pain uniting them.

Finally, Roan broke the silence as he pointed to a small slanted shack in the corner of the clearing. "That's the shed where you can sleep. It's not much, but it'll keep you dry and warm. Go ahead and check it out while I get some blankets." Roan scaled his ladder easily and Aran ambled over to the shack. *I wonder what he's been through,* Roan thought as he grabbed the few extra furs from his house and dropped them to the ground.

He looked to the edge of the clearing and saw James walk emerge from the darkening forest. "Over here," he yelled and waved his hand. The young boy acknowledged the wave and made his way to the shack.

"How'd you make this?" asked Aran as Roan dragged the furs over to the shack.

"What, the shack?"

"Yeah, it looks like the wood was all burned up,

but... on purpose."

Roan chuckled, "That's one way of saying it. I did burn it into shape. It's my power."

"You can control fire?"

"I don't know if *control* is quite right, but I try to. What about you? What's your power?"

"I've got control of water. I don't think it's quite as useful as fire." Aran smiled at Roan, then looked over his shoulder and said, "Oh boy, he's still got that thing with him."

Roan looked around and saw James close by. "What thing?"

"You'll see it soon enough."

Aran was staring at James' shoulder and Roan looked closer. He took a sharp breath at what he saw. "James, why have you got a rat on your shoulder?"

Aran chuckled, but James frowned. "He's not a rat. He's a mouse, and his name's Henry."

Roan was speechless.

"I told you you'd find out," Aran whispered.

Roan shook himself to his senses. "I guess that's fine then. You're James, right?"

James nodded, "The one and only, and you're Roan. Thanks for letting us stay here." Any frustration or anger at the mislabeling of the mouse was gone, and he glanced around before his joy-filled eyes returned to Roan. "Aren't you excited? We're gonna save the world!"

Roan turned to Aran and looked at him questioningly. Aran smiled and shrugged. "Don't ask me. I've just been with him a couple of days."

The awkward conversation that was sure to follow was luckily stopped as Corbin and Kael arrived. The previous melancholy that had settled on the old man had all but disappeared. "Glad to see you're all becoming friends so easily." He looked at them, beaming with pleasure at the success. "And it looks like Roan's already gotten you some bedding. Good, good." He paused for a moment and looked at the rapidly darkening sky, "It's getting late. You should all get some rest."

Kael nodded in agreement and James said, "You're right, I almost forgot how tired I was during all the excitement."

Roan looked at the boy curiously again and Aran laughed, patting him on the shoulder. "You'll get used to it," he said before he grabbed a few blankets, the other boys following his lead.

Roan looked toward Corbin, but he was already on his way to the house. "Well, I guess I'll see you guys in the morning then."

"Sounds good," said Aran.

"Night, Roan," James said.

"Goodnight, James." Roan glanced at Kael, but he seemed to already be asleep.

James was right. I forgot how tired I am. The same weariness that had weighed on him so heavily before began to seep back into his bones, and he yawned as he turned back to his house. *It's gonna be a long day tomorrow,* he thought to himself as he climbed the ladder and made his way to bed.

XV:

The Moon's Glade

The sun was making its descent toward the mountains; rays of light spewed off it and struck the world as it slipped into darkness. The last of the light even managed to strike, sharp and clear, through the thick canopy of leaves that hid Ferox and Lyria from the rest of the world. The glowing beams of pure sunlight shone like pillars in the otherwise twilight-filled forest, catching the air and turning it hazy as they passed by. *It's beautiful,* thought Lyria, entranced by the thick rays and their ethereal substance. *I've never seen anything so pretty.* She sighed, lost in thought as she stared at the light.

Come on, Lyria, Ferox barked in Lyria's mind, and she sensed the wolf's urgency. *We've got to find somewhere to sleep before nightfall.* Ferox stood a few feet in front of her, his body tense as he looked behind them warily. *We've still got three days of traveling before we reach Copper Town and the Forest King told us we have to hurry.*

"Where's the next cave?" Lyria started to jog as Ferox turned back to the small, nearly hidden trail they had been following.

Not far, just past a clearing at the end of this trail, but the sun is setting and I don't want to be in the woods after dark. I've got a bad feeling in my stomach.

Lyria jogged faster after the wolf, careful not to trip over roots or other undergrowth. She kept both eyes on the ground as they continued onward, too many missteps and falls to let her feel comfortable looking straight ahead. It had been two days of hard, fast traveling since they had left the comfortable glade of the Forest King. Trallger had said his farewells and told them not to worry about food; he would make sure that the forest provided it for them. Each night, squirrels or other woodland creatures dropped nuts and fruits for them before scurrying off into the trees.

At first, Lyria had been worried about Ferox, but he had reassured her that he would be fine and loped off into the woods as she ate. He would return with a satisfied look on his face and a small spattering of blood around his maw. Lyria had insisted that he let her wash it off before she let him come into the cave. At first, Ferox had argued that he preferred to wear his kill with pride, but eventually Lyria's stubbornness won out and he let her wash him every night.

The rest of their journey had been uneventful, the only scenery the massive trees and vast swathes of undergrowth that surrounded them at all times. *And I wouldn't have traded it for anything else,* Lyria thought as she looked back on the past few days of travel. The forest had always been her second home and the journey had only increased her love of the dark, peaceful place. *I wish I could stay here forever, let the rest of the world figure out how to fix itself, and just get lost in the trees.* She sighed longingly at the thought, then felt the cold weight of reality rush onto her. She grimaced as she remembered her heroic role. She shook her head, brought her attention back to the present, and pushed the hard thoughts away.

The sparse light in the forest waned and Lyria was forced to strain her eyes to see the path, her pace slowing as she picked her way along. Ferox whined in fear as the slivers of light faded away, the shadows taking up more and more of the path.

Hurry, hurry, hurry! He thought as his fear grew.

Lyria's heartbeat rose and she started to stumble over unseen branches and obstacles, Ferox's fear spreading over to her.

The forest grew eerily quiet as the last of the light faded, leaving the woods in utter darkness. The bugs and other small creatures were silent as they headed toward their homes, the forest left strangely empty as it waited for the creatures of the night to wake and begin to populate it with sound again. Even the wind seemed to ebb into nothingness as the transition from day to night commenced, leaving Ferox and Lyria the only creatures in the dark purgatory between day and night. Ferox dropped back next Lyria and she felt his muscles tense as if he was about to bolt, an instinctual fear that was rooted deep in his mind.

It's alright, nothing is going to happen, she told herself, but the fear still managed to tear at her mind with each step she took.

Eventually, they slowed to a brisk walk and finally to a slow and silent plod as the path was completely hidden from view. Lyria clung onto Ferox's back as he led the way. They stumbled through the darkness, stopping and squinting into the shadows at the slightest rustle.

After what seemed like hours of careful and silent traveling, a soft light showed through the trees in front of them. Ferox began to relax, his muscles finally easing out of the stressed state.

That's the clearing, he said in a whisper, even though Lyria was the only one that could hear him talk. *Just a little farther to go.*

Lyria was still too frightened to risk making a sound and simply nodded acknowledgment. Slowly and carefully, they made their way out of the thick woods and into the small clearing.

A small pond was situated on one side of the clearing, fed by a stream that trickled out of the woods. The burbling water calmed Lyria and she took a deep breath before she admired the rest of the clearing, its beauty and tranquility sinking in. It couldn't be compared to Trallger's glade; it wasn't nearly as grand as that, but it was equally beautiful in its own small way. The moonlight sparkled and reflected off the water, illuminating the whole area in a peaceful glow. The grass brushed gently across her legs as she slowly made her way across the small meadow.

"It's so pretty," she said to herself, the fear of the

dark forest completely gone. Though they'd already been through a vast stretch of the forest, nothing she had seen on the journey was nearly as intimate as this place.

Sensing her admiration, Ferox said, *You'd be hard-pressed to find a clearing like this anywhere nowadays.*

"What do you mean?" Lyria looked curiously at Ferox. "I know it's beautiful, but is there something special about it?"

It's one of the last Fohe glades. Ferox looked up at her to see if she knew what he was talking about and Lyria shrugged in response. *The Fohe glades were made long ago by the moon. They were places where anything could come and be safe from all harm, no matter who or what it was. Many years ago, they were common, scattered throughout the world and occupied by various fantastical creatures in search of safety. But that all changed after the Shadow King started his rule. He couldn't stand the Fohe glades because of the peace they represented, so he started to hunt them down and destroy them. He hated them so much, he would personally come to each glade and burn it to the ground. The moon saw this and was outraged, but she had made a promise to not interfere with mortal affairs and had to sit and watch her creations be destroyed. The only thing she could do was hide the glades. She managed to successfully hide nineteen glades, a sad number compared to the hundreds that once filled the world.*

Lyria was silent for a moment, trying to comprehend why anyone would want to destroy something as beautiful as this clearing. "Why couldn't the moon make more glades? The Shadow King was gone for thousands of years, and I'm sure that everyone would have been happy to see more places like this."

Ferox shook his head. *The moon is the oldest and the strongest of the old gods, their queen, you might say. A thousand years is the blink of an eye for her; she couldn't bear making the glades to watch them be destroyed moments later.*

Lyria mulled over the idea for a few moments. "I guess that makes sense. I don't think I could bear having something as beautiful as this destroyed twice in my lifetime."

Ferox nodded and a warm silence fell over the glade. The two relaxed, letting the stress of reality fall off of them as they made their way across the glade and basked in the moonlight. The moon smiled down on the two travelers as they passed through her glade, as if happy to see it being used again.

I wonder what she's like, thought Lyria as she looked up at the moon.

Then, just as suddenly as they had entered it, they left the clearing. Lyria followed Ferox toward the cave. It was a few hundred feet away from the clearing and Lyria was happy to find that night had at last fully settled over the forest, the chirping of crickets and the hooting of owls filling the previously sound-deprived woods.

At the entrance to the cave, they stopped to look at their home for the night. Lyria smiled as Ferox looked back at her, puppyish delight in his eyes. *Here we are: home sweet home.*

The cave was small but tidy, enough room to safely shelter its inhabitants from the weather without being large enough to hide any frightening beasts or monsters. Near the entrance, a small pile of fruit and nuts had been carefully placed; the creatures that had delivered them must have scattered as night fell.

Moonlight filtered in from the clearing and through the canopy far above, dappling the cave and surrounding woods with soft silver light. The change in atmosphere from the nerve-racking pitch black to the greyish-silver tones that now filled the forest was stunning. *As clear as night and day.* Lyria smiled at the truth of the saying as she absorbed the calm peace of the night. It wasn't the same feeling that the glade had given her, but she was able to relax and let her guard down momentarily.

Lyria walked into the small cave and sighed deeply, breathing in the smells around her. She sniffed at the earthy smell. She missed the scent of her old house. *I'll probably never see it again.* The realization dawned on Lyria and she felt a solemn sensation wash over her.

Ferox perked his ears up and listened for any sign of danger then went back to sniffing the ground in search of prey. Lyria slumped to the ground. She grabbed a few handfuls of nuts from the small pile of food, the melancholy still heavy on her shoulders.

Ferox's voice probed through her thoughts. *I'm going hunting. I'll be back soon.*

"Alright, but wash off *all* the blood in that stream before you come back."

Ferox looked at her with puppy dog eyes, which looked ridiculous on his massive face. *Can I leave a little bit?*

Lyria stifled a laugh at his absurd face, her melancholy momentarily lifted. "No. You know I can't sleep with the smell near me."

The innocent puppy look vanished in an instant,

replaced by a fierce snarl. *Fine, then. I'll just bring you back a bone.* Ferox darted into the night before Lyria could argue.

"Hey! Get back here!" she yelled, although she knew full well that the wolf wouldn't listen to her. She sighed and rolled her eyes before going back to munching on a small wild apple. She resigned herself to having to get rid of any nasty substance that Ferox would bring back, wriggling in her skin at the thought of touching a gnawed rabbit leg. Lyria tried to get the image out of her mind, focusing instead on her dinner. Unfortunately, that distraction didn't last long. The meager supply of nuts and fruits were gone in no time.

She sighed and rolled onto her back, looking up at the canopy and thinking of her old life, the memories heavy and pain-laden. *It's no use, I might as well move on,* she thought as she pictured her father. His image flickering between standing happily in front of her and the dried-up corpse from Ferox's memory.

A sliver of moonlight slid over her face and distracted her from the painful image. The light filtered through the trees and danced along the ground, making patterns that were so complex she labeled them as indecipherable. She sat up again and smiled as she watched the performance, happy to have an excuse not to think about her father.

"I might as well practice while I'm sitting here," she said to herself.

She closed her eyes and breathed deeply, the barriers around her mind slowly falling away. She reached out with her mind as she breathed deeply, but immediately retracted it as she pressed against a presence too massive to comprehend.

What was that?

She tried to reach out again, but couldn't get past the barriers that had risen to protect her. Her breathing was short and a knot of fear and curiosity formed in her stomach.

She pressed against the walls and yelled at them to come down, but they remained. She screamed internally with frustration. *What good is having this power if I can't even use it?*

A soft chuckle rolled through her mind, so quiet she wasn't sure she heard it.

"Hello?" she spoke softly, worried that whatever it was wouldn't be friendly.

She heard the chuckle again and turned to face its origin. The sound came from the path they had taken to get to the cave and, though she strained her ears, she couldn't hear anything.

"Hello," she repeated, louder this time.

She heard the laugh again, followed by a faint voice. *Come find me.*

Lyria gulped at the words and pretended she hadn't heard them. Fear won out over curiosity as she turned toward the cave and started to make herself a bed out of the soft moss that lined the floor. *If I ignore it, maybe it will go away.*

I won't hurt you. I just want to talk.

She tried to blot out the voice and hummed an old song her dad used to sing to her.

The voice was quiet while she sang, and after a few minutes she stopped, ready to lay down and try to sleep. *That was pretty,* the voice spoke again. It was definitely female. *I know a song, too. Do you want to hear it?*

Lyria heard a distant sound. The tones overlapped and threaded through themselves in patterns too complex for her to understand. She felt the rhythm tearing at her mind and put her hands to her ears to no avail. The sound continued to echo in her mind.

"Stop it! I can't take it!" The noise grew louder, threatening to destroy her world.

There was a pause and then the voice came again. *If you want me to stop, then you'll have to come find me.*

Lyria refused to respond and, after a moment, the sound returned and beat down on her harder than before. “Fine, I'll find you,” she relented. “But you'll have to tell me where to look.”

Lyria's mind was quiet save for her own thoughts and she sighed, the ember of anger starting to fade.

I guess that I could tell you. The voice sounded close at hand, then far away. Whatever it was playing games with Lyria. *But that wouldn't be any fun.*

“Where's the fun in me just sitting here and leaving you alone?” asked Lyria in response.

I guess that's true.... The voice faded, but Lyria could still feel the presence at the edge of her mind and she waited patiently for some sort of response.

I've lived for thousands of years but never seen the sun. I've talked to gods and walked among men as equals. I'm farther away than anything in this world, but you can still see me.

Lyria thought about it for a few minutes, then an idea began to form in her mind. “Give me a second, I think I can find you.”

Best make it quick! I haven't got long to talk. The

presence faded, leaving Lyria to try to decipher the riddle.

Lyria started to leave, then looked back at the cave. *I should leave something to tell Ferox where I'm going,* she thought, *but what?* She looked around for something to communicate her plans to the wolf, but couldn't find anything.

Hurry, hurry, hurry. I don't have forever, you know, came the voice, echoing in Lyria's mind.

She sighed. *Sorry, Ferox, but if everything goes well, I'll be back before you return from hunting.*

She started to run through the trees, all guilt at leaving without telling Ferox soon lost. It was a short journey, no more than a few hundred yards, but she sprinted through the warm summer night air. A smile crept onto her face as the mystery of the adventure pulled at her curiosity, her pace quickening as she got closer to her goal. She noticed the faint light of the clearing and looked up from the trail.

At that moment, she tripped on a root in the path and fell, only able to get out a partial squeal before she hit the ground. She rolled ungracefully into the clearing, startling a deer that had stopped by the stream to drink. As the deer bolted into the trees, the voice came back.

I see you've found your way to my glade. I hope your journey wasn't too eventful. Laughter was evident in its thoughts.

Lyria clutched her side and scrambled to her feet. She felt a rush of excitement. "Your glade?" she asked, victory rushing through her veins as she realized her guess had been right.

That's right, I'm happy you figured it out so fast. Most people nowadays are much too dull to even hear me talk. Disdain was obvious in the Moon's voice as she said the last line. *But you're not like the rest of them. You're very special.* She chuckled as Lyria looked up in surprise. *Oh, I knew long before the rest of those buffoons down there. Sometimes I wish I hadn't sworn off meddling in the affairs of the world.* The Moon sighed, like light drifting over dry grass. *But I did what I had to, didn't I? Anyway, I guess you're wondering why I wanted to talk with you.*

"Yeah, I was wondering what a goddess would want with me."

The Moon laughed lightly. *I guess that's fair enough. I forget it's been millennia since the rest of them went to sleep and I stopped my visits to your world. But no matter. I don't have time to tell stories. You must hurry to Copper Town and find Corbin, otherwise, He might catch you.*

"Who?" asked Lyria, fear in her voice. "Who might catch me?"

I don't have time to tell you everything, nor should I be meddling at all, but just know that he is the first of the strætae and a deadly enemy. You have to hurry, for if he finds you, I'm afraid not even your wolf friend could fight him off. And if you die... The Moon paused ominously. *Then the world dies. You must live, so you must hurry.*

"I'll make sure I get there before he catches me."

Good. Now I must go, before he sees me.

The great consciousness began to fade and Lyria felt as if part of her mind was drawn into it as it left. A hollowness remained in her mind where the great entity had been. She turned back toward the cave and began to walk, her mind full of wonder and fear.

I'll have to tell Ferox as soon as I can, she thought. *I don't like the idea of being hunted.*

She stepped out of the glade and felt a great exhaustion sweep over her, her mind numb and tired. She yawned and slowly stumbled back to the cave, falling over more than once on the return journey. Her eyes were drooping closed as she finally arrived at the cave. Ferox wasn't anywhere to be seen. Lyria walked to the back of the cave and sat down, forcing her eyes open as her head nodded.

"Got to stay awake. Got to tell Ferox."

It was no use. the exhaustion took her mind and the world faded into darkness as she fell into the realm of sleep.

XVI:

The Bright Side of the Mountain

The sun crested the distant peaks, its light scattering across the vast valley. Mist hovered above the thick canopy of leaves, the bright green trees hidden beneath the shadow it cast. Brianna looked down from the heights of the mountain, sipping hot tea that Shriggus had told her would help prepare her for the journey that lay ahead. She gazed at the rising mist in disappointment, for, although it was beautiful, it meant that traveling was going to be damp. She was sitting cross-legged on a patch of grass, a shawl draped around her shoulders to ward off the cold morning air. Under the shawl, she wore a pair of soft, warm pants, a pair of boots, and a silky tunic. She felt the odd fabric again. *I wonder what it's made of?* she mused. Shriggus hadn't told her, only that it was much better at regulating temperature than normal cloth.

Brianna gazed out over the fog-veiled valley and toward the narrow gap in the mountain range for a few more minutes before she stood and walked back to the cave. Erik was leaning on the doorframe, ready to start the journey. His face masked unreadable thoughts. He was dressed similarly to Brianna, but wore a long cloak and carried his axe at his side, his hand comfortably resting on the pommel. Although he was almost half a foot shorter than Brianna, he still managed to carry himself in a way that made her respect him. She gave him a friendly nod. He merely glanced at her for a moment, then turned his attention back to the valley, his eyes glazed over as hidden thoughts flowed in his mind.

I know how he feels, Brianna thought as she moved by, leaving Erik alone to think. She walked into the cave and bent her head to make it through the arched doorway. The musty smell of brewing elixirs and potions, along with a slight scent of a stew boiling in the background hit her when she first stepped into the cave. It was an oddly pleasant aroma and smiled as she saw Shriggus hunched over the small fire, stirring his stew.

"What amazing dish have you cooked up today, Shriggus?" she asked, genuinely interested. Shriggus didn't turn away from his creation, entranced in his work. Brianna chuckled to herself. *He really isn't used to having visitors, is he?* "What are you cooking, Shriggus?" she said, louder.

Shriggus jumped and turned around, startled. He saw Brianna and sighed, "Sorry, I forgot you were here. I guess I really am getting old. Anyway, it's a mixture of goat, potato, garlic and a few special ingredients that you'll have to guess."

Brianna walked over to him and squatted down, peering into the pot. She inhaled deeply, the delicious smell infiltrating her nose. "It smells fantastic."

Shriggus grunted in response, already focused on his work again.

She sighed contentedly, the warm air and heavenly aroma gave her a sense of serenity. She stood up and picked her way through the cluttered cave toward her small side room, careful to avoid the hanging braids of garlic and other various herbs. She appreciated the sheer quantity of ingredients that were in this room alone. She pushed aside a curtain made of the same silky material as her shirt and stepped into her room.

The small room that she had slept in for the past few days was bare compared to the rest of the cave; its contents neat and organized rather than spread haphazardly all over the place. It had a small cot, a table, and a tiny fireplace. Other than that, it was empty. She sat on the bed and checked through her bag, making sure that the extra clothes and thick cloak that Shriggus had given her were still there. She felt around in the pack for her journal, found its spine, and gently removed it. She fondly brushed a small patch of dust from the ragged leather cover. The journal traveled everywhere with her, including when the dwarves had captured her. It was her father's parting gift and the only physical reminder of her parents. *I miss you,* she thought as she lovingly opened the first few pages and ran her fingers along the fine paper.

She carefully put the book back into her bag, fastened the straps, stood up. *I know I've only been here for a few days, but I'm gonna miss this place.* She silently waved goodbye before she turned and walked through the curtain.

In the larger room, Shriggus had ladled out three bowls of the thick stew. Steam rose off the bowls, sweet and enticing. Shriggus looked up at her. "Good, I was just about to call you. Go ahead and take a seat. I'll go get Erik."

"Alright, but don't take too long. I'm starving."

"Don't worry, I'll be back before you know it." Shriggus hustled out the door to find Erik.

Brianna set down her pack and flopped in a chair near the fireplace, her mouth-watering at the delicious aroma emanating from the bowl of stew. *I won't miss these chairs,* she thought as she tried to squeeze her legs into the small space the short chair gave her.

"... he'll be there, I'm sure." Shriggus led Erik into the room as Brianna finally found a comfortable position in her chair.

"How do you know? What if he isn't there, what then?" Erik's gravelly voice was full of uncertainty and brewing anger. "I know you think he'll be there, but how sure are you?"

Shriggus threw his hands up in frustration. "You're right, you're right. I can't be sure he's going to be there. If he isn't there, you don't come back here and stay with me. You don't have time for it."

"What're you talking about?" asked Brianna, although she was fairly certain they referred to Corbin.

"Nothing important. And let's not argue about it over our last meal together," Shriggus answered gruffly and looked accusingly at Erik who mumbled something under his breath before sitting down at the table.

"Alright, let's eat." Shriggus sat down abruptly.

Brianna felt the tension in the air and was quiet as they ate, content to leave it alone and enjoy the stew. It was delicious, flavored with various herbs and spices from around the country.

Brianna finished first, pushed her bowl away, and sighed contentedly. "I think I'm gonna miss your cooking more than anything, Shriggus."

The old heiren nodded with pride. "And so you should. I was the king's personal chef for a while, you know."

Erik chuckled at the comment. "I've no doubt about that. Your cooking could satisfy a dragon." He pushed his empty bowl away and stood up, a look of finality in his movement. "We should go now, before it gets too hot."

Shriggus nodded. "You're right! I wouldn't want either of you dying from heat exhaustion. Do you both have everything?"

"My pack's just outside the door," Erik said.

Shriggus looked at him and Erik sighed. "I'll go check that everything is there. Brianna, when you're ready I'll be outside."

Shriggus shook his head and turned to Brianna,

smiling. "Watch after him for me. He's a good person, although a little bit too much of a worry-wart."

"I thought that he was supposed to be watching me."

"Brianna, you are so much more powerful than you think. Believe in yourself and you can accomplish anything. Never forget that."

Brianna smiled, not letting the few tears that had welled behind her eyes flow. "Thank you, Shriggus, I won't forget it."

Shriggus smiled and walked over to her, arms outstretched. Brianna crouched a little bit and hugged him. They stayed that way for a few seconds, like grandfather and granddaughter.

"Promise me one thing," Shriggus said, moving away from the embrace. "Promise me you won't forget what you have to do. No matter how hard times get, no matter how much you might want to quit, remember what's on the line."

Brianna nodded, afraid that she couldn't control herself if she spoke.

Shriggus gazed fondly at her one last time, his old eyes filled with kindness, sorrow, and hope. He turned toward the door and Brianna followed, swinging her pack onto her shoulders and heading out of the cave.

Erik stood stoically outside, face grim and shoulders set back.

"I guess this is goodbye," Shriggus said and walked to Erik, his hand outstretched. Erik shook it, then brought the ancient man in for a bear hug, startling Brianna who was afraid Erik might crush him on accident.

"It's not goodbye, just see you later. But I think later might be longer than we want." Erik managed to keep his face set grimly as he spoke, but his eyes were watery with emotion.

Shriggus smiled and grasped the young dwarf by the shoulder, almost like a father. "It might be sooner than you think." The look in the old man's eyes implied softness and deep affection.

Erik sniffed and hugged the old man once again, whispering something Brianna couldn't hear.

"It's alright, Erik, I know you'll be fine." Shriggus patted Erik's head as he spoke, then gently pushed him away. "Now go ahead and get going, the sun's already too high for my comfort."

"You're right." Erik wiped his eyes quickly. "You ready?" he muttered gruffly to Brianna. She nodded and stepped to join him. Shriggus stayed back and waved them off as they made the slow descent down the mountain

They walked in silence, the winding path slowly leading them to the edge of the forest. Brianna wondered what powers had created the range of mountains spread before them; the beauty of the peaks' regal height amazed her, even after days of admiring the peaks. The mountains narrowed abruptly until they came to a steep valley that separated Copper Town, Ardell, and the few other small cities on the far side of the mountains from the rest of the world.

Brianna couldn't see it, but she knew that a river flowed out of the valley toward the far, curving side of the mountains. It was fed by two tributaries, both snaking down each side of the mountains. Where the tributaries met, a small trading village had sprung up. The people who had settled there had found the ground rich with copper ore and had, very creatively, named the settlement Copper Town. The river formed by the two tributaries had also been creatively titled Copper River and was the main means of transportation for many goods in and out of the world beyond the mountains.

This is the first time since Mom died that I've been

this side of the mountains, Brianna thought, the realization only now hitting her. She looked across the verdant forest with new appreciation. The view stirred a few memories of her youth.

The forest was a dark green gash across the open land It spread from the edge of the mountains into the distance, as far as the human eye could see. Brianna remembered playing hide and seek in the woods with her parents as they traveled from town to town. She remembered her father and mother laughing as they told stories around the campfire, each one filled with comfort and joy that Brianna had thought would last forever. The forest she now faced seemed darker and more forbidding than the one she remembered.

Erik walked slightly in front of her. He stood tall, despite his short frame, and walked with purpose in his step. *There's more to him than meets the eye.* The stout dwarf moved with innate pride obvious in every step. *I wonder how--* She stumbled over a loose rock in the path and fell forward.

Erik moved as soon as he heard the slight movement, and caught her before she hit the ground.

"Careful." His tone was brusque. "You never know when one wrong step could end everything. Try to keep your mind on the trail."

Brianna nodded, embarrassed at the fall. "Sorry, I will."

Erik grunted.

They walked in silence, following the curve of the trail.

"What were you thinking about?" Erik's question surprised Brianna.

"Nothing. I mean, I was just wondering how you and Shriggus met."

"Why do you want to know?" Erik's voice was rough, unwelcoming.

Brianna held up her hands defensively. "No reason, just curious. You don't have to tell me if you don't want to."

Erik sighed. Moments of silence passed awkwardly.

"It's just not something I talk about often. Since we'll be traveling together for a while, you might as well hear it… As long as you promise to stay focused on where you're putting your feet."

"Right."

Erik paused again. Brianna walked as carefully as she could, not wanting the sound of her feet on the rocky trail to distract him.

"It's not a very exciting story," he began. "I was young and stupid. Very stupid. One day, I thought it would be a good idea to climb to the top of Kingspire Mountain." He chuckled darkly at the memory. "Kingspire is one of the deadliest mountains in well over a hundred miles. Plenty of venomous snakes and flaky ledges. A lot of the mountain is impossible to climb, but that didn't stop me. I thought I was invincible, like all young climbers, I guess, and decided to tackle the mountain head-on." Only the sound of their footsteps filled the long pause in his story.

"Well, what happened?" Brianna finally blurted impatiently.

Erik took a long, deep breath and continued. "Exactly what you would expect. I fell. My foot slipped as I was crossing a ledge and I fell into a ravine. My left leg bore the brunt of my fall and it shattered. The rest of my body was only bruised. I was lucky to have survived the fall. After realizing that I would die if I didn't try to help myself, I dragged my body out of the ravine."

Brianna's toe caught on a rocky protrusion. She saw Erik's body flinch as he heard the sound. They walked quietly. Brianna tried to make everything about her movements quieter and more controlled.

"Everything was red with pain. I don't know how I managed to make it out of that place. I lost all sense of direction and barely knew who I was. When I finally reached the edge of the forest, I collapsed. I was so disoriented from pain and loss of blood, I thought the old man in front of me was a hallucination. He could have left me to die, but he took me home and healed me. That was almost seventy years ago. He saved my life and gave me a chance to walk again. I doubt there is anyone in the entire kingdom who could have healed my leg as perfectly as he did. He worked with me for months, teaching me to walk without a limp, strengthening muscles and rebuilding bone."

Brianna waited for a few moments, hoping he would add more. The silence stretched uncomfortably. "I see why you two are so close now," she said.

Erik grunted. "That's part of it."

Brianna waited, anticipating more, but he didn't elaborate. *I still don't really know him, but it's a start.* She brought her attention back to the path. She was determined not to trip again.

The trail had dipped into a blanket of mist. She felt more than saw the moistness they passed through; its soft, cold hands caressed her, leaving a sheen of fine droplets like silver webbing over her entire body and Erik's hair and pack. The mist gradually dissipated as it was burned away by the rising sun. The bright ball of light showed itself above the rugged mountains. *It's beautiful,* she thought.

The trail turned from narrow and rocky to a wide, soft dirt path through shrubbery and an occasional patch of grass. Erik looked back at Brianna and nodded confidently, a bright sparkle of adventure flicking in his eyes. "It's a wonderful day to be traveling," he laughed and started to jog down the path.

"It's fantastic!" she agreed and started to run after Erik. The stress of focusing on every footstep lifted and left her giddy with relief.

Erik must have felt the same. He laughed and shouted an incomprehensible word over his shoulder. Brianna looked up at the sky and let out a long laugh, enjoying the cool breeze that blew past her as she ran down the last gentle shoulders of the mountain.

Panting and grinning, they reached the bottom of the path and Erik stopped at the fringe of the trees. Brianna followed suit and examined the forest in front of her.

"It's bigger than how I remember," she said.

Erik nodded but didn't say anything as he caught his breath.

Underneath the massive tree branches, the sun's light faded into near-nothingness, the few rays that made it through the thick canopy above creating flashing shadows.

"You ready?" Erik asked, his voice once again somber.

"Yes," Brianna nodded, pushing away frightening memories of the Shadow Realm as she watched the dancing shadows beneath the trees.

Without another word, she followed Erik into the dark forest.

XVII: The Dark Side of the Mountain

On the other side of the mountain range, the sun had yet to rise, leaving the fog to thicken in the trees. It lay heavy and wet, a dense blanket of moist air that filled every cranny and crevice of the forest.

The wall of mist stopped abruptly at the pass and formed a menacing barrier in the shadows. The fog was the front of a great ocean of dark grey that hid the land from the sun. In the depths of the forest, the combination of fog and the thick leafy canopy managed to blot out all light; the forest below left in a deep shroud of darkness.

This mist-fueled darkness was weighty and took on the properties of a liquid, oozing across the ground like cooling tar. It sprawled among the roots of trees, a thin oily layer of shadow that infected the inner heart of the forest. Low-dwelling creatures crept like snakes through the tar-like layer of shadow. This was a world of suffocating darkness, where shadows took on a muted life of their own.

The oozing shadows felt a disturbance, not from a light source or the slowly rising sun, but from something cloaked in a deeper shadow. The dark mist shied away from this creature, afraid of what the pure shadow might want. The shape walked calmly through the forest, unhindered by the lack of light. The shadows that wrapped around it were pure black and had a velvety quality about them, making the oily darkness that lay on the ground seem like a child's plaything. The creature moved gracefully, not lurching from side to side as one would expect from something so darkly layered. It seemed at peace in the surrounding sea of night. The creature would've stayed in the shadows forever if the sun hadn't finally reached over the mountain peaks.

Shards of light shattered the fog, breaking its unified quality and making it take on its normal grey hues. However, the figure stayed the same shade; its cloak of shadow retained its plush texture and the hood covered its face.

The scattered beams of light started to make their way into the depths of the forest. They forced their way through cracks in the shattered fog and dense forest canopy. The creatures that had come out during the night slipped and oozed into their homes, crawling from the day. The dark-cloaked creature continued on its path, sidestepping the occasional pillar of light and moving calmly onward. The mist rolled away fearfully from the creature's steps and gave the shadow-being a radius of clear air that shimmered like a heatwave.

The sun's whole body had risen above the craggy tops of the mountains, and he reached down with his bright hands, breaking apart the last of the fog and unveiling the land. The leaves above the cloaked figure saved him from most of the light. Only a dappling of sunshine sifted through the foliage. The figure's smile turned to a scowl as he tried hopelessly to dodge the constantly moving beams of light. A soft breeze rose from the north, bringing with it the fresh, cold scent of autumn. The wind touched the dark figure's body and altered its course, creating the same heatwave effect as the mist.

The figure laughed harshly. "So, we meet again," he said in his smoky, hissing voice.

The wind's only response was to hurry its way past

him, stirring a pile of fallen leaves momentarily to life.

The dark creature laughed again and threw back his hood, unveiling a smokey shadow for his head. The head appeared to shift in place while remaining solid, the illusion itself enough to make even the hardiest of sailors seasick. Two glowing embers stood in what could only be his face.

He took a deep breath and inhaled the scent of the day. He frowned for a moment, trying to identify a new smell that wafted lazily into his nose. Slowly, the frown flipped into an evil grin as he realized what the scent was.

It was a girl.

More than that, the smell had a distinct scent of magic, more powerful than any he had felt in many years. He flipped the hood back onto his head before starting to trot down the path, not caring if the light touched him anymore.

His prey was near and he couldn't be bothered with slowing down for anything. As he set out on the trail, he released a guttural screech so unnatural that the trees themselves seemed to shrink back.

Railin, the Shadow King's right hand, the first stræntae, and the bane of light, was on the hunt.

XIII:

Training with Friends

The early morning mist had just lifted when James awoke to the smell of frying meat. He scrambled out of his bed and looked at the other two boys, still basking in dreams beneath their blankets. *All the more for me,* he thought, salivating at the scent of bacon.

He made his way out of the woodshed, careful not to wake the others. He heard a soft squeak and turned around to see Henry staring at him with beady eyes.

"Come on, Henry, but be quiet."

The mouse hopped onto James' shoulder.

"You're a dork," James said and rubbed the little creature's head.

The morning was cold and James quickly made his way toward the tree. His breath came out in frosty puffs. *I wonder what'll happen today. Will we fight all kinds of magical creatures and other exciting things?* James' mind was brimming with fantasy; the prophecy had filled him with excitement.

"I bet you never thought I'd be a hero, did you, Henry?"

The little mouse shook his head and squeaked sarcastically. James grinned and grabbed onto the ladder leading to the treehouse door. "Just you wait and see. I'm going to be a legend someday."

"What do you mean we have to leave?" James paused at the sound of Roan's voice. "You said that there were five of us, and the last time I checked I only count four."

"It's actually only three. Kael doesn't have any power."

"Hmph. All the more reason to wait for the other two to get here. I would think you'd agree with me, unless… what are you hiding?"

James heard Corbin clear his throat. "You're right, we should wait, but I have a bad feeling about the three of you being together. I could feel the energy shift when you were all together in the tavern yesterday. It was obvious, like a flare of energy. I'm afraid that the Shadow King might be able to feel it as well and find us. It's safer to be on the move. It makes our location more difficult to pinpoint. I don't think that I could take on a strætae in my old age."

A somber silence followed Corbin's statement.

James took the opportunity to knock on the door, his earlier thoughts of being a hero overcome by a sense of danger. He heard a commotion, then the trap door opened, framing Roan's face.

"Good morning. Did I interrupt something?"

Roan shook his head and tried to smile. "Nothing at all. I just didn't know you were awake. Let me help you up." He offered his hand and James took it, hoisting himself up into the small room.

James looked around and was surprised to see how large the house looked from the inside, with plenty of space for Roan, Corbin, and him to sit comfortably.

"How'd you sleep last night?" Roan asked as he plated up thick strips of bacon and a rustic mixture of roasted potatoes and eggs.

"I slept great, thanks. A lot better than the boat." James decided not to bring up the argument he had heard between the two. "Did you make this whole place by yourself, Roan?"

Roan smiled proudly, some of the distress dropping from his face. "Yep. A lot of work, but it was worth it.

You can sit on the bed if you want. Sorry there isn't another chair." He gave James the plate and pointed toward the pinewood bed.

"Good morning, James," Corbin said and smiled.

James smiled, but was almost completely distracted by the mouth-watering food in front of him. He sat and began to ravenously tear into the bacon and hash. He passed an occasional morsel to Henry who whined and nuzzled him constantly.

"What's the story with the mouse?" asked Corbin.

"Who, Henry?"

Corbin nodded, a curious expression on his face.

"It's kind of a long story." James took another bite of food and wolfed it down. "Do you mind if I eat first? It's been a while since I've had such good food. Thanks, by the way."

Corbin chuckled and grinned at Roan. "I think that'd be fine. Roan, can you pass me my dish. Now I'm interested to see how good it really is."

Roan grinned and passed a heaping plate to Corbin. The three sat in silence as they enjoyed the breakfast, the early morning sun illuminating the room with cheerful, bright light. James swallowed the food messily, a habit from his years on the streets and in the orphanage. He finished long before the others.

"That hit the spot. Thanks, Roan."

Roan nodded, concerned with his own meal, and made motioned toward the mouse sitting on James' lap.

James looked down at Henry. "Oh, right. We met a long time ago. He actually found me, back when I was fending for myself on the streets. He was the first creature to show any kind of care for me in my life, so I guess I couldn't bear the thought of leaving him. Ever since then we've been connected at the hip. I mean, the shoulder." James smiled and patted the creature's head fondly before he continued, "Anyway, we looked after each other on the streets and in the orphanage. He's basically the only family I've got. It's a little silly, I know."

"I wouldn't say it's silly," said Corbin. "I know from experience that some animals can be a better family than people. I also know that not all creatures are created equally and I'd wager that this is a very special mouse. Why'd you choose Henry as his name?"

James looked at him questioningly.

"I mean, does the name have any significance?"

James considered the question, trying to remember what he was thinking when he had first named the mouse. He glimpsed a vague memory of something he had seen when he was just a small child. He reached for the memory, but it was just beyond his sight. He shrugged. “I’m not sure. It just kinda was what I thought it should be.”

Corbin nodded and leaned back in his chair, thoughtful.

James looked at Roan, but the older boy’s face was inscrutable. Uncomfortably, James turned his attention back to Henry. He playfully batted the mouse’s tail and smiled as the mouse tried to nip his fingers.

Roan coughed. “Do you mind if I ask why you were on the streets?”

James hesitated before answering. He felt the intensity of Corbin and Roan’s focus. “My parents left me alone when I was a baby.” James owned up to it; he never knew his parents and didn’t think of them as anything more than a couple of random people. “That’s all I can remember. I never met them or any other family members. I don’t even know if I have any family.”

Roan sat in silence and mulled over the information. James went back to playing with Henry.

No wonder he's so happy about this. He's had it hard and it seems like a break to be a hero, Roan thought. *Then again, I guess many would say the same about me.* He shook his head and pulled himself back into the cheerful room.

"Well, I guess I'd better go wake up the others."

"Good idea. I'll dish them up some food," said Corbin.

"Sounds good. I'll be back in a few."

Roan looked over to make sure James was alright and the boy smiled and gave him a thumbs up. Roan grinned at the childish expression and slid down the ladder.

I'm happy I met him, he thought, the grin still on his face as he pictured the young boy playing with his mouse. Roan walked through the grass with almost no noise. His years in the forest had given him the ability to move quietly. He neared the shack and peeked in, his eyes quickly adjusting to the dim light inside the cabin as he searched for the boys. Both of them were asleep in a far corner, covered in furs and snoring softly.

This could be fun. Roan silently approached Kael and shook his shoulder.

Kael woke immediately and looked around panicked,

his breathing fast and scared. Roan felt guilt seize his stomach as he saw the pain he had caused.

"It's ok, it's just me. You don't have to worry."

Kael's breathing slowed back to normal and he gulped down his fear. "Sorry, I just… I was having a bad dream."

Roan patted his shoulder. "No worries, I get it. James is already in the house eating breakfast. You'd better hurry up before it's all gone."

Kael nodded and began to collect himself. Roan watched as he slowly unrolled himself from the ball of blankets. *He's entirely different than James. So scared and timid. I wonder what his story is.* Roan mulled over the question, thoughts about Kael's life circulating through his head like leaves falling around a tree in autumn.

Next, Roan knelt and shook Aran's shoulder, doing his best not to suddenly wake him like he had Kael. It wasn't any use. Aran woke almost instantaneously, flying to an upright position and nearly hitting Roan in the process.

"I didn't mean it! I don't know what I was thinking!" Aran yelled and then curled into a fetal position, shivering intensely.

Roan sat back on his heels, unsure of what to do. Roan glanced at Kael, but the younger boy only shrugged, obviously as confused by the odd behavior as Roan.

"You alright?" asked Roan. He gently laid his hand on Aran's back.

Aran stiffened at the touch and mumbled something incoherent.

"What?" Roan leaned closer to try and hear what Aran was saying.

"I said, don't touch me." There was a note of steel in the voice and Roan quickly pulled his hand off of Aran's back. He leaned back onto his heels and waited, the tenseness in the air palpable. "Go. Go away."

Roan opened his mouth to speak, but a soft touch on his shoulder stopped him. He looked up and saw Kael's shy face looking down on him.

"Let's leave him alone," Kael said softly.

Roan nodded and followed Kael out of the shack. A backward glance revealed Aran, still curled into himself, a tight knot of self-defense.

Aran breathed unsteadily as he heard the footsteps

slowly fade away, his knees damp from tears. The same image replayed again in his mind and he flinched at the sight of his dad's broken and battered body.

"I didn't mean to," he whispered to himself. "I just lost control."

And what if you lose control with your friends? What then?

Aran fought the thought. "I won't. I don't want to hurt them."

So, you wanted to hurt him? You wanted to hurt your own dad?

"I didn't mean that I just…"

He was met by a smug silence in his mind; he couldn't argue against the voice in his head.

He clasped his legs tighter in anger and pain. "I won't hurt them."

There was no response, and he sat there with tears streaming down his face. At last, he took a shaky breath, uncurled, and stepped out of the shack, the painful thoughts still heavy on his mind.

Instead of heading straight for the house, he turned and wandered through the foggy field. *I can't let them see me like this. Roan and Kael probably already think I'm crazy.* He walked to the edge of the forest and found a faint path leading into the woods. He followed it and breathed in the misty morning air to try to calm his mind. He covered the painful memories and thoughts deep inside the recesses of his brain, hidden behind walls that he had become all too familiar with constructing. As he did this, his feet wandered along the path until he reached the edge of a small stream. The sound of the water lulled him into a trance-like state where he forgot all his problems and he sighed deeply.

After a few minutes standing near the water, he turned back and made his way to the treehouse. His mind was calm and steady, like the small stream by which he had just been standing by and he was ready to face his companions. *I just hope that they don't ask what that was about.* He shook his head at the thought. *They won't ask about it, and if they do, I'll just say I had a bad dream or something.* He nodded, happy with his plan as he broke out of the thick forest and into the clearing. The sun was getting high in the sky and he felt the air grow humid and hot around him. An irritable itch formed between his shoulders and he felt his calm, clear mind began to cloud in the moist air. He frowned and tried to shake off the feeling as he crossed the clearing. *I really don't need this right now.*

He reached the bottom of the ladder and started the climb, pausing just before he opened the door at the sound of voices.

"Do you have any idea why he might have been acting like that?" Roan's voice was clearly audible.

"It doesn't matter why. We all have our own pasts," Corbin said. "If he wants to tell us, then he will. If not, then we don't need to pry."

Aran held onto the ladder silently, afraid that someone might disagree with Corbin, but the room remained quiet.

At last, Roan said, "I guess you're right. I won't ask him."

Aran sighed, the stress of telling his story lifted from his shoulders. He didn't pay attention to the rest of the conversation. Instead, he gave a firm rap on the pinewood door and heard someone hurry over. The door opened and Aran grinned at Roan's dark black eyes, raising his arm for help up. Roan smiled back, not a convincing smile, but a smile nonetheless, before he helped Aran into the cramped room.

James and Kael sat on the bed in the corner of the room, Henry on James' shoulder nibbling a piece of bread. Aran waved at them. "Morning, boys, I'm guessing everyone slept great."

Kael smiled in his shy way and nodded before he hid his face behind his hair.

"We did!" James exclaimed, grinning broadly. "I slept so well that I nearly forgot about Henry when I woke up."

"What do you mean, almost?" Corbin laughed. "He had to come find you before you remembered him."

Roan chuckled and a rosy shade of pink spread across James' features.

Aran looked at the furry creature who continued to eat the bread. He smiled at the simplicity of the situation, the calm and comforting way the group interacted.

Everything's gonna be fine, he thought. "Where's the food? I hope you guys didn't eat everything."

Roan moved to the clay oven and pulled out a pan brimming with thick chunks of cured venison. "I think you're looking for this. I hope there's enough here for you."

"There's plenty for me, but…" he looked around. "Do you have a plate or something? I don't want to offend you by eating it with my hands."

Corbin chuckled and Roan smiled. He pulled a plate from a shelf hidden from Aran's view. "Here you go.

Now, eat up."

"Thanks." Aran piled the plate high with food. James gaped at the mountain and looked up at Aran, an expression of pure disbelief on his face that forced Aran to burst out in laughter. "Don't worry, James, I'll be fine." The others looked at the boy's open mouth and chuckled. James' face turned red again and he shut his mouth. Aran smiled and continued to eat.

The sun was above them when Corbin forced them out of the hut. "Come on, it's time to start."

Roan groaned at the prospect, the weight of the situation falling back onto his shoulders.

The others seemed to feel an electric and jittery excitement run through their bodies. James was the first out, practically throwing himself to the ground while Henry held on for his life. Kael followed close behind, although his climb to the ground was much more cautious. Aran was about to start down the ladder when Corbin said, "Aran, stay back for a second, I want to talk to you in private." Aran gulped inwardly but nodded in assent. Roan looked at the two, then slid down the ladder, leaving them alone.

"What do you want?" Aran looked at Corbin, hoping for the best and fearing the worst.

"I just want to know why you're hiding it from them."

Aran looked at the man in confusion "Hiding what?"

"I know that you didn't just jump on a boat for no reason. I don't have any right to ask, but they do. They're your friends.

"I can't talk about it. They wouldn't understand it at all."

"I think they might be more understanding than you expect. They've all been through a lot."

"I know they have," he said softly. "But I did something… I did something I can't forgive myself for. Why should I ask them to do something for me that I can't do?"

"I'm sure you did what you had to," said Corbin reasonably. "But I can't be sure unless you tell me."

"You wouldn't like me much if I told you."

"I don't think you can say anything that would make me think you are an awful person. I've seen plenty of awful people…" Corbin trailed off for a moment, caught up in a distinctly painful memory. He shook his head and continued, "You aren't like any of them."

"That's what you say now, but if you heard what I did…" He felt the pain from the memory pressing against the walls he had put up and took a shuddery breath. "I can't even talk about it."

Corbin nodded and grasped Aran's shoulder, "I get it, but you should tell them. You all have to be able to trust each other. Now, let's go get to work. I trust you'll tell them when you're ready to. Talking about it will help. Trust me. Tell them."

"I will," he said. "But not at this moment. It's still too… fresh."

"I know you'll tell them soon. Now go on down that ladder and get ready for hell." His smile turned devilish and Aran felt a shiver of fear run down his spine. He looked around and saw the others standing a few feet away from the tree.

"What was that about?" Roan asked.

Aran smiled and looked around before he whispered conspiratorially, "He told me he thinks James is crazy for having that mouse."

Roan couldn't help but chuckle. "You better not let James know that."

"I'm not planning on it, but you better keep quiet, too."

"You're going to be running today," said Corbin. All the boys looked at him, "Roan, lead the way around the track."

Roan groaned at the thought.

"And then you're all going to run until I tell you to stop."

Roan's face fell even farther as he thought of running the long route over and over again.

Corbin looked at him and made a gesture. "Well, go on, then."

Roan sighed and looked at the boys. "I'll take the first one kinda slow to show you the route." Roan saw James' excited expression and shook his head. "Let's go."

He started to jog into the woods. Corbin looked after them as for a moment, then turned and peered into the other side of the forest. A dense cloud covered the sun and the shadows under the trees darkened.

"Something's coming," he whispered softly to himself.

XIX:

Danger in the Woods

Lyria pushed away a dangling creeper, staying a few steps behind Ferox. Her mind was distracted by some hidden thoughts nagging at it, something important that she couldn't remember. *Maybe it's the reason I was so tired last night,* she thought. The only thing she remembered from the previous night was a wave of exhaustion that had washed over her after Ferox had left. He said that he came back from his hunt to see her curled up in the back of the cave, softly snoring. Lyria stumbled as she tried to remember what had happened, almost face-planting on the forest floor.

What's wrong? asked Ferox.

"What do you mean?"

The wolf sighed and looked at her accusingly. *You've been tripping and falling over everything today. Something's wrong.*

Lyria felt her face flush red with embarrassment. "Nothing. I just have this feeling… Like I forgot something really important."

Hmm. Any idea what it might be?

"No, but I think whatever it was happened last night."

Does it have to do with the moon? In your sleep, you kept saying you'd been talking to the moon. I didn't think anything of it at the time.

Lyria stumbled again as the mention of the goddess sparked her memories. "We've got to go faster," she whispered, suddenly afraid.

What do you mean? Ferox's eyes narrowed.

"I remember what was so important. We have to go!"

Why? What was so important?

"I'll have to tell you the whole story, otherwise you won't believe me, but we have to keep going while I talk. Come on!"

Fine. Ferox increased his pace to a loping run. *Start talking.*

Lyria jogged behind the wolf, her breath coming too fast for regular talking. *I was just sitting there and then I heard a voice…* Lyria related her story as they continued through the forest. The sun rose menacingly above the trees. The air slowly became humid as the remaining water evaporated into the air, creating a heavy atmosphere that pressed uncomfortably against the two travelers. All the while, Lyria stumbled through her story. The heat and her broken memory continued to make her thoughts slip.

The day wore on and the heat rose steadily. Ferox began to pant, his tongue lolling out of his mouth at an odd angle, while the sweltering sun above distorted the humid air. Beads of sweat rolled down Lyria's face and she felt the exhaustion from the past few days of traveling catch up with her. She was bitter with anger as they pushed on through thick underbrush. The heat was under her skin and she couldn't rid herself of the chafing feeling. Finally, she spit out the last of her story, her words harsh and venomous as the heat overwhelmed her. "Then she told me to hurry, something bad is coming."

And you didn't ask what? Lyria could feel the sharp tone in his mind and bared her teeth in anger.

"Of course I did! What do you think I am? A child?"

Well you are, aren't you?

"I am not! I wouldn't talk to me that way if I were

you."

Is that a threat? They had both stopped in their tracks.

"I guess it is." Lyria crossed her arms and looked haughtily at the wolf, unwilling to give up her position. They stood there at odds, neither willing to back down. The sun continued its path through the sky until it was almost directly above them, the air stagnant and quivering in the heat. Eventually, the tension grew too great and one of them had to give up. Ferox was the one to do so. He sighed and turned back to the path, resentment and anger obvious in his steps.

You can think whatever you like, but we can't waste time sitting here and arguing. Let's go. He started to walk away. Lyria huffed, flipped her hair, and followed him. They walked in silence, the tension still present even though the fight was over. Lyria refused to give in to being wrong.

Why should I apologize? she thought to herself. *I wasn't the one who started it.*

The midday heat began to fade and the anger that had burned so vehemently in Lyria's veins slowly dissipated. Still, her pride didn't allow her to take back anything she had said to Ferox. *It was stupid, but why should I tell him that?*

They picked their way through a dense patch of brambles and various other spikey undergrowth. Lyria winced as she felt multiple spines lacerate her bare flesh, but the heat had drained all her energy for arguing.

Ferox stopped suddenly, cocked his head, lifted an ear, and listened. Without a word, he turned to a thicker patch of thorns, shoved his way through, and left a clear trail for Lyria to follow. She sighed at the seemingly unnecessary detour but followed without complaint.

The brush grew thicker and taller along this path; their progress slowed to a crawl. One upside of the trail was that the trees also grew taller and cast cool shadows through which to walk. Lyria pushed past a spiny bush and paused, closing her eyes and listening.

She heard a faint bubbling sound in the distance and frowned. *Is it water or something?*

A low growl from Ferox pulled her back to the path and she continued to follow the wolf's footprints. The sound grew louder as they proceeded, the air cooling as they moved more deeply into the tree's shadows.

Soon, Lyria was wading through waist-high brambles and ferns, the burbling now a soft rushing. *It's a stream, for sure,* she thought and did her best to keep up with Ferox. The idea of wading through cold water was enticing. Along with the rushing sound came other noises: the happy chittering of squirrels, soft scurrying sounds in the brush from small creatures, and chirping from dozens of little flitting robins and sparrows.

The stand-off between Lyria and Ferox faded until it was a distant memory, disappearing along with the intense heat of the day. In the deep forest, the silence between them slowly turned to the friendly quiet they had enjoyed over the past weeks of their journey.

Ferox stopped in front of a massive wall of brambles that grew well over Lyria's head. *It feels... nice here.* He turned and looked at her, checking to make sure she was willing to make one last push through the brambles.

A half-smile showed on Lyria's face, and Ferox turned back to breaking a new trail. He set his shoulders back and the muscles rippled down his back as he forced his way through the thick brambles. Lyria felt her toes curl in her soft leather boots as she saw a faint line of dark, wet fur appear from where one of the longer spikes had cut his back.

He really is strong, she thought as he forced a hole big enough for her to fit through in the tangled mess of brambles. She ducked through the hole and was greeted by a wonderful sight.

They were in the deep forest, a place filled with shadows and cool air, and right in front of them lay a small stream. It wound its way through the forest, burbling happily as it made small waterfalls and pools on its trip.

Lyria took a deep breath and sighed, the faint feeling of anger and pride left from the heat of the day cleansed by the calm forest. She looked at Ferox and felt guilt wash over her. "Hey… About what I said back there, I didn't mean it. I'm sorry." She looked at the ground, afraid of what his response would be. She heard him sigh.

No. I never should've called you a child. I'm sorry.

They were both quiet afterward, momentarily taken away from the harsh reality of life by the calmness of the deep forest. Lyria absentmindedly took off her boots and let her feet dangle in the gentle coolness of the water. Ferox joined her and lay down in the cool stream, washing off the faint trail of blood from his battle through the brambles. They sat there together, enjoying the beautiful world they had stumbled upon and their rekindled friendship; the heat of the day and their insane journey was forgotten.

"My da used to sit next to rivers like this with me," Lyria spoke quietly, trying not to focus on the fact that he was gone. "I would play in the stream while he told me stories. Anything I wanted him to tell me, he did. I remember looking up at him as he told me about fey folk, dwarves, heroes of men, and all the other races." She felt her eyes moisten and stopped talking, the moisture traveling down her cheek and falling into the water below.

She felt Ferox's soft, damp nose nuzzle against her and she smiled, looping her arm over the great wolf's neck.

Why don't you give it a shot? Try telling me what happened last night again. Maybe we can figure out what the moon was talking about.

"I'll do my best."

She took a deep breath and started from the beginning again, her words smooth and flowing this time around. The story was more quickly told this time, unhindered by the muggy air and anger from before. "The last thing she said was that she had to go before he saw her."

I wonder who he is?

Lyria shrugged. "That's what I'm trying to figure

out." She sat in puzzled silence while a horrible idea grew slowly in her mind. "You don't think it could be the Shadow King, do you?" Ferox's hair bristled and he growled at the name.

I hadn't considered it before, but now that you mention it-- He was interrupted by a flock of birds that flew overhead.

Lyria waited for them to pass, but the sound only intensified. She looked up. Sher jaw dropped in astonishment. There weren't just a few birds, but hundreds of them. They all screamed in fear, fleeing something.

We need to go! I don't want to see what they're running from.

"You don't think it could be what the moon was talking about?"

I don't know, but it's something bad. Let's go!

With that, Ferox got up and started to trot down the stream. It wove its way back slowly into the normal trees and undergrowth, following a much less painful path than the one they had taken to reach it. As they left the deep forest for the younger edge of the woods, Lyria saw that the sun had sunk to the low horizon, its light barely managing to illuminate the surrounding forest.

There's no way that it's already too late. Her breath caught in her throat as she remembered the terrible time before it was full darkness. She didn't want to be stuck in that darkness with whatever was chasing them. She pushed on, faster and faster after Ferox.

The sound of the birds had faded, and she looked up to see the sky was empty, the only sound the wind whistling through the trees. She shivered as she felt something cold and dark press against her mind. It was like the moon's mind, but instead of being a wise conscious, it seemed the presence was void of any feeling at all: blank and immense, like a great wall of nothingness.

Lyria shook her head. *It does have one feeling: hate.*

As the thought crystallized in her mind, she realized that her growing dread came not only from the encroaching dark, but from the pure malice emanating from the mind.

We don't stand a chance against it. She knew it was true and felt the knot of fear in her stomach grow tighter as she ran faster in an attempt to escape the creature.

We have to go faster, Ferox! Her mind was yelling; his only response was to run faster than before. Trees flew past and the sun sank lower and lower, the forest now in a twilight haze.

Lyria glanced behind her shoulder and almost froze in terror.

Behind her, a creature as dark as night was rushing over the ground, slowly gaining on them. She turned back to running, her mind spinning. *It can't be,* she thought, even though she already knew it was.

The creature behind her was a stræntae. She remembered her da telling her stories about them, and she didn't relish the idea of trying to fight one. She pressed on with new determination, her feet pounded against the ground and the only thing she could hear was her heart crashing against her chest as adrenaline and fear took over her body.

We're almost there, Ferox said. His mind-voice was edgy with fear.

He charged on, the last few rays of sun illuminating the path. They burst through a line of trees and found themselves in a small clearing. Lyria wished she had time to admire it, but the stræntae was close behind them. She only managed to catch the briefest details: a shack filled with logs, a house in a tree, and a group of boys in front of her. There were four boys, around her age or a little older, and an old man who stood slightly apart from them. The man took one look at Ferox and Lyria, then glanced behind them into the forest. Lyria noticed his eyes, bright and stern. *He's seen this before*, she thought wildly as she ran headlong toward the small group.

"I think we'll have to cut training short. It looks like we've got unwanted company." The old man was still looking beyond Lyria and Ferox, into the dark shadows of the forest. An inhuman shriek came out of the woods and everyone but the old man balked and stepped back fearfully. The old man grimaced but held his ground. Any sign of fear within him gave way to steely determination.

XX:

A Meeting of Friends, New and Old

The sun was making its descent as Roan led the group along the final length of the lap for what felt like the thousandth time. Aran followed closely behind, panting and sweating like a dog from the exertion. James and Kael trailed farther back from the older boys, each grimacing in pain. They had started strong, but by now an ache had developed in their sides and Henry's constant chatter wasn't helping their mood. While they all wore similar pained expressions, Roan was considerably less exhausted than the rest of the group. *I guess my training really is paying off,* he thought as he glanced over his shoulder and saw Aran panting in exhaustion behind him. They jogged past a group of young trees clustered closely together, a key landmark on the five-mile route, and pressed onwards, all of their energy put into this last push.

Roan burst out of the forest and ran toward Corbin, followed soon after by the rest of the boys.

"Alright, you can stop."

Roan gasped for breath. Corbin watched them with obvious joy in his eyes

I'd like to see you do it. Roan would've said the words out loud, but he barely had breath to stand, let alone speak.

"Go ahead and go get some water. You've earned it." Corbin nodded at the boys, clearly pleased with their efforts.

Roan looked at the others and motioned for them to follow. "It's just through those trees."

The others nodded their thanks, then started to trudge drearily in the direction Roan had pointed. After a moment, Roan followed, his muscles screaming at every step he took.

Corbin chuckled softly to himself. "So this is what it's like on the other side. I always wondered how it felt."

Roan couldn't muster any response and focused on forcing his legs to pull him toward the water. By the time he had broken through the trees, the other boys had already flung themselves into the small creek and were groaning in pain.

"How is it?" asked Roan

Aran looked over with an exhausted grin. "It feels great." He turned his head to the sky and closed his eyes, enjoying the simple coolness of the water.

Roan quickly stripped before he got into the water. He sighed as the cool liquid embraced his burning body the group stayed there in silence, the only sound Henry's occasional squeak.

"Is it normally this bad?" asked Aran after a few minutes.

Roan thought for a moment before answering, "Yep. Sometimes it's worse, actually, but your body kinda gets numb after a while."

Aran groaned. "Well, I guess that means we'll be sleeping pretty sound for a while."

Roan laughed from exhaustion but grasped his sides in pain. "Laughing hurts."

Aran started to laugh then stopped abruptly as he came to the same conclusion as Roan. "You're right, no more jokes."

They wordlessly enjoyed the blissful relief from the blistering heat of the sun and their exertions.

Eventually, James broke the silence. "I thought being a hero was going to be more fun."

"I think that Corbin has a different definition of fun than we do," Roan said.

"I guess so."

It was quiet again, then Kael spoke up. "What's it like... to have powers?"

"What do you mean?" asked Aran.

"Well..." Kael was quiet for a second as he tried to think of how to phrase his query. "I mean, what does it feel like when you use them?"

Roan spoke first. "I'm not sure how to describe it. For me, it's kinda like a barrier deep inside me breaks and releases some sort of… something." He finished, grasping for a better word.

"Yeah, but it doesn't feel like it's something that's mine, more like I'm borrowing it for a while," James agreed.

Aran nodded. "Exactly. Like something wild."

Kael listened, smoothing his jet-black hair against his head and letting the water stream down his back, the motion fulling revealing his normally half-hidden face. "I thought it would be more... powerful, I guess."

"Maybe we all wish it felt that way, too," Roan spoke

for James and Aran who nodded in agreement.

"I guess that makes sense," Kael smiled.

They sat in companionable silence, content to let the water smooth as much pain as possible from their ravaged muscles. Roan lay back in the shallow creek and closed his eyes, basking in the sun's heat and the water's refreshing coolness.

"It's a nice day," he commented.

"No kidding," said James. "I wish we could stay here for a few hours."

"I wouldn't be so ready to relax," Corbin's voice came from the bank.

Instinctively, Roan's eyes flew open. He had just enough time to see Corbin toss a rock his way. Using his split-second advantage, he dodged the flying projectile. The other boys were not so fortunate, and he heard cries of pain and surprise rise up from the water.

"What was that for?" Aran cried as he touched the welt that had already formed on his side.

"I've still got things to teach you and you've been sitting here for almost an hour now." Corbin shook his head and tried to hide his grin.

"But did you have to throw rocks at us?" James quivered, his voice shrill with insult. He looked at the dark bruises on his ribs. "You could have at least thrown them a little more gently."

Corbin's grin turned to a wide smile. Kael followed Roan's example and climbed out of the stream without complaint.

Roan glanced from the grumbling Aran and James to Kael. He rolled his eyes. "You're a fast learner, aren't you? They'll learn quickly enough not to argue with Corbin."

A trace of a smile flickered across Kael's face. "Aran might, but I'm not so sure about James. He isn't exactly the brightest."

Roan snorted. "Maybe you're right. If that's the case, he's gonna get a few more bruises and bumps."

Kael's barely noticeable smile grew into a full-fledged grin, but he remained quiet.

Roan pulled up his trousers and patted Kael's back before he turned to face Corbin. "What's next?"

"History, your favorite."

Roan groaned.

Kael quickly dressed and Aran followed closely behind, still muttering under his breath. James was last. He whistled for Henry who jumped onto his leg and scrambled up to his shoulder where he perched comfortably.

Corbin made sure they were all ready before leading the way back to the treehouse.

When they reached the clearing, Corbin told them to sit on the ground around the base of the tree where he had put a chair from the wood shack. They obeyed, having learned their lesson from the river.

Corbin made himself comfortable on the chair before he began. "Who here knows about the treaty between the shadow plane and our world?"

He was met with blank stares.

"How about the crowning of the first human king, or the war between elves and dwarves?"

Again, their faces were blank and empty.

"I see," Corbin sighed. "Well, then, let's start from the beginning. At first, the only two beings in existence were the sun and the moon…" Corbin went on to regale the boys with stories of the creation of the earth and the great battles and the first kings' laws and government.

The sun sank lower and lower behind the trees, and its rays barely made it past the mountain range. Even without the sun there to fuel it, the heat of the humid day still hung in the air. It left the boys itchy and uncomfortable throughout Corbin's lecture. Occasionally, he would pause and ask them questions with no repercussions if they responded incorrectly.

As the web of stories grew, night began to spill into the forest. It gathered among the trees first, slowly polluting the clearing and reaching under the tree. Corbin felt a chill run down his back and paused, looking for the source of the feeling.

"What is it?" asked Roan.

Corbin shushed Roan. He cocked his head and listened.

The group held their breath in anxious anticipation. Sweat from the hot day had begun to cool off. They all felt a shiver of coldness.

Then they all hear it: the sound of brush being trampled.

Corbin grabbed his staff and leaped to his feet. "Get up. Something's coming." Corbin spoke in a monotone that didn't allow argument.

Immediately, the boys got up and stood behind the old man. They assumed fighting positions, hands back and ready for anything. Corbin felt a thrum of pride in their bravery. "Stay back," he whispered fiercely.

"Whatever it is, you're too valuable to take any risk."

The crashing drew closer. Darkness and shadows thickened around them. The forest was now fully cloaked in shadow. Corbin stood straight and tall, holding his walking stick like a staff.

Suddenly, the crashing sound was right in front of them and a creature burst out of the forest, skidding to a halt in front of Corbin.

The boys all gasped and stepped back in shock. It was a giant wolf. He stood about half as tall as Roan and his mouth was so large that he could easily fit one of their heads in it.

Past the wolf, a second figure burst from the night forest. This one was a young girl, no older than James and Kael. She was dressed in torn clothes and her arms were marked with scratches and scrapes from her dead sprint through the forest.

"Who are you?" Corbin maintained his calm reassuring tone.

The girl looked at him as she gasped for breath. "No time… have to go… Bad things."

What she means to say is that we have to move, a strætae is close on our heels. The wolf spoke and Corbin nodded.

"How much time do we have?" asked Corbin.

The wolf shook his head. *We don't.*

Corbin nodded gravely. "Take them as far and as fast as you can. I'll deal with the strætae."

The wolf nodded and turned to nuzzle the girl into movement again.

Corbin turned to the boys. "You have to follow the wolf. He'll get you to safety. I'll join you as soon as I can." He looked at them. "Do you understand?"

They nodded and spoke in unison, "Yes, sir."

"Good."

The other boys had started to move, but Corbin drew Roan aside. "Roan, if I don't make it out of this, then you have to promise me you'll remember to go west to the temple of the moon and find Anna." He grabbed Roan by the shoulders, "Promise me."

Roan nodded and gulped, his throat dry, "I promise. But you'll be back."

"We can only hope." Corbin smiled sadly, then wrapped Roan in a hug. "Now, go. GO!"

The wolf was already on the other side of the clearing with the girl standing next to him. James and Kael turned without a second thought. Aran stayed a moment longer, looking at the old man in concern before he turned and followed. Roan was the last to go.

He looked at Corbin in fear and anguish. He knew enough about the strætae to fear the worst. "Promise me you'll do everything you can to make it back to us."

The sad smile slipped from Corbin's face, replaced with stubborn determination. "I will. Now go."

Roan looked back once more before he fled after the others. Corbin watched them disappear into the thick brush before he turned around and prepared to face the monster that was quickly approaching.

He closed his eyes and started to tear down the barriers he had made around the spring of power that welled deep in his mind. As more layers of the barrier fell, the power began to trickle out like a stream. Soon it was a steady river of energy that filled Corbin with youthful exhilaration. He tore down the last wall and opened his eyes to the darkness that lay in front of him. His eyes were alight with blue fire that poured out from spiderweb cracks, fierce and unyielding as he stared into the shadows before him. He stood steadily, his staff held in one hand, with blue symbols lit up along its length.

A bright light began to emanate from the staff as Corbin directed the river into it, the lettering becoming brighter and a bulb of white fire forming at its tip. The darkness recoiled, confused by this retaliation. The shadows swirled in strange patterns. Corbin willed the light to grow brighter and a sudden flash of brilliance illuminated the surrounding forest. It flung the shadows into the deeper woods and created a barrier against any more of the creeping darkness.

The light continued to grow; soon it filled the clearing with a harsh luminescence. It wasn't warm or yellow, but pure white that brought into sharp clarity the contrasts that existed in all parts of the meadow. It sharply outlined each blade of grass and turned every shape a shade of greyish white, bright enough to blind any normal creature. Corbin was unaffected by the light; the glowing blue energy that filled his eyes protected him from any ill effects of his powers.

He felt something press against the edge of his barrier of light, pushing and prodding for a weakness. He pushed back and tried to find out how powerful it was. His first prod was met by a vast nothingness that swallowed anything that fell into it. The shadows felt him reach out and attacked, preying on his momentary weakness. Effortlessly, they started to penetrate his light.

Corbin grimaced. *It's strong, alright.*

He willed the light to intensify and force the

shadows out of the circle. They lay just out of sight, hiding behind the first line of trees and waiting for their master to aid them.

Corbin had fought strӕntae before and he knew that there would be worse to come than the darkness that preceded them. He held his ground, saving his strength until the real battle began. The shadows continued to pound away at his shield, wave after wave wearing his energy down slowly.

Where is it? Corbin cast around the meadow, searching for the master even as he continuously deflected the smaller shadows.

Then, he felt it.

Something was fast approaching the circle of light, something more powerful than he had expected. He felt it reach out with its mind, tendrils snaking their way toward the barrier he had created.

Corbin stood his ground and pushed back as the first tendril of darkness slammed into the edge of the light. The dark mind paused in its charge and pulled back the tendril as if to retreat, but Corbin knew better and used the momentary lull to harden the barrier in preparation for a stronger attack.

He felt the dark creature move forward, slowly at

first, then at a full sprint until it rammed into the wall. The impact created a wedge of darkness that broke the ring. Corbin grunted and strained against the attacking force, barely managing to push back the shadow that invaded the ring. Next came waves of tentacles that smashed relentlessly against the crack in the barrier. Corbin was so overwhelmed by the sheer power of the thing that he had no choice but to let the circle of light shrink.

He closed his eyes and leaned heavily on the staff as the darkness slowly started to close in on him. He was forced to retreat. The strӕntae pushed onward, its shadowy minions running tirelessly into the wall.

Corbin knew he couldn't maintain the barrier in the face of this powerful onslaught. He opened his eyes and looked behind him. *I'm sorry. I wish I could've bought you more time,* he thought before he let the circle of light close into an area only a few feet around him.

The darkness flowed around him, surprised by his sudden retreat. It waited, confused, for its master's orders. Corbin searched the shadowy blackness for his opponent, his vision focused in the direction of the forest's edge which had been clearly visible seconds ago. He felt the strӕntae move forward before he saw it, a ripple of some greater shade in the darkness.

Corbin peered into the gloom but saw nothing, save the shadowy outlines of a tree or two.

Then he saw it. A human-sized blackness moved gracefully out of the forest, across the grass, and stood next to the orb of light that surrounded Corbin. The being was pitch black, darker than a starless night, and more menacing than an angry bear. It looked at Corbin and he saw two dull glowing red dots in the swirling shadows.

"Who are you that can stand against my might?" It spoke in a distinctly male voice that slithered and spun like smoke on a stormy night.

"I'm a teacher." Corbin stared at the creature in front of him, unafraid. "Who are you?"

"A teacher, you say? Where are your students?" The wraith hissed like a snake.

"They're not here, but you haven't answered my question. Who are you?" asked Corbin, unwavering.

The shadow laughed, low and murky. "I am a strænta."

"Yes," replied Corbin matter of factly. "Anyone could see that, but who are you?"

"You don't know who you're talking to! I am the left

hand of the Shadow King. Does the name mean anything to you?"

Corbin shrugged. "I've heard of you, but I don't remember what you did to get the name."

The strӕntae cackled, his smokey voice rising fitfully between the trees. "That's all? You don't know anything about my power?"

Corbin's face twitched as the darkness around him grew, forcing itself against the shield of light.

The strӕntae drew closer to the orb. "You're a worthy opponent. What's your name?"

Corbin smiled devilishly back and whispered, "My name is-" He didn't finish the sentence, instead he sent out a blast of energy that surprised the strӕntae.

After a moment, it recovered and started to fight back, the two forces equally balanced. They remained in a standoff until Corbin managed to pool enough energy for an attack.

He collected his thoughts and held up the barrier with one hand, spinning a fiery ball of energy into existence with the other. He tossed the spear of light across the line and watched as it slammed against a shield the strӕntae had managed to create just in time. The strӕntae retaliated with his darting tendrils that snaked into the light-filled area and exploded a few feet from Corbin.

Corbin stepped back slowly, his breathing heavy as he deflected the black tendrils of slimy darkness that penetrated his dome of light. *He's too strong,* he thought. *I'll have to outsmart him.* An idea began to form and he started to execute it with the hope that the rest of it would come together as needed. With a sudden burst of energy, he threw the ring of light out around him in a dazzling display of sparks and lightning that flitted through the air.

Railin closed his eyes, blinded by the flash, and Corbin used the opportunity to slip out of the clearing, away from the strædntae.

Corbin heard the roar from the trees as he flitted nimbly through the brush toward Copper Town. *Only a fool would've fallen for that.* He heard crashing behind him and felt the onset of cold, but the adrenaline that rushed through his body combined with his iron will was enough to stop fear before it could form. A crash sounded close behind and to his left; Corbin shot his hand back, a bright spear of light streaming toward the source of the sound. The crashing paused momentarily, then the creature redoubled its speed, enraged. Corbin felt a sense of unease growing in the back of his mind as the strӕntae warded off his blows as if they were nothing more than pine needles. *Maybe he's more powerful than I thought.* He patted the hidden pocket in his shirt and frowned. *I hope it doesn't come to that.*

Corbin broke out of the brush and saw the town in front of him. He sprinted toward the center, caught his breath, and waited for the strӕntae to emerge. Darkness began to ooze into the barren ground of the town center and climbed stickily over houses and sheds. Corbin grimaced as he thought about what he had brought to these innocent people. He hadn't been thinking about them when he had come up with the plan to run. As the shadows crept toward him, he looked behind his shoulder across the river where he imagined he could see five figures as they ran quickly up the base of the mountain range that surrounded the town. *They won't make it if I don't stop him.* He turned his attention back to the approaching darkness.

The shadows had almost reached halfway across the well-trodden ground. *That's far enough.* He initiated a barrier, similar to the one in the clearing but strengthened by threads of moonlight. He closed his eyes and concentrated on weaving the beams from the freshly risen moon into his wall of light before the grasping hands of darkness could start to tear it apart. A cold fog crept about his feet, but Corbin paid no attention to it as he continued to build his barrier. At last, he finished and opened his eyes.

Around him was a sea of darkness that scratched and clawed against the dome of light he had created. Inside the blackness, he saw a darker shadow moving slowly and calmly toward him.

"Quite impressive." The smokey voice of the strækntae echoed out of the darkness. "It's been some time since I've had a challenge like you, and I thank you. But now I'm going to kill you."

Corbin chuckled. "Do you really think you can kill me? You asked me my name, but I never gave it to you. Would you like to know now?" Corbin paused only long enough for Railin to open his mouth before he continued. "My name is Corbin. I've killed kings, brought kingdoms down before me, saved beautiful maidens, and killed wretched beasts. But my greatest accomplishment went down in legend." He paused again for effect before he continued. "I ended the tyranny of an ancient titan from another realm, a creature still spoken of thousands of years later. Some would even call him a god. Do you know of whom I speak?" Corbin's gaze was fierce. "I was the one who single-handedly took down your Shadow King."

Railin and his shadows stopped, awestruck by this new information. Realization dawned on the strædntae as he called back ancient memories. "I know who you are and I know what you've done, but that was long ago and time seems to affect you just like the rest." His smokey voice did not mask the ripple of doubt that ran through his mind.

"We'll see about that." Corbin made a ferocious push against the dark mass of shadow minions and managed to get them back near their master. They screamed in horror as the barrier of light slammed into them at full force, an ear-splitting sound that shattered the glass windows in some of the richer houses. Corbin winced and looked around only to see a few faces in the windows. *I'm sorry,* he thought before returning his attention to the battle at hand. The strædntae had recovered as well, stringing together a formidable defense. Both stood still, Corbin's face grim and the strædntae's red eyes narrow slits of concentration.

More people began to wake and look at the spectacle. Many of them clutched at pieces of metal and muttered prayers. A baby cried and his mother shushed him quickly before she went back to sprinkling a fine powder over her windowsill. Dark slimy vines of darkness thrashed against Corbin's shield of light, each with enough force to shatter trees, but Corbin still stood strong, one hand gripped firmly around his staff and the other resting calmly at his side. He felt at peace, a leaf riding a warm current of air higher and higher during a storm, untouched by the madness that swirled around it.

Corbin felt a tug at the back of his mind and glanced upwards to see a mass of dark clouds approaching the moon. He looked back at the angry dark and grimaced as he tried to formulate some sort of plan before the cloud reached the moon. Much of the energy in the shield was supported by the moonbeams that he had so cleverly woven into it. Without the moon, his defense would be full of holes.

Corbin's only option was going on the offensive, so he did. He raised his hand and, reaching into the spring of energy in the back of his mind, started to form a spear of light in his hand. The spear grew. Its shaft thickened and the weak tip grew into a large, broad, sharp triangle.

The strӕntae was so focused on the barrier that he didn't see the great spear of light until it was too late to stop it. Corbin heaved the stick of pure energy forward with a grunt and watched it fly along the intended path. The spear went easily through the few puny snakes of shadow that the strӕntae had managed to pull together as a defense, leaving a trail of light in its wake. The strӕntae tried to move out of the way, but it was caught off guard. The spear struck him just to the right of his heart.

The strӕntae screamed in agony, the shadows around him squirming and writhing in pain. Corbin closed his hand and twisted it to the right, forcing the spear deeper into the strӕntae, whose only response was louder cries of fear and pain. The circle of light began to expand until it encompassed over two-thirds of the town. The shadows gave way easily now, their master greatly weakened.

Corbin stepped calmly forward until he was in the center of the square. He looked with pity at the creature who writhed before him, just outside of his luminous sphere. "This is where your story ends." Corbin spoke with a sense of finality, his voice sharp and unforgiving. He turned his fist until it was upside down before he opened it. The spear exploded in a brilliant flash of light that shattered the darkness around the strӕntae. The dripping shadows that enveloped the creature were the last things to go; they clung helplessly to the lifeless stræntae until they were stripped away, one by one.

The body that remained was someone very frail, aged almost beyond recognition. Corbin bent down and looked at the face, the wall of light chasing the remaining shadows into the forest. "Who are you?" he asked. The face that looked back at him was almost familiar.

The fragile man's only response was to groan and crumpled, like an old pile of sticks on the ground.

Corbin inspected the face more closely, then stumbled back in shock. "Railin?" Corbin struggled for words; the face of his old friend rendered him speechless.

The frail man let out a maniacal laugh. "You thought wrong, old friend."

Corbin stumbled back in utter shock, and the dark clouds that had threatened to cover the moon swept forward to cut off all moonlight. In the absence of the moon, the shadows regrouped and forced their way back into the town, gathering again in Railin's broken body.

Corbin struggled to regain control of his shield. He managed to stop the shadows about halfway into the square. The dripping, pure darkness had reformed itself around Railin and had transformed the broken sack of bones back to the dark humanoid strætae. This time, however, the shadows didn't blanket all of his features; they left a hole around his face and used Corbin's surprise to their advantage.

"Corbin." Railin's voice changed from smokey and scratchy to a deep, rich voice of a young man. "I thought you'd died long ago. I didn't even connect the person that bard was talking about with you."

"Rai, how could you?" Corbin was even more astonished by the face, now that the darkness had somehow managed to restore it to the one he remembered from his youth.

Railin grinned wickedly. "Power, my old friend, power." He reached out with a shadow-cloaked hand. "You still could join us. The Shadow King would be happy to have someone like you on our side."

Corbin shook his head. "I would never join him. You know that."

The grin fell, and Railin shrugged. He lowered his hand. "Have it your way, then. Let's see how well you fare without help from your precious moon."

The shadows launched themselves against the barrier, pounding against it harder than ever. Corbin gritted his teeth and gripped his staff with both hands, barely managing to keep the force back.

Railin laughed. “Not so strong now, are you?” He pushed harder and slowly the shadows began to gain ground. Inch by inch, they moved advanced.

Corbin closed his eyes and did his best to halt their progress, but it was no use. He reached slowly for the hidden pocket in his shirt and pulled out a bright glimmering stone. He looked over his shoulder toward the mountain. “I’m sorry Roan,” he whispered.

Railin saw the movement and peered curiously at the small spot of light. “What have you got there?”

Corbin refused to answer as he brought the stone to his face, fighting for every inch while he deflected the attack of the darkness around him.

“I’m sorry, Roan,” Corbin said, letting it echo out toward the mountain and the young boy. For a moment, he closed his eyes, preparing himself to do the thing that he had hoped he would not need to do.

He lifted the stone higher and felt a tear leak from his closed eyes. When he opened his eyes, the blue fire leaped from them for the last time. “So long, old friend. I wish things could have been different.”

He dropped the stone as the realization hit Railin. It

wasn't just a stone; it was a bomb of energy that Corbin had gathered over many years. Railin screamed and attacked with more power than before, forcing the barrier of light to collapse inward.

Time slowed as the stone fell; the shadows reached out with dark tentacles and Corbin smiled sadly as he focused his remaining energy into a small shield around the rock. Darkness rushed forward and consumed him, but the stone remained untouched. It twisted once and a rainbow of color flashed from it before it struck the ground. The world went still for a moment. The shadows halted in their pursuit as the outer shell of the stone began to crack and shatter.

The stone shattered. A blast of energy radiated outward, incinerating the shadows, houses, ground, and anything that stood in its way. The people at the edge of town were awake and saw it coming, but didn't feel anything as they were turned to ash instantaneously by the wave of energy. The Drunken Cow disappeared. The town vanished. A circular arc of the forest ceased to exist.

Then it was over. The blast of light faded gently away, leaving darkness. Gradually, the moon's pale light returned and revealed a swathe of stunned emptiness.

XXI:

Saying Goodbye

"**F**erox says we should hurry up!" yelled the girl, obviously frantic.

The others took her word for it as they heard a loud boom from the town below. James and Kael were a few steps behind Lyria, and Aran was still farther in the rear. Still Roan came last, Corbin's final words running repeatedly through his mind. An invisible hand tugged at him. He slowly turned to look back at the town, afraid of what he might see.

He stopped and stared in awe. Half the town was shrouded in shadows, the other filled with a blinding light. He squinted against the bright light and managed to make out two figures in the middle of the town staring at each other. *Corbin!* He was filled with joy to see the old man, but he frowned as the shadows begin to encroach on him. The ball of shadows surrounded him.

"NO!" The others stopped at Roan's painful cry.

Roan stood frozen in place. Everything around him disappeared except for the miniature scene playing out below. He heard the whispered words: *I'm sorry.* It was Corbin's voice. Tears rolled down Roan's face as he felt the pain and anguish in his teacher's words. Then, a burst of sudden luminescence covered the town, blinding Roan and his companions. Roan felt the remnants of the voice slip away. The burning memory of his parents' death reverberated through his mind as he remembered the old man fondly. He hadn't known him long, but Roan had grown to think of Corbin as a grandfather. He hated the feeling of loss that once again infected the pit of his stomach.

Tears streamed down Roan's face. He sank to his knees and sobbed into his hands. "I forgive you," he managed to whisper before he was consumed by the magnitude of his loss. His hometown and part of the forest he had lived in had disappeared from existence. As if from a great distance, he heard the girl gasp. She felt his pain leaking from his body. He grimaced. *I have to be strong. I can't let my pain affect the rest of them. It's what Corbin would have wanted.* Still, Roan couldn't bear to move and stayed huddled in a ball. The girl made her way to him and he felt her presence gently comfort him as he wept.

Eventually, the companions recovered. The place where Copper Town had been was illuminated by the silvery light of the moon. A crater stood in place of the town, almost a mile in diameter. A thick layer of ash rested in its base and on the surrounding land. The only trace of the town was the road that led into the empty, barren pit. The group silently absorbed the enormity of the event they had witnessed.

Aran's already numb mind began to shut down further, but he forced himself out of the shell and looked for Roan.

He found Roan doubled over with the girl comforting him, her arm wrapped around him like a mother. Aran made his way to the two of them and crouched down, laying his hand on Roan's back and staring at the remnants of the small town. He opened his mouth, then closed it. *What do I say… What can I say?*

Soon enough, James and Kael sat next to the rest of the group and Aran hugged the young red-haired boy. "It's going to be alright," he whispered, more to himself than to anyone in particular. No one else spoke.

Eventually, Roan wiped his eyes and started to get up.

"Sorry. We need to get moving." His voice was strained from the force of his lamentation. He cleared his throat. "And, thanks..." He looked at the group of people gathered around him, hopeful that they understood what he meant. "I need all of you."

Aran nodded. "We all need each other now."

The rest of them nodded. James and Kael were still too shocked to speak.

After another moment of rest, Aran voiced the question on the other boys' minds. "Who are you?" He looked at the girl.

The girl looked up, her face still wet with tears. "Me?"

Aran nodded and she gulped, glancing at the wolf before continuing. "My name is Lyria. He's Ferox. We've come a long way to find you and Corbin, but...." She left the sentence dangling.

Aran was quick to reply. "Well, we're still here. But how did you know his name was Corbin? I don't remember any introductions." His previously foggy mind had started to clear and a bit of the quick thinking from his years of trading began to come back to him. *And what about the wolf? She said that he told us to hurry up back there. Since when do wolves speak?*

Lyria shook her head. “No introductions. I found out from Roan.” She pointed at Roan.

Roan glanced up, startled to hear his name from her lips.

“And, Aran, before you ask, let me explain.” The girl spoke quickly and with confidence.

Aran’s mouth was open, so he shut it and nodded, his mind full of questions.

Lyria sighed. “You’ve probably already guessed, I’m like the rest of you. It’s my power. It's like... like,” she waved her arms around, in a failed attempt to show some sort of ability. “I can read minds, but only sometimes. For example, I don’t know how, but I… felt...” she paused, unsure if it was the right word before continuing, “I felt Roan’s thoughts and now I know what he knows about all of you.”

Aran saw her glance at the wolf. He saw the creature make a motion very similar to a shrug. “I think I get it,” Aran said slowly. After a long pause, he once again voiced the unspoken question of the whole group. “What now?”

Roan began to move, his mind returning from a familiar dark place. "Now? We go west, to the temple of the moon. It's the last thing Corbin told me." He spoke with such conviction that even James and Kael seemed to thaw a bit from their shocked state.

Roan scanned the group with a look that suggested he wasn't in the mood for answering questions. "Unless anyone else has a better idea."

No one spoke.

"Then it's decided. We go west."

Lyria was the first to stir into motion. "Ferox says he can show us the fastest way. Let's get going."

Ferox started to climb again, followed closely by Lyria. Aran looked at the rest of the group, then back at the crater for a moment. He shuddered. He headed after the enormous wolf. Roan followed. His body moved robotically while his mind wandered aimlessly inside itself. James met Kael's eyes and they silently agreed to never talk about this moment again, then they fell into line, Henry riding on James' shoulder, solemn for once.

They didn't make it far before they had to stop and rest. The adrenaline of the night had worn off and everyone was deeply exhausted. Ferox located a small cave where they could sleep.

After making sure that everyone was at least partially comfortable, Aran approached Roan. "Are you alright?"

Roan shook his head. "No. There's nothing you can do to help."

Aran spoke gently, "I know. It's gonna be alright, though."

Roan shrugged and held his head in his hands.

Aran sighed. *I hope he gets better.* He lay down near the others, but in his sleep he wrestled with dark thoughts that had broken free and tumbled wildly through his dreams.

Roan was the last to fall asleep. After speaking with Aran, he walked outside to sit in the moonlight. In the pale, silvery light, his deep melancholy hardened into a thick shell that compartmentalized the memory of Corbin's death. The shell allowed Roan to hold onto the good memories but shielded him from the sorrow. He knew he would have to examine Corbin's death later in order to understand its full meaning, but the time for grieving would have to wait. He turned his tear-stained face up to the moonlight and accepted the strong, silvery shell the moon's gentle light crafted. He understood that it was temporary, but he was grateful he could find a place to contain the suffering with which he was stricken. Eventually, he wandered to the cave and fell asleep curled between Aran and Ferox.

XXII:

A New Family

A light wind was blowing from the north when James woke up the next day. It brought the hints of fall and winter, leaving the air crisp and chilly. He felt a slight tap on his shoulder and saw Kael standing there, motioning for him to follow.

Before James could ask what was wrong, Kael turned and walked away. *I'd better see what's up.* James rubbed his eyes sleepily then gathered up Henry without waking him, rolled, with more than a little regret, out of his sleeping pad, and followed after his friend.

They walked a short way into the forest before Kael sat down at the base of a stump. James sat next to him in silence for a few moments; he knew that he couldn't push Kael to tell him anything he didn't want to.

"I shouldn't be here." Kael's hair hid his face.

"What do you mean?"

Kael shook his head. "All of you have these powers and I'm just… me. Why should I be here?"

James sighed. He had known the question was coming. He looked up at the trees, trying to formulate an answer. "I'm not sure why any of us are here. Everyone's happy to have you here, anyway, even if you don't have powers."

Kael shook his head. "That's not what I meant. I know that they don't care, but you all have to save the world. You know better than anyone that I'm not the kind of person meant to save the world."

James was quiet for a long time. When he finally spoke, it was slow and steady. "I think you're here because you want to be. I know you better than anyone, and I know that even if you say that you're afraid, you would still be the one to help others before yourself. Maybe you don't have any special "powers," but you always think of others first. And if you're asking me, that's more of a power than the rest of us combined."

Kael lifted his eyes hesitantly. "Do you really think so?"

James grinned and softly punched Kael in the shoulder. "I do, I really do."

Kael smiled and let his hair fall back over his face.

Without seeing his face, James knew that he was pleased.

They sat there for a while longer, enjoying the feel of the cool air and the scent of the forest. The crisp breeze from the north continued. It cleared the shards of the previous night from their minds and blew them far away, toward the mountain range and the plains beyond.

James was the first to stand up. "We should get going before the others start looking for us."

Kael nodded. James offered him a hand up. Kael took the outstretched hand and the two friends walked back to the cave where they found the rest of the group just starting to stir.

Roan sat up and rubbed his eyes. The wind seemed to have brought hope with it and swept away the immediate pain and grief that he had felt the night before. He smiled at James and Kael.

"Morning, boys, you ready for a day of walking?"

They both groaned and he laughed. Then he met Aran's thoughtful gaze. "Thanks for taking charge last night," he said with full sincerity.

Aran shrugged. "Someone had to."

Roan paused, noting a hint of bitterness in the other boy's tone. Then Aran grinned and Roan nodded, relieved that boy's sour attitude had been nothing but a joke.

Lyria and Ferox were up and stretching. He wasn't sure what to think of them yet, but he felt like he could trust Lyria. Last night, when she had looked through his mind, he had felt her presence. It was confident, yet gentle. *I trust her,* he thought to himself as he watched her pet the massive wolf.

Roan nodded to the wolf. "Ferox, right?"

The wolf met his gaze and bent his head somberly.

"Thanks for what you did last night."

Ferox growled and showed his teeth in what Roan believed to be a grin.

"He says it's no big deal," Lyria translated. "He also says that we should get going."

"Well, the big wolf has spoken. Let's get moving." Roan looked at the rest of the group. "Everybody, get your stuff together and eat on the way. I don't want to stick around any longer than we have to."

A chill ran through the air and no one objected to the idea.

They started to make their way hurriedly through

the forest. The great pines and maples towered high above them while the lesser alders and myrtles spread their branches closer to the ground. The breeze slowly died as the sun climbed higher above the mountains, raining down warmth. It was a much drier and more pleasant warmth than the previous day's. They trooped along quietly, content to walk in companionable silence, their minds reeling from the recent events.

They reached a small stream and followed it until it joined the larger river, the water smooth and fast-flowing. Despite the weight of responsibility on Roan's shoulders, he couldn't help but feel a sense of adventure as he gazed at the sleek water. A bridge crossed the river and they ran across, sharing a wordless fear that someone or something might see them on its exposed planks. They gradually gained altitude and the trees began to thin. The mountains drew closer.

"Ferox says this is the pass through the mountains," Lyria said, the first words spoken since that morning. "He says we'll be through by nightfall."

Roan nodded. "Let's keep going." He glanced around and saw affirmative looks from the rest of the group. He motioned for Ferox to lead the way.

The great wolf flicked his tail before he continued

to lead the group through the forest.

The sun was almost a quarter of the way to the horizon when Roan began to feel an ache in his stomach. The meager food he had eaten during the day wasn't nearly enough to support the combined stress and physical exertion of the journey. Roan looked around and saw James grimacing and looking hungrily around. *We're gonna have to stop soon.*

As if on cue, Lyria spoke again. "Ferox says we can rest in a clearing just ahead."

Roan heard James exhale in relief. *He's a tough kid, but he's still just a kid,* Roan thought. They were in the clearing shortly. Ferox stayed only long enough to see that everyone had made it safely. Then, he turned and bounded away.

"Where's he going?" asked Aran

Lyria shrugged. "He said he was going hunting."

"Hopefully he brings some back for us," grumbled Aran. Roan could tell that the lack of food was getting to him.

Before anyone else could complain, Roan took charge. "Before we all settle down, let's get a proper camp ready. I'll take care of the fire if you guys can go find some wood."

He heard a few groans, but no one verbalized their objections. *Good,* he thought as they left to search for wood. *I don't need to get in a fight with anyone right now.* Truth be told, he had barely slept the night before and was completely exhausted. Still, he willed himself to get together his bundle of sticks and gather enough energy to ignite them with a small, blue flame. The world became fuzzy as the wood began to burn. He cut off the energy before he completely collapsed. *Gotta be careful, can't do something stupid.* He felt dizzy and his mind was foggy. He sat down to try and rest while he waited for the others.

Lyria came back to camp with a small bundle of logs. She hadn't been able to find much, but she hoped it was good enough to prove she was useful. She saw the boys sitting around the fire and tried to remember all their names. *Red hair, that's James. And then Roan is sitting on the ground next to the fire, so the other two are...* She thought for a moment, then remembered. *Kael is the one next to James and Aran is the taller one.* She smiled at herself for remembering the names, then composed herself and brought her bundle over to add to the rest.

Aran looked up. "You can put that over there. Roan just about fell asleep while we were gone." He grinned and pointed to a pile of wood.

"Is he alright?" Lyria set her contribution of wood atop the growing pile.

Aran glanced at Roan. "Yeah, he's fine. It's been a long couple of days for him and I think starting the fire took just about everything he had left." He pulled an apple out of a sack and tossed it to her. "Eat up. I don't want the wolf to think we aren't taking care of you." He chuckled at his joke and pulled out an apple for himself.

"Thanks." Lyria took a bite of the apple and enjoyed the taste for a moment before she completely devoured the small fruit. She looked at James and Kael playfully batting at each other, Aran looking into the fire, and Roan sleeping peacefully. She smiled. *It's just like a family,* she thought as she settled in to wait for Ferox to get back.

Brianna and Erik were nearing the end of their second day of travel and could see the pass. The mountains crashed down to a small gap, the edges fringed with dark trees from the encroaching forest.

"We'll stop here for the night. We'll get to Copper Town early tomorrow morning," said Erik.

Brianna nodded, tired from the long days of walking. She was amazed at the dwarf's dexterity and fortitude. She followed him to the beginning of the pass, her legs lead-heavy and her mind foggy. Even so, she saw the tell-tale plume of smoke that Erik pointed to as he spoke. "Wouldn't hurt to go and see if those travelers have room for us. I don't feel like starting my own fire when there's one so close."

Brianna snapped out of her daze. "Are you sure? I mean, what if they are bandits or something?"

Erik snorted. "Bandits are smart enough to find wood that won't smoke. These are probably just travelers who don't know much about the woods."

Brianna considered his logic and relented. "Sounds good enough for me." She was exhausted and she had to admit the thought of an already-lit fire was appealing. "Lead the way."

Erik harrumphed and they made their way toward the smoke. Soon Brianna saw a light and Erik pushed his way through the brambles as stealthily as he could. Needless to say, he wasn't very successful in this endeavor and Brianna cringed as she heard the racket from his pushing. *They'd have to be deaf not to hear us,* she thought. Luckily, the travelers didn't notice their approach.

Brianna and Erik stopped and peered into the clearing. Brianna counted five figures seated around the fire. Two boys laid lazily on mats, sound asleep as far as Brianna could tell. A slight girl was seated to one edge of the fire, and two more boys sat on the far side. One of these lay slumped against a log and Brianna had not seen him at first.

"What do you think?" whispered Brianna.

"Not sure."

With that, he stood up and stepped briskly into the clearing, leaving Brianna to ignore the knot of anxiety that formed in her stomach as she cautiously followed.

The figure seated on the far side of the fire was the first to react. He stood up and looked directly at them. "What do you want?"

"Relax," said Erik in a reasonable tone. "We're just going to see some friends in Copper Town and we wondered if you'd like to share your fire for the night."

The boy looked from Brianna and Erik to the girl and back again. The girl nodded, and the boy said, "Feel free to join us." He motioned for the two to come and sit.

"Don't worry about them." He pointed at the sleeping bodies. "It's been a long day."

The slight girl walked over and shook the other boy awake.

"I understand that. We're pretty tired ourselves. If you don't mind my asking, what's your name?" Erik asked as he strode quickly to the fire and sat cross-legged.

The boy looked over his shoulder at the boy and the girl. The boy was rising groggily and the girl looked up and gave a brief nod again. "My name's Aran."

Brianna followed slowly and uneasily behind Erik, sitting like a doe ready to bolt.

"Wait a second. You're a dwarf, aren't you!" Aran exclaimed excitedly. "I haven't seen one in ages."

Erik couldn't help but chuckle at his enthusiasm. "I am. Where do you come from?"

"We came from over the river." Aran lost all of his enthusiasm at the question. "What about you?"

"I heard that a friend of mine was in Copper Town and was going to visit him."

"What's his name?" The previously sleeping boy asked the question quickly and quietly, with too much intensity for casual conversation.

Erik looked at him and paused. "Well, for starters,

what's your name?"

The boy didn't smile. "I'm Roan. This is Lyria, and those two are Kael and James. Who are you going to see?"

Erik narrowed his eyes and Brianna felt tension build in the air. "We are going to see Corbin," she blurted out.

Erik glanced at her, his eyes narrow slits.

"Do you know him? We understand that he's in Copper Town." She looked from face to face anxiously.

Roan's body slumped, exhaustion evident in every limb. "I knew him." He looked down at the ground for a moment. "You won't find him in Copper Town."

"What do you mean?" asked Erik, his eyes still narrowed suspiciously.

"I mean, he's gone. It's gone." Brianna couldn't see his face, but she could tell that the boy was on the verge of tears.

"What do you..." Erik's eyes widened.

She grabbed Erik's arm, interrupting him. "What happened?"

"It's a long story," said Aran. He looked over at his friend. "Roan, I can tell it if you don't want to."

Roan shook his head. "No. It'd be better if I told it." He looked up and Brianna saw his eyes were red-rimmed. She had a sinking feeling that whatever he was about to share was going to be bad. “I do have one question first. What are your names?”

Brianna started as she realized that she hadn’t introduced herself. “Sorry, of course. I’m Brianna and this is Erik.”

The dwarf growled, but Brianna punched him and he was quiet.

“Now, please tell us what happened to Corbin.”

Roan took a deep breath, then began.

Brianna and Erik listened intently as Roan related his part of the story, Aran occasionally butting in to tell of his adventures and Lyria listening patiently in the background. At one point, the girl walked away and returned with a massive wolf.

“What in the blazes is that?!” shouted Erik as he saw the wolf enter the clearing.

“This is Ferox,” Lyria smiled. “Don’t worry, he won’t hurt you.”

“Not worried,” Erik mumbled. “Not worried at all.” Erik narrowed his eyes at the wolf, who feigned a lunge, then fell to the ground, tongue lolling like he was laughing. Lyria reprimanded him and Roan cleared his throat.

"Sorry about that, we haven't quite gotten to his part yet." He looked at Lyria curiously. "As a matter of fact, I don't think any of us have heard your side of the story."

The girl blushed. "Yeah… Sorry, there hasn't really been a good time yet. I suppose now is as good as ever." She paused and looked at the wolf, cocking her head as if listening. "But first, Ferox says he's got a deer for everyone."

Everyone's spirits perked at the thought of food and a quick effort was made to wake James and Kael and haul the kill back into camp. Afterward, the two young boys were properly introduced and Lyria began to tell her story as they cut the deer and started to cook some of the choice cuts.

Soon, the sad story of Copper Town and Corbin had been told and the group sat in solemn silence.

"I'm sorry," said Brianna. "He seems like he was a fantastic person."

Roan nodded. "He was. I just wish he could have told us more." He looked at Brianna then, his eyes full of questions. "What about you? What's your story?"

"It's not nearly as exciting as yours, but it's something." She told them about her time, careful to leave out the Shadow Realm, as she didn't want to talk about it more than she had to. As she spoke, the venison was cooked and passed around. Everyone ate hungrily. Brianna ate slowly, telling her story and satisfying her appetite at the same time. Eventually, she came to the end and spread her arms out in an all-encompassing gesture. "And now we're here." She looked around the group. It was a much more comfortable and welcoming atmosphere than when she had first entered.

"Well, I guess we should decide what to do next," Roan looked around at the others for ideas.

"You said that Corbin told you to head west, right? We could go straight through these woods and reach the dwarven capital in a day or so. We could get supplies there before looking for the Temple of the Moon," suggested Erik.

"The dwarven capital? You mean Drunmal?" asked Aran excitedly. "I've always wanted to see the legendary city and meet the crafters that live there."

"I wouldn't mind going to a big city and getting a cloak before winter," mused Roan and Lyria nodded in agreement. Henry squeaked, and James looked at Kael before throwing his vote in for going to the city.

The only one who disagreed was Brianna. "We could go see Shriggus. I'm sure he would have supplies for us. He could give us advice as well."

The others looked at her, weighing her suggestion.

"But Shriggus lives to the north and is farther away than the city. Besides, he told us we didn't have much time." Erik said, raising his eyebrows and shaking his head.

Brianna nodded. "I guess you're right, but still he might know more about what to do."

"How about we have a vote," Aran said. "All in favor of going to Drunmal raise their hands."

Everyone's hands went up except for Brianna, and Ferox, of course.

Aran looked around. "Well, then, I guess it's settled. We're going to Drunmal."

Brianna sighed and shrugged away the feeling of dread that had settled in her mind.

"In the meantime, we should all get a good night's sleep so we can get an early start tomorrow," Erik stated and the group nodded in agreement.

The small company was soon spread comfortably around the fire, warm and filled with roasted meat. Eyelids drooped and breathing relaxed until nearly every one of the travelers was asleep. Ferox alone stood guard, his regal head resting on his great paws, but one eye open and his ears alert to the smallest noise.

Still doubting the wisdom of their upcoming plans, Brianna lay awake trying to put her finger on the source of her anxiety. She noticed Roan slumped by the fire, his eyes gazing intently into the flickering flames. *He's different than the rest of them,* she thought before she drifted off into a troubled sleep.

XXIII:

Traveling to the City

The travelers awoke early in the morning and began the long trek toward Drunmal. It was a cold day. The sun was hidden behind dark clouds of autumn. Ferox and Erik led the way, each stoic and focused on the path. The trees surrounding them were tall and dark; their foliage absorbed what little light made it through the clouds long before it could brighten the forest floor.

Even so, the group maintained high spirits, and as they began to come fully awake, conversations broke out despite the darkness and the somber attitude of Ferox and Erik.

"So… you said you're from Erindale, right?" Roan asked Brianna. "What's it like there?"

"Boring." Brianna looked at him and smiled softly. "What about you? What was it like living out in the wild by yourself?"

Roan felt something about her smile tug at him. "It was hard. But it was nice to not have to deal with anyone."

Brianna raised an eyebrow and Roan felt his stomach churn. "Are you saying I'm bad company?"

Roan shook his head and threw his hands up defensively. "No! I just meant it was nice to be able to..." he trailed off and Brianna laughed.

"I'm just kidding. I get what you mean." She paused. "Anyway, what's it like controlling fire?"

Roan was glad to be on familiar ground and started to talk about his power. The two drifted into amiable conversation and they progressed easily through the rest of the day. There was no sign of bandits or stræntae and by the time they stopped for lunch, Erik said they were halfway to the city.

"If we keep up this pace, we'll be there before nightfall," the dwarf said as he gnawed on a piece of leftover venison.

"Then let's get going," said Aran. "I don't feel like spending the night in this forest."

"I agree," said James. Kael nodded in agreement.

"I have to admit, it'd be nice to sleep in a real bed for a change," said Lyria. "No offense, Ferox." The wolf nodded and she patted his enormous head.

Roan looked at Brianna and she shrugged. "I'm fine either way, although a soft bed does sound nice."

"What's the soonest we can get there, Erik?" asked Roan.

Erik thought for a moment, then said, "If we pick up the pace a little, we should get there in a few hours, just before dusk."

Roan looked around and saw his friends' faces, eager to get to the city. "Well, then, let's get going."

The dwarf nodded and turned back to the path. Everyone got up and started to follow after him into the deep forest. Roan tried to walk next to Brianna and continue talking to her, but she had moved close to Lyria and the two were discussing something in low voices.

I wonder what they're talking about, he thought, then shook his head. *I shouldn't care about it.*

"She's cute." Roan jumped as he heard Aran.

"I don't know what you're talking about," he said, a blush coming to his cheeks.

Aran laughed and punched him in the shoulder. "Yeah, sure you don't. Anyway, James and I were wondering if you'd be down for a game of toads and flies when we get to Drunmal?"

"Toads and flies?" asked Roan. "What's that?"

Aran looked at him, shock obvious in his eyes. "You've never played before?"

Roan shook his head.

Aran grinned. "Well, we're going to have a good time when we get there, I'm sure." He went on to explain the rules and gameplay of toads and flies, but Roan wasn't really paying attention. Instead, he thought about what they were heading toward. He occasionally nodded and pretended to be interested in what Aran was talking about, but his thoughts drifted. He thought about reaching Drunmal, about the journey to the temple of the moon, of the woman Corbin had mentioned: Anna. More than he liked to admit, even to himself, he also thought about Brianna. Then his thoughts began to drift back to the previous day's events.

I should've stayed. Maybe I could have done something. The thought played through his mind repeatedly as the distance to the city shortened. At some point, Aran gave up explaining the game and dropped back to talk with Kael and James. Roan felt guilty for not listening to his friend, but he couldn't help it. *What if I'd stayed? What if… What if…* The thoughts ran through his head until he felt someone touch his arm. It was Lyria.

"You should stop thinking about it," she said. "You can't change anything you did. Don't think what you might have done. Your mind will get stuck in a loop." She had a sad look on her face. "Trust me. I've been there."

Roan looked at the slight girl's sad face and felt a weight lifted from his shoulders. "Thank you." He took a deep breath and let it out slowly. "You're right. It's just hard to let go."

"I know." She smiled wistfully at him. "You're not the only one who's lost someone."

Roan felt sorrow spread through his heart. *I won't let her get hurt.* It was a promise, and he knew that he would do everything he could to keep it. He touched her arm gently. "Well, then, I guess we both should move on." He smiled. "Besides, this is my first adventure, and I'm guessing it's your first one, too."

Lyria nodded. "I should go check on Ferox."

Roan watched her move over to the wolf's side. He felt a strange connection to her, like she was his long-lost sister. Before he could think any more about the connection, a change in the surroundings caught his attention. The dim sunlight had started to increase in intensity, the trees were spaced farther apart, and the path had become wider and more visible. Roan looked around at his companions. They all had noticed the change and there was excitement in the air as they approached the end of the forest.

I wonder what it'll be like, he thought as the last of the trees fell away and the full force of the setting sun illuminated the landscape. The rays caught on the tall grass, turning it golden. A few small houses dotted the cleared land. Dominating the view was a massive walled city. Gold and marble-topped structures glowed and shone in the light, blazing beacons of hope and adventure to the group.

Erik turned around and grinned. "That's Drunmal," he said gruffly. Roan smiled, looked at the eager faces, and started to quicken his pace toward the impressive city.

XXIV:

Drunmal

Roan looked up at the great wall that stood before him, mouth agape. “It’s amazing.”

The wall rose hundreds of feet into the air, great spires marking the locations of the guardhouses. The soldiers walking along the wall were distant specks.

“That’s Drunmal for you,” Erik said in his gruff voice. “The last ancient stronghold of the dwarves.”

Roan glanced at the dwarf and saw the pride emanating clearly off him before he turned his attention back to the city. The gate was large and there was a flood of people rushing in and out, guards positioned along the massive iron gate.

“Ferox says he’ll meet us on the other side in two days,” said Lyria.

“That's a good idea. We don’t need to draw any unnecessary attention to ourselves.” Roan looked back as he spoke and saw the great wolf trot off into the fringes of the forest, instantly disappearing in the undergrowth despite his massive size. *I'll never get used to that,* thought Roan as he strained his eyes to see any sign of the wolf.

At last, he turned his attention to the rest of his companions. Aran was sitting on a log, his head cocked to one side as he examined the impressive wall. James and Kael were huddled nearby, engaged in whispered conversation.

"Isn't it fantastic? I can't wait to see the actual city," James was saying, his voice enthusiastic but hushed.

"I don't know. It reminds me a bit of home," Kael responded hesitantly. Their conversation fell back into whispers and Roan smiled at the intimate friendship the two had, then looked toward Lyria. She was standing close to Erik, her eyes wide as she stared at the wall before her.

"I've never seen anything so… grand," she said, as she noticed Roan looking her direction.

Roan nodded. "I know what you mean. It's kind of scary."

Lyria nodded vehemently. "It really is!" she said, then tried to compose herself. "I mean, it's not that scary.

I'm just nervous because I'm excited."

Erik snorted and Roan raised an eyebrow. "I'm sure," he said and chuckled at the affronted look that rolled across Lyria's face. "No offense, I'm just playing."

Lyria huffed and crossed her arms, tilting her chin. Roan heard a light laugh and turned toward Brianna. She looked radiant, even in her plain traveling clothes and he felt his palms begin to sweat as she looked at him with her piercing blue eyes. His normally sharp mind went blank and he struggled to keep from shaking in embarrassment and awkwardness as the silence grew longer. She gave him a quizzical look and Roan felt compelled to say something.

"What do you think?"

"About what?" A playful light played through Brianna's eyes as she responded. "The weather? The city? The mission? The sky? There are a hundred different things I could be thinking about."

Roan blushed with embarrassment. "I meant about the city." He could feel the odd looks from the rest of the group as he struggled to recover. Aran gave a snort of laughter but tried to disguise it as a cough.

Brianna smiled brightly. "Oh, I'm excited to see what it's like. I've heard they have all kinds of herbs and potions, unlike anything else in the world."

Roan felt the embarrassment and awkwardness slowly slide off him and he sighed inwardly. "Alright then, I think it's time we see it up close."

"I second that," Aran said as he stood up. "No sense waiting here for another strætae to attack us."

The jovial tone that had been present among the group moments before was immediately replaced by somber dread as the thought of the shadowy warriors ran through their minds.

"You're right, let's go," Roan's voice was gruff and hard as he spoke. The rest of the group looked at him, but he didn't notice, wrapped in despair as he turned toward the city.

Aran felt the shockwave that his words had created and cringed inwardly at his abruptness. *What was I thinking?* He quickly caught up with Roan as the group made their way to the city. "I'm sorry, man. I wasn't thinking when I said that."

Roan brushed the comment aside. "It's fine. Let's just keep moving."

Aran fell back and sank into melancholy thoughts.

I'm such an idiot, he berated himself. *Why did I say something so stupid? Now everyone is going to think I'm some jackass jerk.* He glanced around and saw everyone's gloomy eyes. Even Brianna's face was downcast and she had never even known Corbin. Aran felt tears of shame slowly creep toward the edge of his eyes and he fought with himself furiously as they neared the gate. *I'm just feeling sorry for myself. Just like Dad used to say.* But beneath the embarrassment, he felt panic. *What if I turn these people against me? Maybe I don't deserve to have good friends like this. Maybe I don't deserve them because I'm not a good person. I'm not a good person. I'm not, I'm not.* The dusky light illuminated the surrounding landscape of desolate grasslands and failed farms, the occasional stubborn weed the only greenery. Aran wrestled with his tortured thoughts, but slowly relaxed as more and more people came alongside the group. He was distracted from his foolishness by the variety of folk gathered around them.

He saw dwarves, humans, and the occasional gnome or elf. *So this is what a real city is like,* he thought to himself, awed by the sheer number of faces around him. *I never thought I'd see anything bigger than Arrdell. I'm glad I was wrong.* Despite the former gloom that had pressed on him so heavily, he couldn't help but gain optimism from the city. *So many people, so much happening!* He glanced behind him and saw James smiling happily.

"It's amazing," he said to the red-headed boy.

James nodded enthusiastically. "I know! I was just thinking the same thing! It's so much bigger than where I grew up, and there are so many more people!"

Aran could tell that James was in love with the city and felt a sense of joy spread to his own heart. He turned away from James and caught a glimpse of Kael out of the corner of his eye. The boy was watching him, suspicious and intent. Aran did a double-take to try to catch him mid-act, but the boy had already hidden his gaze by the time Aran turned to look at him.

I don't understand that kid, thought Aran. Then, a tendril of doubt nagged at his mind. *Maybe he knows that I'm not worthy to be James' friend. Maybe he knows I'm not a good person.* Aran shook his head and forced his attention back to the crowd. *It's no use focusing on negative things like this. I have to keep myself going forward, stay positive.* Their small group had slowly pushed its way through the throngs and to the gates, leading to many complaints from the surrounding people. Aran looked up to admire the tall, arched gateway and ornately carved designs that flowed seamlessly along the arches. He thought he saw some sort of flurry of movement in one of the guard towers and turned in time to see one of the dwarves run out of sight in a hurry. He frowned. *I wonder what that's about. Maybe a crisis in the guardhouse.* He shrugged off his sense of foreboding and soon forgot about the sight altogether.

The trip through the gate was faster than he'd expected and they were inside the wall within a few minutes.

"Well, that's that," Lyria said, her relief obvious.

Erik chuckled. "Dwarves are quite a bit more efficient than humans. No point in having everyone walk single file through a massive gate like that, especially when it was built wide enough for ten carriages full of goods." He shook his head. "I've been to plenty of human cities that are just wasteful with space. Such a shame," he sighed at the thought.

"Well, whatever the reason, I'm glad we didn't have to spend too much time with all those people," Lyria said.

"I agree," said Brianna. Roan and Kael nodded along with the rest of the group.

Aran looked at James and saw the confusion he felt mirrored on the boy's face.

"Now, let's get moving and find a place to spend the night. Erik, you lead the way." Roan looked toward the dwarf and he grunted before moving to the front of the line, the others filing in close behind him. Lyria stayed close behind Erik, her hands close to her chest and her eyes darting about, ready to bolt at the first sign of danger. Behind her, Roan and Brianna walked close together and talked quietly, their awkwardness bringing a smile to Aran's face. Finally, James, Kael, and Aran took the rear of the group.

"What'd you think of the gate?" Aran asked James.

James turned to him, his eyes bright with excitement. "There were so many people! And dwarves! And I thought I even saw a couple of elves!" Then his eyes became downcast. "I'm not sure why everyone was so excited to get through there. I would've liked to stay and talk to everyone."

Aran smiled. "I know what you mean."

"Really?!"

Aran nodded as James looked toward him. "Yep. I was thinking of all the stories they would have, and the food and trinkets. It would have been awesome to talk to even a few of them."

James smiled and nodded excitedly. "I know! I hope that we can see plenty of people at the market tomorrow."

Aran rubbed his red hair playfully. "I'm sure we will, and I'll make sure we get to talk to as many as we can."

James laughed and knocked Aran's hand away. "Thanks, man, I can't wait." He turned to Kael and smiled. "I bet we'll hear some wild stories tomorrow."

Aran saw Kael force a smile across his face as he replied, "Yeah, I'm sure we will."

The three walked in companionable silence, taking in the city. The streets were cobblestone, wide enough for ten men or more to walk abreast, and lined with smooth, granite sidewalks. The buildings that lined the street varied from cut stone to creations that appeared to have been made from a single boulder, each lined with their own unique set of ornate carvings. One such building that caught Aran's eye was a massive, single-slab house with golden dragons carved around the frame, almost as if they were chasing each other. He was so entranced by the house that he barely managed to stop himself from running into Roan.

"Why'd you sto-" Aran stopped mid-sentence as he saw the battalion of armed dwarves standing in front of Erik. "Oh." He quickly looked around and saw other guards behind him.

"Rathenfoth, what do you want?" Erik asked.

A dwarf in silvery chain mail stepped forward, sword in hand. "Erik, it's been a long time. Too bad we had to meet in such an unfortunate circumstance."

Erik grunted.

Rathenfoth smiled grimly. "You always were the silent type. I'm here under orders of the King to arrest you and your companions."

"What for?!" Roan asked, confused.

Rathenfoth turned toward him and the grim smile was replaced with a harsh frown. "Erik and the girl next to you are both convicted of injuring the King's nephew, Grimsvor."

"But he was trying to capture me and sell me into slavery!" exclaimed Brianna. "I was only defending myself."

Rathenfoth shook his head. "That sounds like an admission of guilt. Whether or not you're telling the truth, you are both wanted criminals - you and anyone you happen to be traveling with. Now you can either come peacefully or in pieces."

Aran was about to say something, but Erik turned back to the group and shook his head. "I wouldn't try anything. They've got a thousand or more warriors here."

Aran growled and reluctantly harnessed his temper, glaring at Rathenfoth.

Rathenfoth nodded, pleased. "Good. Now, follow me and I won't have to hurt you."

Roan felt a coal of hot anger burning inside him as he let himself be handcuffed. He tried to open the gate and let his power rush out, but something stopped him. He looked at Brianna and mouthed, "I can't use my power."

She looked at him, confused. She closed her eyes and furrowed her brows in concentration. A moment later, she opened them and mouthed back, "Me neither."

They looked at each other, terror in their eyes as they realized they were helpless. Roan looked around the rest of the group and saw the realization slowly come over the rest of their faces.

"Move it," Rathenfoth said harshly and Aran felt the

sharp jab of a spear in his back. Reluctantly, he started to move, his mind overwhelmed by his inability to use his power.

The dwarves lead them through a twisting maze of back alleyways and main streets, all the time the same thought echoed through Roan's mind: *Why? What's happening?* He couldn't tell where they were when they finally stopped, the only marker a large, menacing square building in front of them. Rathenfoth opened the gate and the guards prodded each of the group into the building and down a flight of stairs.

Five guards grabbed Roan and pulled him away from the rest of the group. "Wait, where are you taking them?" he asked and strained against his captors.

One of them pressed the spear into his backside again. "None of your business. Now, move it!"

Roan struggled once more, but felt the hard steel bite into his flesh and grimaced, letting the dwarves lead him away. He walked down another flight of stairs, then another, and felt the air grow dank and musty around him. The only light this far down came from the occasional torch on the wall, and the air smelled of rot and smoke. He wrinkled his nose as the leader of the procession stopped and opened a cell door.

"Get in," he said and the other dwarves forced Roan into the cell, shoving him so that he fell onto the hard ground before they closed the door.

Roan pushed himself to his feet and looked around the small cell. In one corner was a pile of hay and in the other was a bucket. *At least they were kind enough to give me that,* Roan thought. He knew there were plenty of cells with just a dirt floor and nothing else. He heard a knocking at his door and went to investigate.

"Howdy, patn'r," came a voice from Roan's left.

He turned to see who the speaker was, but could only make out a pair of crazy eyes surrounded by matted and spiked hair. "Hey, what is this place?"

The man laughed maniacally. "Why dis ol place is the greetest prisn to ever be made. Stretches miles 'n miles underground, thousands o' pounds o' rock all 'round it, impossible to 'scape. The folks outside call it som'en fancy like Drunmal jail or som'en. But down here we just call it The Clang, cause all ye can hear is the crazy ones tapping at their cells." As he said the last words, he hit his cell repeatedly with long, grotesque fingernails. "You'd best git comfy. I don't spect you'll be leav'n anytime soon."

Roan felt fear creep up his spine. "Thanks." He made

his way to the hay in the corner and sat down, overwhelmed with the turn of events.

He heard the man tap on the bars again and sing a tune, the words harsh and shrill in his odd dialect:

"It's harsh and cold and it smells like mold,
Down in the clang where we bang,
We bang and the bars go clang,
Clang clang clang,
Down in the clang where we bang bang bang,
It's dark and it's cold as we sit here and mold,
Down in the harsh and cold and smells o' mold,
And we never get free
Down in the clang,
The clang clang clang...."

Epilogue:

The Fallen Shadow

Night had fallen over the dead forest, leaving eerie shadows to dance across the ground. One of these shadows scurried into a cave that dripped darkness and smelled of death. The shadow crept furtively deeper and deeper into the cave, afraid of what lived there. It grew darker and darker; the shadow became a beacon of light in the gloom and had to feel his way along the cave, groping at the walls. Eventually, he reached a formation of rocks and knelt before it, bowing his head in fear and shame.

"I have failed, Master." The shadow's voice was thinner and smokier than it had ever been before, a permanent whisper.

Out of the gloom, a deep voice hissed, "You have. But you have also succeeded. You must remember, young Railin, that some losses are victories. You have rid this world of the old man and made my job that much easier. Now you must rest and regain your strength. Join me and I will wake you when the time is right."

Railin nodded, got to his feet, and walked into the gaping mouth of the innermost cave where he joined the Shadow King.

Author's Note

If you made it this far, I just want to say thank you. Thank you for helping make my dream a reality. You don't need to read this, I know that I don't most of the time, but if you want to, then go right ahead.

You stuck around? Well, I guess you might want to know a little bit about me. I'm really just a kid who's always lived in my own world, constantly creating stories out of the world around me. It's a pretty easy thing to do when you grow up 45 minutes away from a town, don't have T.V. or internet for the first twelve years of life, and are surrounded by forests, rivers, and mountains.

My grandma gifted my parents our property when I was two years old and my mom and dad built our house. I want to thank them both here, because no matter how much shit I gave them about living so far away from my friends, I doubt that I would have been able to write this story without the inspiration (and isolation) that my home provided me.

I don't know what else to put here. At 17 years old, I don't have any accomplishment that I'm proud enough to list and don't think that most of my life story is that interesting to tell, but I guess I should find something else to say in these last few pages for the few readers that make it this far.... How about I tell you how this all started?

I started writing this in eight grade as a project in my English class, the teacher of which happened to be my mom. We were assigned the task of writing a creative story and I decided to take on the challenge in full. I started out thinking: Oh I'll only write a short story; it won't be too long. But as the term went on and the story got longer, I knew that I couldn't put it down. I remember talking to my mom about it at home and how ecstatic she was, the glee plain in her eyes as I told her that I wouldn't be turning in a full story, only the prologue and first chapter of what would eventually become a book.

Needless to say, it took a lot longer than I expected. I spent a good portion of that summer writing, but with my undeveloped attention span and less than stellar writing skills, I barely managed to get five pages done in a day. I put down the project for a while just to enjoy my last summer before high school, but I never gave up on the idea.

Throughout my freshman and early sophomore year, I continued to write, and started to really get into it. I managed a few pages a day, characters, lore, and story arcs running through my head. I even wrote while we were on vacation. I started by writing just about half a page an hour, but by the time I finished my first draft, I could crank out three to four pages in that same time. That's not to say that those pages were all the same quality writing. That realization was soon to come to me as I started to tackle the monumental task of going back through and revising the story.

This was the point where I started to feel dejected for the first time. I was rereading old sections that I remembered thinking were good but seeing absolute garbage. The writing was a mess, gerunds were all over the place, and the word choice was just terrible. I slowed down a lot during this phase; the process of editing and revising was not fun.

Luckily, my mom stepped in and helped, editing the sections that I revised so that I could focus on the story and not get so caught up in the grammar. It took a long time, it wasn't pretty, and it definitely wasn't fun all the time, but as my junior year came to a close and I was locked inside due to the Coronavirus pandemic, I finally finished writing the book and was on my way to publishing.

Now a few answers to questions you might have. Will there be a second book? Yes, there will be, and I'm already working on it. What or who inspired my characters? Most of them don't have any specific person that I decidedly picked, but Lyria was developed after one of my good friends in middle school who was always smiling and supported my crazy dream of writing even back then. If you're reading this, Paige, I just want to say thank you so much. Henry, the mouse, is named after my younger brother Henry and I think does a pretty good job of representing his character. Ferox was also a character that I created to represent my dog, Penny, but he doesn't do her justice. He evolved into his own character. I think that's probably the best way to describe most of the characters, actually. They all started as someone or something, but then they grew into themselves and I was just a scribe writing down their story.

Finally, I wanted to tell you a little bit about what inspired me to write. I was a big fan of fantasy fiction as a kid if you couldn't tell already, but there were a few books in particular that made me want to pursue writing my own. The first of these was *Eragon,* a book written and published by Christopher Paolini when he was sixteen. I saw the book and immediately knew that I wanted to do something like it. Another big influence was Patrick Rothfuss' *Name of the Wind* which was and still is my favorite book of all time. It taught me a lot of lessons about writing, but it also made me appreciate good writing even more and made me strive harder to make my book better.

I guess that's that, that's the end of this book. I hope you enjoyed it and I want to thank you one more time for supporting this dream of mine. I hope that any aspiring writers reading this are motivated to keep going. Just remember, it may be hard, it may be boring, but it is also wonderful and fun, and at the end of the day telling a story is one of the most rewarding things in the world.